*"I know I'm probably the last person you want to talk to,"* Tamara said. *"But I have questions I have to ask. About the crime scene."*

Déjà vu washed over Clay as he stared at her. She was still the same beautiful woman he'd married, fought with, made love to. He drew a deep breath, wiped away perspiration and jammed his Stetson back on his head. "Sure."

Tamara pulled out a notepad and wet her lips. Colt looked at her mouth, and heat that had nothing to do with the summer day flashed through his blood.

A picture of Tamara from long ago flickered in his mind. Sitting on a fence rail at the rodeo. He'd captured her cheeks between his hands and leaned in to steal his first kiss from her. The first of thousands of kisses they'd shared.

But he'd lost the right to kiss her years ago....

Dear Reader,

I was honored to be asked to participate in THE COLTONS: FAMILY FIRST, especially when I learned the esteemed authors who'd be collaborating on the series. I had a great time writing the reunion story for sexy cowboy Clay Colton and his ex-wife Tamara.

They say everything in Texas is bigger, and the Texas branch of the Colton family tree is no exception. Fans of the earlier Coltons continuities will find that the Texas Coltons live, laugh and love in a big way—especially when danger crosses their path!

*Rancher's Redemption* is about making the wrong choices for the right reasons—and second chances to correct mistakes. Reunion stories are among my favorite plots, both to read and to write. When former lovers rebuild their relationship and heal old wounds, their journey is inherently emotional and rife with conflict. Clay and Tamara were high school sweethearts who married young, then let divergent dreams and disillusionment tear them apart. Over time, they learned those dreams lost their magic without someone they loved to share it. But the name of their hometown, Esperanza, Texas, means hope, and hope is where second chances begin....

Welcome to Esperanza, Texas, and happy reading!

*Beth Cornelison*

# *Rancher's* REDEMPTION

## Beth Cornelison

Silhouette®

Romantic

SUSPENSE

Special thanks and acknowledgment to
Beth Cornelison for her contribution to
THE COLTONS: FAMILY FIRST miniseries.

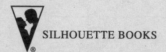

SILHOUETTE BOOKS

ISBN-13: 978-0-373-27602-8
ISBN-10:    0-373-27602-8

RANCHER'S REDEMPTION

Visit Silhouette Books at www.eHarlequin.com

**Printed in U.S.A.**

**Books by Beth Cornelison**

Silhouette Romantic Suspense

*To Love, Honor and Defend* #1362
*In Protective Custody* #1422
*Danger at Her Door* #1478
*Duty to Protect* #1522
*\*Rancher's Redemption* #1532

*The Coltons: Family First

---

## BETH CORNELISON

started writing stories as a child when she penned a tale about the adventures of her cat, Ajax. A Georgia native, she received a bachelor's degree in public relations from the University of Georgia. After working in public relations for a little more than a year, she moved with her husband to Louisiana, where she decided to pursue her love of writing fiction.

Since that first time, Beth has written many more stories of adventure and romantic suspense and has won numerous honors for her work, including the coveted Golden Heart award in romantic suspense from Romance Writers of America. She is active on the board of directors for the North Louisiana Storytellers and Authors of Romance (NOLA STARS) and loves reading, traveling, Snoopy and spending downtime with her family.

She writes from her home in Louisiana, where she lives with her husband, one son and two cats who think they are people. Beth loves to hear from her readers. You can write to her at P.O. Box 52505, Shreveport, LA 71135-2505, or visit her Web site at www.bethcornelison.com.

To my family—you mean everything to me.

Thank you to my critique partner, Diana Duncan, for her input and encouragement.

Thank you to Heath at Cooper Veterinary Clinic for answering my questions about equine diseases.

Thank you to Brenda Mott for her help answering ranching questions.

Thank you to Wally Lind and the crime scene writers listserve for answering CSI questions.

Thank you to Marie Ferrarella, Justine Davis, Caridad Piñeiro, Carla Cassidy and Linda Conrad, who collaborated on THE COLTONS: FAMILY FIRST, for making this series such fun to work on!

And thank you to Patience Smith and the rest of the Harlequin editors who worked on this continuity for the opportunity to write Clay and Tamara's story.

# Chapter 1

He had a trespasser.

Clay Colton narrowed a wary gaze on the unfamiliar blue sedan parked under a stand of mesquite trees. This corner of the Bar None, Clay's horse ranch, was as flat as a beer left out in the Texas sun, and he'd spotted the car from half a mile away.

He tapped his dusty white Stetson back from his forehead and wiped his sweaty brow. Finding a strange sedan on his property didn't sit well with him—especially in light of the recent trouble his sister, Georgie, had endured. He still got sick chills thinking how a woman had broken into his sister's home, stolen from her, passed herself off as Georgie.

A shiver crawled up Clay's spine despite the scorching June heat. Esperanza, Texas, his home for all his twenty-six years, had always been a safe place, no real crime to mention. He clicked his tongue and gave his workhorse, Crockett, a little kick. His mount trotted forward, and as he neared the car, Clay saw that the Ford Taurus had crashed into one of the mesquites, crumpling the front fender. A fresh sense of alarm tripped through him.

"Hello? Anyone there?" Clay swung down from Crockett and cautiously approached the car. Visions of an injured, bleeding driver flashed through his mind and bumped his blood pressure higher. "Is anyone there?"

He peered into the driver's side window. Empty. The car had been abandoned.

Removing his hat, Clay raked sweaty black hair away from his eyes and circled to the back of the sedan. The trunk was ajar, and he glimpsed a white shopping bag inside. Using one finger to nudge open the trunk, Clay checked inside the bag.

His breath caught.

The bag was full of cash.

Intuition, combined with fresh memories of Georgie's recent brush with identity theft, tickled the nape of Clay's neck, making the fine hairs stand up. A wrecked and abandoned sedan with a bag of money meant trouble, no matter how you added it up. He stepped back and pulled his cell phone from the clip on his belt. He dialed his friend Sheriff Jericho Yates's number from memory.

"Jericho, it's Clay. I'm out on the southwest corner of my land near the ravine, and I've come across an abandoned Taurus. The car hit a mesquite and banged up the front end, but I don't see any sign of the driver."

Sheriff Yates grunted. "You don't see anyone around? Maybe the driver tried to walk out for help."

Clay scanned the area again, squinting against the bright June sun from under the rim of his Stetson. "Naw. Don't see anybody. But it gets better. There's a bag of money in the trunk. A lot of money. Large bundles of bills. Could be as much as a hundred grand."

He heard Jericho whistle his awe then sigh. "Listen, Clay. Don't touch anything. Until I determine otherwise, you should consider the car and everything around it a crime scene."

"Got it."

"Read me the license plate."

Clay rattled the numbers off.

Through the phone, Clay heard the squeak of Jericho's office chair. "Thanks. I'll run a check on this plate, then I'll be right out."

Clay thanked the sheriff and snapped his cell phone closed.

Gritting his teeth, he gave the abandoned sedan another once-over. This was the last thing his family needed. After returning his cell to his hip, Clay climbed back on Crockett and headed toward his original destination—the broken section of fence at the Black Creek ravine. Regardless of where the car and money came from and what the sheriff determined had happened to the driver, Clay had work to do, and the business of ranching waited for nothing.

Several minutes later, the rumble of car engines drew Clay's attention. He looked up from the barbed wire he'd strung and spotted Jericho's cruiser and a deputy's patrol car headed toward the abandoned Taurus. He laid his wire cutters down and shucked his work gloves. Grabbing a fence post for leverage, he climbed out of the steep ravine and strode across the hard, dry earth to meet the sheriff.

Even after all these years, it felt odd to call Jericho "sheriff." Growing up together, he and Jericho had spent hours fishing and hanging around the local rodeo stables where Clay worked whatever odd jobs he could get. Though they'd never spoken much about it, Clay and Jericho had shared another bond—single-parent homes. Jericho's mother had left his family when he was seven.

Though Clay had known of his father, Graham Colton, the man had been an absentee father throughout Clay's childhood. When his mother died, Clay had finished raising his brother and sister while working odd jobs on neighboring ranches. The success both Jericho and Clay had achieved as adults was a testament to their hard work and rugged determination.

Jericho met Clay halfway and extended a hand in greeting. "Clay."

Shaking his friend's hand, Clay nodded a hello. "Afternoon, Hoss. So what did you learn about the car?"

Jericho swiped a hand through his hair and sighed. "It's a rental from a little outfit up the road. Reported stolen a few days ago."

Clay arched a thick eyebrow. "Stolen?" He scowled. "Guess it figures. So now what?"

Jericho squinted in the bright sun and glanced toward the stolen Taurus where one of his deputies was already marking off the area with yellow police tape. "Chances are that money didn't come from someone's mattress. Heaven only knows what we could be dealing with here. I'll call in a crime scene team to do a thorough investigation. Probably San Antonio. They'd be closest."

*A crime scene team.*

The words resounded in Clay's ears like a gong, and he stiffened. *Tamara.*

He worked to hide the shot of pain that swept over him as bittersweet memories swamped his brain.

Clay had two regrets in life. The first was his failure with Ryder—the brother he'd helped raise, the brother who'd gone astray and ended up in prison.

His second was his failed marriage. Five years ago, his high-school sweetheart had walked away from their three-year marriage to follow her dream of becoming a crime scene investigator. Clay blamed himself for her leaving. If he'd been more sensitive to her needs, if he could have made her happier, if he could have found a way to—

"Clay? Did ya hear me?" Jericho's question jolted Clay from his thoughts.

"Sorry. What?"

"I asked if you'd altered anything on or around the car before you called me. Say opening a door or moving debris?"

Clay shook his head. "I nudged the trunk open. One finger, on the edge of the trunk hood. Didn't touch anything else."

Jericho jerked a nod. "Good. I'll let the CSI team know. Be sure to tell your men this area is off-limits until we finish our investigation."

"Right." Removing his Stetson, Clay raked his fingers through his unkempt hair. "Guess I'm just on edge considering what Georgie's been through with that Totten woman."

"Understandable. But there's no reason at this point to think there's any connection."

"Yates." The deputy who'd arrived with Jericho approached them.

The sheriff turned to his officer and hitched his chin toward Clay. "Rawlings, this is Clay Colton. Clay, my new deputy, Adam Rawlings."

"Hey." Clay nodded to the neatly groomed deputy and shook his hand.

"Sorry to interrupt, Sheriff, but I found something. Thought you should take a look."

Jericho faced Clay, but before he could speak, Clay waved a hand. "Go ahead. I need to get back to work, too."

Pulling his worn gloves from his back pocket, Clay strode back toward the ravine where his fence had been damaged and got busy stringing wire again. He had a large section to repair before he went back to the house, and all the usual chores of a thriving ranch to finish before he called it a day. Unfortunately, though fixing the damaged fence was hot, hard work, it didn't require any particular mental concentration. So Clay's thoughts drifted—to the one person he'd spent the past five years trying to get out of his head.

His ex-wife.

If he knew Tamara, not only had she achieved her dream of working in investigative law enforcement, but she was likely working for a large city department by now, moving up the ranks with her skill, gritty determination and sharp mind. Once Tamara set her sights on a goal, little could stand in her way of reaching it.

*Except a misguided husband, who'd foolishly thought that ranching would be enough to fill her life and make her happy.*

A prick of guilt twisted in Clay's gut.

Why had he thought that his own satisfaction with their marriage and the challenge of getting the Bar None up and running would be enough for Tamara? Ranching had been his dream, not hers.

Why hadn't he listened, truly heard her, when she spoke of her hopes for leaving Esperanza and her dream of working in law enforcement? Because of the newlywed happiness in other aspects of their relationship, he'd too easily dismissed signs of her discontent and her restless yearning to achieve her own professional dreams. Soon even the honeymoon stars in her eyes dimmed, and her unhappiness began eroding their marriage.

He'd ignored the warning signs until the night they'd argued over the right course of treatment for a sick stud, and he'd returned from the quarantine stable to find her packing her bags. His heartache over having to put down his best breeding stallion paled beside the pain of seeing his wife in tears, pulling the plug on their life together.

Renewed frustration burned in Clay's chest. Failure of any kind didn't sit well with him, but failure in his personal life was especially hard to accept. His broken marriage was a blemish in his past that marred even the success of the Bar None. His single-minded dedication to building the ranch was what had blinded him to the deterioration of his relationship with Tamara. Until it was too late.

He gave the barbed wire a vicious tug. His grip slipped, and the razor-sharp barb pierced his glove.

"Damn it!" he growled and flung off his glove to suck the blood beading on the pad of his thumb.

Stringing wire might not take much mental power, but letting his mind rehash the painful dissolution of his marriage didn't serve any purpose. Tamara was gone, and no amount of regret or second-guessing could change that. Besides, he was married to his ranch now. Keeping the Bar None running smoothly was a labor of love that took all his energy, all his time. He'd scraped and saved, sweated and toiled to build the Bar None from nothing but a boy's youthful dream.

But today the sense of accomplishment and pride that normally filled him when he surveyed his land or closed his financial books at the end of the day was overshadowed by the reminder of what could have been.

Clay squinted up at the blazing Texas sun, which was far lower in the sky than he'd realized. How long had he been out here?

Flipping his wrist, he checked his watch. Two hours.

Crockett snorted and tossed his mane.

"Yeah, I know, boy. Almost done. I'm ready to get back to the stables and get something to drink, too."

Like Jack Daniel's. Something to help take the edge off. Revived memories of Tamara left him off balance and had picked the scab from a wound he'd thought was healed.

He snipped the wire he'd secured on the last post and started gathering his tools.

"Clay?"

At first he thought he'd imagined the soft feminine voice, an illusion conjured by thoughts of his ex-wife. But the voice called his name again.

He shielded his eyes from the sun's bright glare as he angled his gaze toward the top of the ravine. A slim, golden-haired beauty strode across the parched land and stopped at the edge of the rise. "Clay, can I talk to you?"

Clay's mouth went dry, and his heart did a Texas two-step. "Tamara?"

## Chapter 2

Clay climbed the side of the ravine in three long strides and jerked his Stetson from his head. "What are you doing here, Tamara?"

His ex-wife raised her chin a notch and flashed a stiff smile. "I know I'm probably the last person you want to talk to today, but…I have questions I have to ask. About the crime scene."

An odd déjà vu washed over him as he stared at her. She looked just as beautiful as the woman he'd married, fought with, made love to, and yet…she'd changed, too. Her cheeks and jaw were thinner, more angular. She'd grown her hair longer, the honey-blond shade sporting fewer highlights from the sun, and a hint of makeup shaded her blue eyes and sculpted cheekbones—a vanity she'd never bothered with when she worked beside him on the ranch.

He stood there, so absorbed by the shock of her presence and her beauty that it took a moment for her comment to sink in.

She had questions about the crime scene. Not questions about how he'd been, about their divorce, about the five years that had passed since they'd last seen each other, sitting at opposite ends of a table like two strangers in her lawyer's office.

He blinked. Scowled. "You're here with the CSI team from San Antonio."

The instant the words left his mouth, Clay kicked himself mentally. *Brilliant deduction, Captain Obvious.*

Tamara gave him a patient grin, apparently knowing she'd surprised him and cutting him some slack. If she were rattled by their meeting, she didn't show it. But *she'd* had time to prepare.

"I've been with the department in San Antonio since I finished my forensics training. Jericho—" She paused and lifted a hand. "That is, *Sheriff Yates*—called us out to sweep the scene. I need to ask you a few things. This a good time?"

Clay drew a deep breath, swiped perspiration from his forehead with his arm and jammed his hat back on his head. "Sure. Shoot."

Tamara pulled a small notepad from the pocket of her black jeans and wet her lips.

Clay's gaze gravitated to her mouth and froze on the hint of moisture shimmering in the sunlight. Heat that had nothing to do with the summer day flashed through his blood.

A picture of Tamara from high school flickered in his mind's eye. Sitting on a corral fence rail at the rodeo where his mother had been riding. Her silky hair tucked behind her ears. Her blue eyes shining at him. Pure joy glowing in her face. He'd captured her cheeks between his hands and leaned in to steal his first kiss from her. She'd been startled at first. But soon after, her smile had widened, and she'd returned his kiss in kind. The first of thousands of sultry kisses they'd shared.

Yet now, gawking at her mouth like a schoolboy, he felt as awkward and uncertain as he had that day at the rodeo. But she wouldn't welcome a kiss today the way she had back then. He'd lost the right to kiss Tamara years ago.

Warmth flared in her eyes before she averted her gaze and cleared her throat. "When was the last time you were out on this corner of the ranch?"

Clay shook himself from the unproductive nostalgia and focused on her question. "Earlier this week. Maybe Monday. I ride the perimeter to check fences and survey the property every few days. You know that."

She stopped scribbling on her pad and gave him a penetrating glance. "Assume I know nothing and answer the questions as honestly and completely as you can."

Gritting his teeth, he crossed his arms over his chest. "Yes, *ma'am.*"

"Have you disturbed anything on the scene from the way you found it?"

He shifted his weight and cocked his head, studying the pink flush of heat on her cheeks. She never could take much sun on her porcelain skin without burning. "I opened the car's trunk. One finger on the edge of the hood. I already told Jericho all of this." He hesitated. "You want to wear my hat until you finish out here? Your face is starting to burn."

She snapped a startled blue gaze up to meet his. "I— No. I'll be fine." She furrowed her brow as she studied her notes, clearly ruffled by his offer. "Um… You didn't touch the car otherwise?"

"No."

After several more minutes of her rapid-fire questions, he turned and strolled over to where Crockett waited patiently. Flipping open the saddle pouch across Crockett's hind quarters, Clay dug out the small tube of sunscreen he carried with him but rarely used.

Tamara followed him over to Crockett and reached up to stroke the gelding's nose. "Hey, Davy Crockett. How ya doin', boy?"

Crockett snuffled and bumped Tamara's hand as if he remembered her.

Still patting his horse, she asked, "Do you have any knowledge of who might have left the car here?"

"No." Clay uncapped the sunscreen and squeezed a dab on his thumb.

She consulted her notes again. "Do you have any idea where the money came from?"

"No, I don't." He stepped closer to Tamara, close enough to smell the delicate herbal scent of her shampoo, and she raised her gaze.

"When did you first find the—"

He reached for her, smearing the dab of sunscreen on her nose.

She caught her breath and stumbled back a step. "What are you doing?"

"Sunscreen. You're burning."

She grunted and gave him a perturbed glower. "Clay, I don't—"

He reached toward her again, and she backed away another step. With a resigned sigh, she rubbed the dab of cream over her nose and cheeks, then wiped her fingers on her jeans. "There! Okay? Now I have a job to do. Will you please just answer the questions?"

He tucked the sunscreen back in his saddle pouch. "Is all this really necessary? I've already told Jericho everything I know."

Her shoulders sagged with impatience and a hint of chagrin. "I wouldn't be here if it weren't necessary."

She may have been referring to her job duties, but the underlying truth of her statement hit him like a slap in the face. Nothing had changed. Tamara wanted no part of him and his lifestyle.

He braced his hands on his hips and kicked a clod of dirt. "You've made that pretty clear."

Tamara closed her eyes and released a slow breath. "Clay…"

"Forget it. Just ask your questions, Officer Colton." He glanced at her name badge and another jab stabbed his gut. "Sorry, Officer *Brown*. You went back to your maiden name, huh?"

"Clay…" She studied her notepad as if it held the secrets of the universe, and the silence between them reverberated with a hundred unspoken words and years of regret.

Finally Clay took his work gloves from his back pocket and slapped them on his leg. "Well, I'll let you get back to your job." He turned and stuffed the gloves in his saddle pouch.

Tamara didn't move. Didn't speak.

Clay took a sip of water from his canteen. Hesitated. "I'm

happy for you, Tamara. Glad to see you've accomplished what you wanted."

When she glanced up at last, suspicious moisture glinted in her eyes. But she quickly schooled her face and sucked in a deep breath.

"I—" She stopped herself. Glanced away. Flipped her notepad closed. "I'd better get back to work."

As she started back across the dry field toward the abandoned Taurus, Clay watched her long-legged strides, the graceful sway of her hips, the shimmer of sunlight on her golden hair. His chest tightened with an emotion he dared not name. Admitting he'd missed his ex-wife served no purpose, helped no one.

Giving Crockett a pat on the neck, he grabbed the reins and planted a foot in a stirrup. And hesitated.

He angled his gaze toward the scene where Jericho and his deputy stood while Tamara's team combed the area. Tamara pulled her hair back into a rubber band then tugged on a pair of latex gloves. Curiosity got the better of Clay.

He gave the gelding's neck another stroke. "Sorry, Crockett. I think I'll wait a bit before heading back to the stables."

Shoving his Stetson more firmly in place, Clay headed over to the stand of mesquite trees to watch his ex-wife work.

Tamara took out an evidence bag and tried to steady her breathing. She'd known returning to the Bar None and seeing Clay again would be difficult. But nothing had prepared her for the impact his espresso-brown eyes still had on her.

While working in Clay's stables early in their marriage, she'd been kicked by a mare that was spooked by a wasp. The powerful jolt of that mare's hoof had nothing on the punch in the gut when she'd met the seductive lure of Clay's bedroom eyes today. How could she have forgotten the way his dark gaze made her go weak in the knees?

Nothing about Clay had changed, from his mussed, raven hair that always seemed in need of a trim to the muscular body he'd earned riding horses and doing the hard work ranching required. He still wore the same dusty, white Stetson she'd given him their first Christmas together, and he radiated a strength and confidence that hummed with sex appeal.

She pressed a hand to her stomach, hoping to calm the buzz of bees swarming inside her. When she drew a deep breath for composure, she smelled the sunscreen he'd smeared on her nose, and a fresh ripple of nervous energy sluiced over her. A full day in the sun couldn't have burned her more than the heat of his touch when he'd dabbed the cream on her. She had far too many memories of his callused hands working their magic on her not to be affected by even such casual contact.

Her heart contracted with longing. No one had ever held such a powerful sway over her senses as Clay had. Not one of the men she'd dated since her divorce from Clay could hold a candle to the fiery attraction she felt for her first love. Her cowboy lover. The man she'd thought she'd grow old with.

Tamara sighed. She had to focus, get a grip. Emotion had no place in crime scene investigation, and she had work to do. She stepped over to where the team photographer was clicking shots of the Taurus's trunk. "You finished up front, Pete?"

"Yep. All yours. Do your thing."

Tamara pulled out her notepad and circled to the front of the stolen sedan. She noted a small scrape on the side panel and called it to Pete's attention.

"Saw it. Got it," the photographer called back to her.

Tamara moved on. She scoured the ground, the hood, the windshield, the roof and the driver's side before she opened the car door to case the interior with the same careful scrutiny. Any scratch, stain, dent, hair or foreign object had the potential of being the clue that cracked the case. Nothing was overlooked or dismissed.

As she collected a sample of fibers from the carpet, she heard a familiar bass voice and glanced toward the perimeter of the scene where Jericho Yates and his deputy stood observing.

Clay had joined his friend and was watching her work with a

keen, unnerving gaze. Tamara's pulse scrambled, and she jerked her attention back to the carpet fibers. Sheriff Yates made another quiet comment, and Clay answered, his deep timbre as smooth and rich as dark chocolate. Tamara remembered the sound of Clay's low voice stroking her as he murmured sexy promises while they made love. Just the silky bass thrum could turn her insides to mush.

Her hand shook as she bagged the fibers and moved on to pluck an auburn hair from the passenger's seat. She huffed her frustration with herself. She had to regain control, forget Clay was watching her and get back to business. She closed her eyes and steeled her nerves, steadying her hands and forcing thoughts of Clay from her mind.

"What you got?" said Eric Forsyth, her superior in the CSI lab, as he bent at the waist to peer through the open driver's door.

Tamara bagged the hair and labeled it. "Not much. I've never seen such a clean car. It's odd."

Eric shrugged. "Not surprising. It's a rental car. A company typically washes and vacuums the cars after every customer."

"That's not what I mean. I'm not finding fingerprints or stray threads. No footprints or tire tracks around the car. Not much of anything."

Eric scrubbed a hand over his jaw. "What's more, anything we do find is gonna be hard to pin to whatever happened here. God knows how many people have been in this car in the past month." He motioned to the bag in her hand. "That hair could belong to a schoolteacher from Dallas who rented the car two weeks ago."

Tamara sighed. "Exactly why it doesn't feel right. Even with the rental agency's regular maintenance, we should be finding at least traces of evidence. I think someone wiped the scene."

"You're sure?" Her boss adjusted his wire-rimmed glasses.

"The evidence—or lack of evidence—seems to point that way." She frowned. "Which tells me something bad happened here. Something someone doesn't want anyone to know about."

"Wouldn't be the first time. Well, keep looking. Maybe whoever wiped the scene missed something."

Tamara nodded. "Got it."

Clay tensed as the lanky man with glasses who'd been speaking with Tamara walked up to Jericho and shrugged. "My team isn't getting much for you to build a case on, Sheriff. In fact, our professional opinion is the scene has been wiped clean."

Jericho furrowed his brow and stroked his mustache. "Nothing?"

Clay turned his attention back to Tamara as he listened to the exchange between the crime scene investigator and the sheriff.

"Well, we found a partial print on the trunk. A hair on the front seat. A scratch on the front fender—but it looks old. There's already a little rust formed."

"No signs of foul play or a struggle?" Jericho asked.

"Not yet. But we're still looking."

Clay watched Tamara comb the Taurus with a calm, methodical gaze. She moved like a cat, her movements graceful, strong and certain as she inched through the interior, pausing long enough to bag tiny bits of God-knows-what and securing the evidence. Her professionalism and confidence as she processed the scene was awe-inspiring.

He remembered her awkwardness during her first weeks on the ranch as she learned to use the equipment and handle the horses. Though she soon picked up the finer points of ranching— he didn't know of much Tamara couldn't do once she set her mind to it—she'd never had the passion for the daily workings of the Bar None that he'd hoped.

Today, as she scoured the stolen car, her love for her job was obvious. She had been flustered when she questioned him, but seeing her again after five years had thrown *him,* too. Despite the awkwardness, she'd rallied and fired her questions at him like a pro.

"I did an initial survey of the area and didn't find much either," Rawlings said.

"Have you found anything that'd tell us what happened to the driver? Tracks of a second car for a getaway? Footprints leaving the scene? The fact that the money is still here bothers me." Jericho shook his head. "Who'd leave that much money behind unprotected?"

The crime scene investigator with the wire-rimmed glasses gave Clay a wary look then glanced to Jericho. "Good point. And, no. No footprints or tire tracks."

"It's been too dry," Clay volunteered. "Only rain we've had in weeks was a couple nights ago. A squall passed through. Hard and short. Any surface impressions that might have been left in the dust would have been washed away."

"I'm sorry, who are you?" the investigator asked, sending Clay a skeptical frown.

Clay offered his hand, choosing to ignore the man's churlish tone. "Clay Colton. You're on my ranch. I found the car. Reported it."

The man shook his hand. "Eric Forsyth. San Antonio CSI. I believe you already met my assistant, Tamara Brown?"

"Yep. Met, married and divorced." He gave the man a level stare. "She's my ex."

Forsyth arched an eyebrow. "Oh? She failed to mention that."

Clay quickly squashed the disappointment that plucked him. Apparently she'd cut him cleanly out of her new life. Setting his jaw, he angled his gaze to watch Tamara again. She was giving the driver's door a thorough go over, her jeans hugging her fanny as she squatted to study the contents of the map pocket. "She had no reason to mention it. It has no bearing on anything related to this case."

"We'll see about that." Forsyth turned to the sheriff, effectively dismissing Clay.

Clay ground his teeth and did his best to ignore the affront.

"Colton is right," Sheriff Yates said. "About the dry weather and the brief rain on Tuesday night. Whatever slight impressions might have been around before that storm were almost certainly lost to the rain."

Forsyth crossed his arms over his chest and grunted. "Yeah. There's a puddle of water in the trunk with the money. If the hood of the trunk was ajar, we can assume it's rainwater that leaked in."

"Which helps establish a time frame. If the car sat out here in the rain, we're looking at events that happened before Tuesday night." Jericho rubbed his jaw as he thought. "The car was reported missing Wednesday morning when the first shift arrived at the rental place and checked the inventory."

"I'll call the rental agency and ask them to send copies of the images from their security cameras for Tuesday. Maybe the theft was caught on tape," Deputy Rawlings said.

"Good thinking," Jericho said.

"You oughta talk to my neighbor, Samuel Hawkins, too." Clay crossed his arms over his chest as he spoke to Rawlings. "He came out here Tuesday evening to investigate a commotion he'd heard and found one of his longhorns tangled in that fence I was working on."

"Could the commotion have been something besides the steer?" Rawlings asked.

Clay shrugged. "You'll have to ask him."

"Why didn't your neighbor see the car when he was out here?" Forsyth asked.

"It gets mighty dark out here at night." Clay poked his thumbs in his back pockets and shifted his attention from his ex-wife's sultry curves and confident investigative technique to Eric Forsyth.

"The moon would have been behind the clouds, making it even blacker. He was on the lower side of that ravine—" Clay hitched his chin toward the steep drop-off a few hundred yards away "—with his hands full, tending an injured and agitated longhorn. Not surprising he didn't notice anything."

The crime scene investigator narrowed his eyes on Clay, but before he could reply, Tamara called out.

"Eric! Sheriff! I found something."

Clay whipped his gaze back to his ex. She lay on her back studying the underside of the driver's door.

Jericho, Rawlings and Forsyth all trotted closer to the abandoned vehicle. Clay hesitated only a moment before ducking under the crime scene tape and following.

"What do you have?" Forsyth asked, squatting beside Tamara.

"Hand me a swab." She extended her hand and wiggled her fingers.

Forsyth fished a clean cotton swab from the toolbox-like kit on the ground a few feet away and handed it to Tamara. With meticulous focus on her task, Tamara swiped a spot on the door. After rolling out from under the door and sitting up, she held the swab up to the sunlight and squinted closely at the sample she'd gathered.

"That's what I thought," she murmured, then tipped her head back to meet the expectant gazes of the men circled around her. "Our first sign of foul play, gentlemen. This is blood."

# Chapter 3

After bagging the blood sample and wrapping up her sweep of the abandoned car and surrounding area, Tamara collected her equipment and prepared to leave for San Antonio. She was eager to start processing and analyzing the evidence she'd collected.

*Blood.*

Sure, a past driver could have gotten a bloody nose, and the rental company might have missed this drop during their routine cleanup. But coupled with the curious circumstances surrounding the scene—the money, the indications that the car had been wiped clean, the fact the sedan had been stolen—Tamara's bets were on the blood pointing to a violent confrontation involving the missing driver. That was the theory she would be trying to prove or disprove back at her lab.

She had ridden over from San Antonio with Pete, and the team's photographer was loading the last of his equipment into his SUV. Time to go.

But not before she took care of one last item.

She marched across the hard Texas dirt to where Clay stood beyond the yellow crime scene tape talking to Sheriff Yates.

"All finished, Sheriff. We'll let you know as soon as our test results come in."

Clay's gaze stroked her like a physical touch as she offered her hand to Jericho.

The sheriff clasped her hand in a firm grip. "It was good to see you again, Tamara. Take care and thanks for your help."

She pivoted on her heel to face Clay. Her stomach somersaulted when she met his dark brown eyes. Fighting to keep her arm from shaking, she stuck her hand out. "Clay, thank you for your help."

She was fortunate she'd finished speaking by the time he wrapped his long fingers around hers, because the moment he grasped her hand, her voice fled. A tornado of emotions sucked the air from her lungs, and heady sensations churned through her.

"No problem." The intimacy in his tone, the fire that lit his eyes sparked a heated flush over her skin. "If there's anything else I can do to help, don't hesitate to ask."

Was there any hidden meaning behind that offer, or had she imagined the intimate warmth in his tone? Fighting for oxygen, she tried to pull her hand back. But Clay refused to release her. He squeezed her fingers, his hot gaze scorching her, and he stroked the tender skin at her wrist with his thumb. "It was good to see you, Tee."

Her heart leaped when he used his pet name for her.

She nodded her head stiffly. "You, too."

"You're as beautiful as ever." The soft, deep rumble of his voice vibrated in her chest and stirred an ache she'd thought time had put to rest.

"Thank you," she rasped. This time when she tugged her hand, he let her fingers slip from his grasp.

Tamara curled her tingling hand into a fist and wrapped her other hand around it, as if nursing a wound. But her scars were internal, and seeing Clay today had only resurrected the pain she'd worked five years to move beyond.

Spinning away, she hurried to the SUV where Pete was waiting. She climbed into the passenger seat and angled the air-conditioning vents to blow directly on her face. If the summer sun weren't enough to induce heatstroke, the fiery look in Clay's eyes and the warmth of his sultry tone could surely cause spontaneous combustion.

"You okay?" Pete asked as they pulled away.

Not trusting her voice, Tamara nodded. She leaned her head back on the headrest and closed her eyes. The image of Clay's square jaw, straight nose, stubbled cheeks and thick eyebrows flashed in her mind. Her ex was pure testosterone. All male. Grit and determination.

Suddenly Tamara was blindsided by a need to see for herself what Clay had accomplished at the ranch, to revisit the haunts of her married days. She clutched the photographer's arm as he started to turn toward the highway. "Wait, Pete. Let's not go yet. I want to drive through the ranch. See the property, the house, the stables."

"What's up? You thinking Colton might be hiding something?"

She jerked a startled glance to Pete. "Heavens, no! Clay's as honest and forthright as a Boy Scout. He had nothing to do with that money or car."

"And you know this because…" He drew out the last syllable, inviting her explanation.

"I was married to him."

A startled laugh erupted from Pete. "Excuse me?"

"Before I came to San Antonio, I lived here. With Clay." Tamara tucked her hands under her legs and stared straight ahead. "We were high-school sweethearts and got married just hours after he signed the deed to this ranch."

Pete frowned. "Does Eric know? Are you objective enough to work this case?"

"I'm fine. There's no conflict of interest, because Clay's not involved. We can prove that easily enough if you're worried. And Eric knows…now. I heard Clay tell him."

"I suppose you know Sheriff Yates, too, if you lived out here for a while."

She bobbed her head, grinned. "I had a crush on Jericho for a while in tenth grade. Before I started dating Clay. Jericho's a good man. Salt of the earth."

Pete drummed his fingers on the steering wheel. "So what is it you want me to do here?" He waved a finger toward the windshield.

"Go left. I want to see how things have changed…or not. For old times' sake."

Pete complied, and Tamara sat back in the front seat, holding her breath as familiar landscape and outbuildings came into view. They drove past a corral where three magnificent stallions grazed. The horses looked up, tossing their manes as the SUV rolled by. As Tamara admired the striking males, melancholy twanged her heartstrings.

Lone Star had been a beautiful animal, too. After years of feeding and grooming the stud, Tamara had bonded with the best stallion in Clay's breeding operation. She'd been heartsick when she learned he'd contracted strangles, a bacterial disease that affects the lymph nodes, and devastated when Clay had chosen to put the horse to sleep rather than treat him for the illness. She still couldn't understand how her ex-husband could have been so clinical and emotionless about his decision, especially when she'd begged him to save the horse she'd grown to love.

*"Quinn thinks putting him down is our best option,"* Clay had said.

*"Quinn? It's not his decision! He's our horse!"*

*"He's the vet, Tee. His professional opinion counts—"*

*"More than mine? I'm your wife! What about what I want, what I think is best?"*

*"Ranching is a business, Tamara. I have to do what is best for the ranch."*

*"But why can't we even try—"*

*"My decision is made. Quinn knows what he's doing."*

Tamara squeezed her eyes shut as revived pain shot through

her chest. Resentment for the veterinarian who'd held more sway over Clay than all her pleading churned with a bitter edge in her gut. Quinn Logan may have been Clay's friend, but Tamara had no respect for the man's medical choices. Every rancher she'd spoken to after Lone Star was put down told her strangles had a vaccine, could be treated with antibiotics.

Why hadn't Quinn taken measures to prevent the illness in the stud? And why had the vet dismissed the option of treating the animal's illness so quickly? Was he trying to cover his ass? Prevent a malpractice suit? The whole scenario seemed highly suspicious to Tamara, yet Clay had sided with Quinn.

The crunch of gravel beneath the SUV's tires told Tamara they'd reached the main drive to the ranch house. She peeked out in time to see them pass the barn where Lone Star had been quarantined—and put down. A sharp ache sliced through her, and she swallowed hard to force down the knot of sorrow and bitterness that rose in her throat.

What was it about this ranch that brought all her emotions to the surface, left her feeling raw and exposed? In San Antonio, in her lab, at a crime scene, she'd become a pro at suppressing her emotions and keeping a professional distance in her job. Yet a few hours in Esperanza had her dredging up old hurts, recalling the passion she'd once shared with Clay and longing for the early days in her marriage when life had seemed so golden.

"Nice place. How many acres does Colton have?" Pete asked, pulling her from her thoughts. His gaze swept over Clay's spread.

"He started with thirty acres. I'd guess he's up to about three hundred acres now." Tamara glanced through the open door of the building where Clay still parked his 1978 Ford pickup.

*Still runs. Why should I get rid of it?*

A grin ghosted across her lips. Practical, frugal Clay. He still had no use for waste.

Yet, for all his prudence, Clay *had* gotten rid of his wife.

Her smile dimmed.

After three years, their marriage had been damaged. The

incident with Lone Star had just been the final straw. For months, Tamara had felt herself suffocating, her dreams of working in criminal investigation withering on the vine. When they married, she'd put her aspirations on the back burner to help Clay get his new ranch on its feet. But the longer she'd stayed at the Bar None, the dimmer her hope of fulfilling her life's goals grew.

She'd awakened every morning to a sense of spinning her wheels, going nowhere. At night, she'd tumbled into bed, sore and tired to the bone from the arduous labor involved in running a ranch. Even her happy-new-bride glow had tarnished as, time and again, she'd taken second place in Clay's life to his land and his horses. Like the night he and Quinn ignored her opinion and put down the stallion she'd loved.

"Wow. That house is huge!" Pete sent her a wide-eyed glance.

She angled her gaze to the ranch house, a two-story wood-frame structure with a wide front porch and a warmth that had welcomed her home for three years.

She hummed her acknowledgment. "The previous owner had a big family and needed all four bedrooms. Clay and I kinda rattled around in all the extra space. We used the spare rooms for storage mostly."

Fresh pain squeezed her heart. She and Clay had planned to fill the bedrooms with their own children, had dreamed of outgrowing the house as their family multiplied.

Pete slowed to take a long look at the Bar None homestead. "Sweet digs. And you gave it up for a tiny apartment in the city?"

She gave him a withering glance. "We got divorced. Remember?"

"Ever miss the wide-open land and smell of horse manure? Or does the glamour of big-city life and crime solving fill the void?" His tone was teasing, but Pete's jibe touched a nerve.

Tamara scowled. "I've seen enough. Let's go."

The realization that she missed a lot of things about the Bar None caught her by surprise. The night she'd left Clay, she couldn't get away from the ranch fast enough.

But she missed the fresh air, the solitude, the animals…and Clay.

She huffed and shook her head. Fine. She admitted it. She missed her ex.

That didn't mean she was ready to run back to him and beg for a second chance. Nothing had changed between them. He was still a dedicated rancher, and she had her life, her work, her dreams that pointed her in a different direction.

As they bounced down the gravel driveway toward the old farm-to-market road into Esperanza proper, Tamara noticed the foals in the fields, the abundant supply of hay in the barn, the fleet of farm equipment, the full stables. Signs of prosperity and success.

Clay had his dream. His ranch was thriving. Bittersweet pride swelled in her chest. As happy as she was for Clay, she wondered if he ever regretted the costs of building the ranch. Did he ever miss the early days, miss their marriage? Miss *her?*

Chances were, she'd never know.

Clay climbed into the saddle and turned Crockett toward the main stable.

Thanks to finding the stolen car, he was well behind schedule for the day.

He didn't know what bothered him more, the evidence that a violent crime had taken place on his property or the reappearance of his ex-wife in his life. One could mean trouble for the ranch, the other could stir up past events better left alone. As a kid, Clay had learned the hard way what happened when you poked a hornet's nest. The summer after first grade, he'd spent two weeks recovering from that foolish bit of boyhood curiosity. His divorce from Tamara was still too fresh in his memory to dwell on the could-have-beens.

Still, he sighed. Having Tamara at the ranch again had felt natural. As if five years and countless lonely nights didn't stand between them.

He gave Crockett a pat on the neck. "You sure seemed glad

to see her. Bet you thought she had some of those sweet treats she used to spoil you with, didn't you?"

Clay sat straighter in the saddle and rolled his stiff shoulders. The simple joy that had filtered across Tamara's face when she'd recognized Crockett and patted the bay gelding made his breath lodge in his throat. Tamara's love of animals had been one of the reasons he fell for her, one of the reasons he'd believed she'd be happy on the ranch.

One of the reasons she ended up heartbroken. One of the reasons they'd fought the night she left. What would she think if she knew how much it had hurt him to have Quinn put down his prize stallion?

Clay shook his head and scoffed. There he went poking that hornet's nest again.

As they crested the rise at the north end of the main pasture, Crockett saw the shady barn where his evening hay and cool water waited. The bay picked up his pace.

Clay was just as eager to get a cold shower and a hot meal. But before he could call it a day, he had animals to feed and groom, stalls to clean, and financial reports to review. Hired hands helped with the daily chores and a part-time housekeeper cooked for him three nights a week, but ranching still filled every waking hour. Many times those hours extended late into the night if a horse got sick or a mare was ready to foal. Clay couldn't complain, though. Ranching was his life, his passion.

He thought again of the blood Tamara had found on the stolen Taurus and the huge sum of unclaimed money. A chill skated down his spine. Whatever seedy events had happened under the mesquites by the Black Creek ravine, Clay would make damn sure the ripples couldn't touch his ranch. Since Tamara had left him, the Bar None was all he had.

Tamara carefully transferred the partial fingerprint they'd lifted from the trunk to a slide and sent the image to the main computer for analysis. She wasn't holding her breath for a match, but she'd been surprised by what her tests had revealed in the past.

Forensics was a science. Her tests revealed facts and scientific data that had to be reviewed objectively. No amount of hoping the print would lead them to a suspect would change what the computer analysis told her was the cold truth.

Never mind that the crime scene was on Clay's land. Still, the notion that a heinous crime could have happened so close to where her ex slept at night made the fine hair on her neck stand up.

Tamara clicked a few computer keys. The hard drive whirred softly as the program searched local and state police databases for a match on the print. The familiar hum was comforting. Her lab was a safe haven of sorts. She was in her element here, where her logical mind could have free rein and her tender heart was never at risk of being broken. Statistics, patterns and chemical elements provided basic certainties with no room for emotional entanglement. At day's end, she could set a case aside like shedding a pair of latex gloves. No fuss, no muss. No heartache if things didn't work out as you'd hoped.

Not like her years of working the ranch with Clay, where a foal might be stillborn or a case of colic could be fatal or a prize stud could be put down in the name of business.

Tamara rocked back in the desk chair and propped her feet on the drawer. She watched the computer screen click through images, making mathematical analyses, comparing patterns and probabilities.

Numbers. Safe, unemotional numbers.

*Tee, I have a business to run. Even if we could save Lone Star, the treatment would be expensive. He's contagious, and I can't afford for any other horses to get sick.*

Her breath caught, and she slammed her feet back to the floor as she sat up.

For Clay, ranching had been about the numbers.

Her heart performed a tuck and roll. Maybe she and her ex-husband weren't so different after all. Was it possible Clay relied on the numbers, based his decisions on business models because they provided a distance, a safety net for the difficult decisions when a beloved horse was at stake? Was he trying to protect himself from the pain of loss inherent to the business of horse ranching?

Didn't she purposely refuse to think of the evidence she gathered in terms of the people who were involved, the lives taken, and the families shattered by the crimes?

Her computer beeped, telling her its work was done and calling her out of her musings. Rattled by her new insights about Clay's attitude toward ranching, her hand shook as she rolled the mouse to review the results lighting the screen.

Shoes scuffed on the floor behind her, and Eric stepped up to review the fingerprint analysis over her shoulder.

"You get a match?"

Tamara scanned the report. "No. The print's not in the state database."

Her boss sighed and rocked back on his heels. "Got anything on the carpet fibers?"

She spun the chair to face him and folded her arms over her chest. "Yeah. The color is called *basic beige.* It's an inexpensive brand sold by most do-it-yourself home stores and used widely by the construction company that built three-fourths of the new homes in Esperanza in the past twenty years. No help there."

Eric skewed his lips to the side as he thought. "How many homes could have been built in a podunk town the size of Esperanza?"

She grunted her offense. "Hey, I grew up in Esperanza, remember?"

"And you told me you couldn't get out of that two-horse town fast enough, if I remember correctly."

He was right. In high school, she'd been itching to shake the dust of Esperanza from her feet and head to New York or Chicago. But once she'd married Clay, she'd revised her plans for a while. She'd have been happy living in Esperanza with Clay until her golden years, if only...

She squelched the thought before it fully formed.

"I'll have you know, Esperanza had a boom of new houses in the early '90s. Surrounding towns did, too. The guy made a mint building small, affordable homes for the families who wanted the rural life and to be within easy driving distance of San Antonio."

Eric raised a hand. "Okay, so more than five houses with this carpet?"

"Way more. Try ninety to a hundred, if you count the surrounding towns and do-it-yourselfers." Tamara turned back to the computer and clicked a few keys. "I also found nothing on the red hair from the passenger seat. DNA breakdown for it and the blood from the driver's door won't be ready for a while yet. A batch of samples from the Walters case got in before us."

Tamara frowned. "I can't help but think we missed something. I was careful, and I double-checked everything, but…where's all the evidence? The scene was just too clean."

"You can always go back out to Esperanza and take another look. Head down to impound and check the car again. Maybe without your ex-husband watching your every move, you'll find something you didn't notice before."

Tamara snapped her gaze up to Eric's. "Clay didn't— I wasn't—"

"Save your breath. I saw how you looked at each other." Eric headed for the laboratory door. "Just don't let your feelings for your ex get in the way of this case."

She squared her shoulders, pricked by the implication that she still cared for Clay, that she was less than professional in her approach to her job.

Her boss turned when he reached the door. "Go back to Esperanza tomorrow and widen the search grid. I'll sweep the Taurus again and take Pete with me, so be sure to have one of the department cameras with you when you go."

"Right." Tamara swallowed hard. Being close to Clay and her old home had been hard enough the first time.

Maybe she could do her search without alerting Sheriff Yates or Clay. If she found anything significant, she'd call Jericho. If

she were lucky, she wouldn't have to face Clay at all. She hoped
not anyway. Her heart stung badly enough from their unexpected
encounter today.

The next morning, Tamara drove across the drought-parched
pasture at the far end of the Bar None and headed for the
mesquite trees near the Black Creek ravine. After parking her
Accord, Tamara climbed out and lifted a hand to shield her eyes
from the bright sun. She swept her gaze around the field. What
had she missed? The department's camera in hand, she headed
toward the stand of trees where the Taurus had been found. From
there she could fan out, searching in a methodical way, dividing
the land with a grid and going section by section.

After two hours of the tedious work, with little to show for
her efforts, Tamara had reached the edge of the Black Creek
ravine. She thought of Clay, striding up from the ravine yesterday when she'd sought him out for questioning. With his dark
good looks, cool control and muscled body, he personified the
rugged, larger-than-life attitude that made Texas famous.

The trill of her cell phone roused her from her wandering
thoughts.

She checked her caller ID and pressed the answer button.
"Hi, Eric. What's up?"

"You still in Esperanza?"

"Yeah. Why?" She nudged a rock with her toe then moved on,
her gaze sweeping slowly left to right and back again.

"Just wondering how much longer you think you'll be."

"Well, it stays daylight until almost 9:00 p.m., so I'd say I have
eight or nine more workable hours." She lifted a corner of her
mouth, picturing her boss's face.

"The scary thing is, I'm not so sure you're kidding." Eric
groaned. "Don't get me wrong. I love your work ethic. But I don't
need you running yourself down, wearing yourself out. I need
you mentally and physically sharp."

"I just don't want to leave until I'm sure I've covered every-thing this time. I should be finished in a couple hours."

"Well, you got anything yet?"

She sighed. "Nothing that looks promising."

When she finished the call with Eric, Tamara snapped her phone closed and cast an encompassing gaze around the area. Had she made the search grid large enough this time? Was she overlooking something?

As she walked the grid, she flipped her phone open again, and using her thumb, she punched in Pete's number in the photo lab. 5-5-5-3-0—

Suddenly the earth gave way beneath her.

Tamara gasped. Her phone flew from her hand as her arms windmilled and she scrambled to catch herself. The cave-in sucked her down, and she landed with a jarring thud. Terror welled in her throat as gritty dust filled her lungs and scratched her eyes. Raising an arm to protect her head, she winced as dirt and rock pelted her.

When the world stopped shifting, Tamara lifted her head, shook the loose dirt from her. She coughed out dust, and her chest spasmed. Searing pain arced through her torso, stealing her breath. She lay still for a moment, letting the fire in her ribs subside and collecting her wits.

Grit abraded her watering eyes. Blinking hard to clear her vision, she moved slowly, checking herself one limb at a time for broken bones. Every movement made her chest throb. She grimaced. Cracked ribs. Maybe worse.

Adrenaline pulsed through her. Hands shaking, she tried to calm herself without breathing deeply, which would only fill her lungs with more grit. As the dust settled and she could draw clearer air, the putrid smell of rotting flesh assailed her. She wrinkled her nose and squinted in the dim light. How far had she fallen? The sinkhole she'd landed in seemed to be six or seven feet deep. Like a grave.

She shuddered and quickly shoved aside the chilling thought.

Stay calm. Think. Clay and his ranch hands were too far away to hear her call for help. Her cell phone was—

She groped in the darkness, digging with her fingers through the soil and rock.

Fresh streaks of hot pain sliced through her when she moved. Tamara bit down on her lip and rode out the throbbing waves and ensuing nausea. Climbing out of this hole and driving to Clay's house was going to hurt like hell, but what choice did she have?

Holding her ribs, she shifted to her knees. A moan rumbled from her throat, and she gritted her teeth in agony. Before she tried pushing to her feet, she ran her hand over the dirt one more time, searching for her cell phone. She stretched as far as she could and found nothing but hot, crumbled earth. She crawled forward a bit, deeper into the shadows, and again shifted her fingers through the dusty debris.

Her hand bumped up against something large and heavy. When she tentatively brushed her hand along the object, she found it soft, like fabric. Or clothing.

Foreboding rippled through her.

She fished in her pocket for her keys, where she kept a small light on the fob to help her find the ignition switch at night. The bright LED light illuminated a tiny portion of the sinkhole. Holding her breath, she held the light toward the object.

And screamed.

Lying face down, mere inches from where she'd landed, was a man's dead and decaying body.

# Chapter 4

Tamara struggled to regain her composure, find her professional detachment. She'd seen enough corpses through her job to stomach the grisly sight and even tolerate the smell to an extent. But the shock of finding the body so unexpectedly, the eerie shadows her key-ring light cast, having nearly fallen on top of the dead man…

She swallowed the sour taste that rose in her throat. Clenching her teeth to endure the sharp pain, she pulled herself to her feet. Her fingers scrabbled for purchase to climb out of the pit. By using the toes of her shoes to dig footholds, she managed to pull herself out of the sinkhole, one excruciating inch at a time.

Overwhelmed by the pain, the stench of death, the horror of what had happened to her, she braced on shaky hands and knees and retched—which sent fresh paroxysms of pain through her chest. The unforgiving Texas sun beat down on her and made her head swoon. Common sense warned her she had to get to her car, had to get out of the heat, had to get help for her injuries.

She had to report finding the dead man.

She shuddered.

*A body.*

The driver of the stolen car? Maybe. But if so, who put him down in that hole?

After struggling to her car, holding her aching ribs as still as possible, Tamara drove slowly toward the ranch's main house. The idea of facing Clay again hurt almost as much as the jarring bumps and jolts of the uneven pasture and pothole-riddled driveway.

She blasted her horn as she approached the house. Within moments, two irritated ranch hands stalked toward her car, shouting for her to quit honking. Others looked on, clearly curious about what she wanted. She scanned the approaching ranch workers, looking for the one man she wanted most to see and yet dreaded facing.

Finally she spotted Clay, hurrying through the front door of the white house and crossing the wide porch. A familiar beagle rose from his nap on the porch and romped across the yard at Clay's feet.

Tears of relief pricked her eyes, and she blinked rapidly to force them down. She swore to be strong in front of Clay if it killed her. Gaze fixed on her ex-husband, she waved off the ranch hands when they opened her door and offered her help.

The moment Clay realized who was behind the wheel of the Accord, his gait faltered for a second. His irritated scowl morphed into a look of shock then concern. He sprinted the remaining distance to her driver's side door.

Pushing aside one of his workers, he squatted in the *V* of the open car door. "Tamara, what's wrong? Why—"

"I fell…into a sinkhole. Out by the ravine." She closed her eyes and waited out a new wash of pain.

Clay mumbled a curse. "How bad are you hurt? Can you walk?"

Before she could answer, he shoved to his feet and leaned in to check her. Taking her chin in his fingers, he swept her face with his gaze, then touched a scrape on her temple.

Wincing, she grabbed his wrist to stop his ministrations. "I found a body."

Clay's thick eyebrows dipped, his dark eyes homing in on hers. "A body? Where?"

"In the pit. A man. He's been dead at least a couple days, judging from the stink."

Clay stiffened at the news, barely brushing her chest, but the contact sent a fiery spasm through her. She gasped and gritted her teeth.

"Where are you hurt?" he demanded, snatching his hands away from her.

A prick of self-consciousness filtered through her haze of discomfort. She must look frightful, scratched, bleeding and covered in grime. And after baking in the heat for hours, wallowing in a dirt pit, then dragging herself to her car, she had to be ripe.

By contrast, even breathing shallowly as she was to avoid pain, the aroma of sunshine and leather clung to Clay and filled her nose. Her heart gave a hard thump. So many precious memories were tied to his seductive scent. Memories that now left her emotionally raw.

"I…may have cracked…a rib or two. I can hardly…breathe. It hurts…every time I move—"

"Can you walk or should I carry you inside?"

Just getting to her car had hurt like hell. She was tempted to let him carry her, but she hated to seem needy. "I can walk."

"Hobo, get back," he told the beagle, who stuck his nose inside the car to greet the ranch's visitor.

Tamara smiled through her pain at the sight of the mutt, her old friend. She held her fingers out for him to sniff and scratched his head. "Hi, boy."

Clay placed a hand under her elbow to steady her as she rose slowly, stiffly from the car. New aches from the tumble into the pit assaulted her. Muscles cramped, joints ached, scrapes throbbed.

She hobbled a few steps and couldn't stop the groan that escaped her dry lips.

"That's it," Clay said and carefully lifted her into his arms.

She clutched the shirt at his shoulder when pain ripped though her chest. "No, Clay, I—I'm okay." She stopped to suck air in through her teeth. "Really. L-let me down."

He scoffed. "You can barely stand, much less walk."

"But if I move slowly, I can—"

"Don't argue." His penetrating espresso gaze silenced her.

Cradling her ribs, she rested her cheek on the soft cotton of his shirt. Being this close to him again stole her breath. Feeling the power of his arms around her, hearing the thud of his heart left her a bit dizzy. With Hobo barking excitedly at his feet, he strode with smooth quick steps, mindful not to jostle her, and soon had her in the blissful air-conditioning of his house.

He bypassed the living and dining rooms, heading straight down the long hall, through the kitchen and into the family room at the back of the house.

"Marie!" Clay called as he settled her on a cool leather couch.

A Mexican woman came out of the laundry room and appeared in the kitchen. "*Sí*, Mr. Clay?"

"I need the hydrogen peroxide and a damp cloth."

Tamara met the woman's startled expression and gave her a strained smile.

The woman pressed a hand to her cheek and hurried closer. "Oh, my! What happened?"

"I fell in some kind of sinkhole…out in the south pasture." She opted to leave out the detail about the dead body until the sheriff had a chance to investigate.

Clay made quick introductions between Tamara and his housekeeper. If the woman found it odd that Clay's ex-wife had been hanging around one of his pastures, she hid it well.

Tamara winced as she tried to find a more comfortable position.

Marie waved a hand toward her. "Mr. Clay, she needs to see a doctor. She's hurting."

Clay unclipped his cell phone and started dialing. "I know. I'm calling Doc Mason right now."

The older woman shook her head. "But Doc Mason is not here. He went on vacation, I heard."

Clay scowled and closed his phone. "Vacation? Doc never takes vacation. It's hard enough to get him to take off a day to go fishing."

Marie shrugged then hurried toward the hall bathroom.

"Clay, we have to call Jericho…about the body I found," she whispered so Marie wouldn't overhear.

"I will. First I need to make sure *you're* okay. If Doc is out of town, I'll have to call an ambulance, but the nearest one could still take almost an hour to get you to a hospital."

He stroked his stubbled cheeks, and the scrape of his callused palms on the bristles slid over her like a lover's caress. She knew so well the sandpapery scratch of his unshaven chin against her skin, gently abrading her during lovemaking. The sensation was tantalizing, thrilling.

Tamara took a deep breath to clear the erotic memories from her head and was rewarded with a sharp stab from her battered ribs.

Her grunt of discomfort darkened Clay's concerned stare to the shade of midnight. "Try not to move."

She quirked a grin. "Ya think?"

Her attempt at levity bounced off his tense jaw and stress-tightened muscles. He began to pace.

When Marie returned with the cloth and antiseptic, she sat on the edge of the couch and began dabbing the scrapes on Tamara's face. "Call the clinic," she said. "There is a doctor filling in for Doc Mason, I think."

Clay's eyebrows lifted, and hope lit his eyes.

His housekeeper nodded. "That's what I heard at Miss Sue's. Everyone was as surprised as you."

The mention of the local diner brought a smile to Tamara's face. "Gossip central. Is the pecan pie there still as good as it used to be?"

Clay gave Tamara a worried frown, as if her interest in the best pie in Texas were a sign of head injury. Flipping open his cell, he punched redial. His concern for her both touched her and chafed her independence. In their marriage, Clay's take-charge, assume-all-responsibility mode of operation had always been a mixed blessing.

Once arrangements had been made to meet the doctor on call at the Esperanza clinic and Clay had her settled in his pickup, Tamara shifted her attention once more to what she felt was a more pressing issue.

The dead man on Clay's property.

She borrowed Clay's phone as he drove her to town and called Sheriff Yates.

After Jericho assured her he'd start an immediate recovery and investigation of the body, she inquired what he'd learned about the money.

"Nothing yet. The serial numbers didn't turn anything up," Jericho said. "None of the banks in the area have a record of a withdrawal of that size or any other unusual activity. I'm checking the rest of the state now, but so far that money's proving a dead end."

The truck hit a bump, and she inhaled sharply.

Clay winced. "Sorry. No way to miss 'em all on this road."

"Tamara, is something wrong?" Jericho asked.

"Did I mention *how* I found the body?" She explained about her fall and that Clay was taking her to the medical clinic in town.

"Ouch. Broken ribs are a bear. Sorry 'bout that." She heard another voice in the background, heard Jericho reply. "Well, we're headed out to the Bar None now. I'll keep you posted."

"For the time being, you'll have to reach me on Clay's cell." She gritted her teeth as they lurched over another pothole. "But if you find my cell at the scene, I'd appreciate getting it back."

"Sure thing. Take care, Tamara."

When they reached Doc Mason's clinic in Esperanza, Clay helped her out of his truck and into the wheelchair a nurse brought out. He parked the wheelchair in the waiting room and walked up to the desk to check her in.

Tamara was grousing to herself about take-charge Clay's

latest crusade when the clinic door opened and a familiar blond-haired man walked in from the street. He slipped off his sun-glasses and headed straight for the front desk.

"Billy? Billy Akers?" Tamara asked.

Her longtime family friend and former neighbor turned, and when he spotted Tamara, his face lit with an effusive grin. "Well, I'll be! Tamara the Brat! How are you?"

She smiled at his use of the nickname he and her older brother had given her growing up. Billy, who still had the build of a line-backer from his high-school days, hurried over to her and bent to give her a hug.

Tamara held up a hand to stop him. "Oh, uh…don't squeeze." She winced and pointed to her midriff. "Possibly broken ribs."

Scrunching his freckled nose, Billy made an appropriately sympathetic face. "Yikes. What happened?"

She waved his question off. "Long story. Gosh, it's good to see you. It's been years. How are your parents?"

Billy's face fell. "Well…not so good. Mama's been diag-nosed with ALS…Lou Gehrig's disease."

"Oh, no!" Grief for the woman who'd been like a second mother to her and her brother plucked Tamara's heart.

"Seeing her suffering has been hard. Especially on Dad."

Tamara took Billy's hand in hers and squeezed it. "I can imagine. Oh, Billy, please give her my best. Tell her I'll be praying for her."

"I will." He hitched a thumb toward the front desk. "In fact, I'm here to refill one of her prescriptions." When he spotted Clay at the counter, a speculative gleam sparked in Billy's eyes. "Are you here with Clay? Does this mean you two are—" He wagged a finger from Clay to Tamara.

She shook her head. "No, nothing like that."

When she saw her denial hadn't satisfied his curiosity, she tried to work out the simplest explanation that would stave off the rumormongers. "I was on his property when I fell, and his house was the closest help."

"Why were you on his property? I thought you lived in San Antonio now."

"I do. I—" She sighed, then gave him a watered-down version of the truth. Knowing this town, word had probably already spread about the Taurus being found at the Bar None. "So I was looking around his south pasture and…*boom,* fell in a sinkhole. Thus the possibly broken ribs."

A bit of the color leeched from Billy's face. "You fell in a *hole?*"

She flashed a chagrined smile. "Klutzy me."

Clay strolled over and stuck out his hand toward Billy. "How ya doing, Akers?"

Billy shook hands with Clay. "I'm…uh, fine. You?"

"Good." Her ex shifted his gaze to her. "They're ready for you."

Billy excused himself, promising to give her regards to his parents and offering well wishes for Tamara's speedy recovery.

As Clay rolled her to the exam room, Tamara grinned. "That's a small town for you. Can't go anywhere without running into a neighbor or a lady from church or your parents' bowling partners."

"Which is why we always drove away from town for our dates in high school."

"Dates? You mean when we went parking." She wished she could recall the words as soon as she said them. No point reminding Clay of the car windows they'd steamed…or the first time they'd made love.

"Yeah. That's what I meant." His voice had a thick seductive rasp that told her those memories still affected him. Her pulse stuttered. Maybe he hadn't totally wiped her from his life after all.

Doc Mason's nurse, Ellen Hamilton, stuck her head into the hall from an exam room a couple doors down. "Right in here, Ms. Brown." After Clay wheeled Tamara into the exam room, the petite gray-haired woman laid out a sheet and a paper gown. "Would you like help changing out of your clothes, honey?"

Tamara tried to push herself out of the wheelchair and fiery needles stabbed her chest. She muffled a moan. Instantly Clay tucked his arms under hers, lifting her and helping her to the exam table.

Tamara glanced to the nurse. "Yeah. I think I'll need help."

"Fine." Ellen turned to Clay, her expression patient.

Unmindful of the nurse's stare, Clay took Tamara's foot in his hand and unlaced her shoe. After sliding it from her foot, he moved to the next shoe.

Tamara was so stunned at his presumptuousness that she could only gawk. When he gave her foot a soft rub, her breath snagged in a hiss of surprise.

Foot massages after a full day tending the ranch had been one of Tamara's greatest pleasures when they were married, a relaxation treat that often led to full body contact, clothes shed, lusty appetites sated.

Clay's eyes locked with hers, and he grimaced. "Sorry. I was trying to be gentle."

She started to tell him the gasp hadn't been one of pain, but the nurse cleared her throat.

"I meant that *I'd* help her change." Now her expression was challenging. She lifted a sculpted eyebrow and tipped her head toward the door.

Her ex-husband wasn't stupid and wasn't easily cowed. He straightened his spine and set his jaw in a manner that Tamara knew well. He had no intention of backing down.

Tamara almost laughed at the standoff, until she realized that Clay thought he still had a right to be in the exam room with her, that it was natural for him to help her change into the hospital gown. A warm swirl of nostalgia flowed through Tamara followed closely by a shot of irritation.

Clay had lost any claim to such marital intimacies when he signed their divorce papers without blinking, without so much as a tremble of his hand. She, on the other hand, had been shaking so badly she barely recognized the signature she'd scratched as hers.

And now he wanted those privileges of familiarity back? She didn't know whether to laugh or cry.

"Would you please step outside, Mr. Colton?" Ellen Hamilton asked.

A muscle in Clay's jaw twitched. He raised his chin, his eyes determined.

"Clay." His name squeezed past the lump of regret that clogged her throat.

He snapped his rich coffee gaze to hers, and the stubborn glint faded, replaced by a wounded expression, a chagrined acceptance that plucked at her heart. He hid it well. Someone who didn't know Clay and his take-no-prisoners attitude, his stubborn cowboy pride, would have missed it. But Clay had been her husband, half the blood and breath that made her whole. An ache wholly unrelated to her injuries pulsed through her chest.

He ducked his chin in a quick jerky nod of understanding and concession that broke Tamara's heart. "I'll be in the waiting room when you're ready to go."

He left without a backward glance, and the room seemed infinitely colder and more lifeless with him gone.

A moment later, a lean man in his late forties with thinning dark hair stepped into the room and shook Tamara's hand. "Ms. Brown, I'm Frank O'Neal, Dr. Mason's fill-in. I hear you took a nasty tumble."

"You heard right."

The doctor flashed a polite smile. "Well, let's see about getting you all fixed up."

Over the next hour, Dr. O'Neal X-rayed and examined Tamara from head to heel. He taped her ribs, gave her injections for pain and to relax her cramping muscles, all of which made it far easier for her to move unassisted. While the X-rays developed, she redressed by herself, though the process wore her out.

She sat in the exam room alone, remembering Clay's earlier hurt expression, when the sound of raised voices filtered through the door left cracked open.

Concerned that something was wrong, Tamara strained to hear the exchange between Ellen Hamilton and Dr. O'Neal.

"How long…—azine…missing…" Dr. O'Neal groused.

"I don't know." The nurse who'd stood up to Clay sounded shaken.

"…your job to…any idea…hell we could catch if…missing?"

"…well aware…accounting of…narcotic. Doc Mason always…himself."

"Have any…—peared before?"

The nurse's answer was too quiet for Tamara to make out.

The scuff of hard-soled shoes drew closer then hesitated just outside the exam-room door. Tamara looked up, and through the narrow opening, she met the doctor's shaken gaze. The man's brow furrowed, and he rubbed a hand over the nearly bald spot on his head. Appearing agitated, he glanced away for a moment before schooling his expression and entering the exam room.

He plunked two bottles of pills on the exam table and gave Tamara a tight grin. "I want you to take one of these every four to six hours when you need them for pain. The other is a muscle relaxant. Since people react differently to this medicine, it'd be wise for you to have someone stay with you while you recuperate."

She studied the bottle of pills. "I occasionally get migraines. These won't trigger a headache, will they?"

He shook his head. "Shouldn't. This is one of the best pain meds on the market. However some people report getting sleepy, some get loopy, some feel a little dizzy."

Clearly the man didn't want to acknowledge that she'd overheard his heated discussion with his nurse. Tamara took the hint and dismissed the issue.

Dr. O'Neal shoved his hands in his lab coat's pockets. "Do you have a roommate?"

"No. I live alone in San Antonio."

A knock sounded on the door before it was opened. Clay peered into the room. "Ms. Hamilton said to come back, that you were ready to go?"

The doctor nodded. "I was just telling Ms. Brown that the prescription I've given her for pain could make her sleepy or one of several other side effects. She needs to get plenty of rest and to have someone with her for the next couple days until she knows how her body reacts to the meds."

Clay nodded. "She can stay with me."

Tamara shot him a startled glance. "No, Clay, I couldn't… I—"

"I could admit you to the hospital for observation if you'd rather." Dr. O'Neal gave her a teasing grin, but also arched an eyebrow, telling her the threat wasn't idle.

"No, I—"

"Good. Make sure she takes it easy," Dr. O'Neal said with a nod to Clay. "And I'd like to check in with you again in a couple days to see how you're doing."

Holding his Stetson, Clay fiddled with the brim. "When do you expect Doc Mason back?"

The doctor glanced up from scribbling a note on Tamara's chart. "Not sure. He didn't give us a time frame. Just said he needed to get away for a while."

Clay cocked his head. "Well, good for the Doc. He's sure earned a vacation. Can't say I remember the last time he took off longer than an afternoon to fish."

The nurse bustled in with Tamara's X-rays and clipped them on the light board.

Dr. O'Neal stepped over to study the images. "Well, I don't see any fractures. All in all, I'd say you were quite lucky to walk away from a fall like that with no more than bruised ribs and some superficial lacerations. If you take it easy over the next few days, limit your activity and take your muscle relaxants, you should make a full recovery in a couple weeks."

Tamara thanked the doctor, paid the bill, and soon she and Clay were headed back to the ranch.

Staring at her hands as they drove, she considered Clay's invitation to recover at the Bar None. He hadn't so much asked her as declared that was how it would be. Did he really want her there? Or was he motivated by guilt and responsibility because she'd fallen on his property? Either way, sharing the same roof with Clay, even if just for a few days, would be awkward at best.

"Clay, I—" When his dark brown eyes met hers, her argument drowned in their fathomless depths. She fought the mule-kick loss of breath. "I…think I'll be fine at my place in San Antonio. I appreciate the offer, but—"

His brow lowered. "You have someone in the city who can stay with you?"

"Well, no."

"You heard the doctor. You need rest and someone to keep tabs on you."

"I know, but—"

Clay's cell trilled, cutting her off.

"Hello? Hey, Jericho." Clay glanced at Tamara. "Yeah, she's with me. We're headed home from Doc Mason's clinic. Why?" When he frowned, Tamara's pulse kicked up. She didn't need more bad news.

"Maybe. Let me ask her." Clay held the phone against his chest. "Feel up to a short side trip by the south field? Jericho is out there with Deputy Rawlings, and they haven't found the body you saw. They need you to show them where it is."

The injection she'd gotten for pain at the doctor's office was already making her drowsy, but she had a duty to her job and to the deceased man's family. She stroked a hand over her taped ribs. "Sure. I can manage."

Ten minutes later, she and Clay were standing with Jericho and Deputy Rawlings beside the sinkhole. The sheriff shook his head. "We've been down with searchlights. Turns out this hole is an offshoot cave from the old tunnel Clay and I used to play in when we were kids."

"A tunnel? For what?" Tamara asked.

Clay shrugged. "Don't know what it used to be, but the tunnel's been there for decades. When I bought the ranch, I put barbed wire across the entrance of the tunnel so none of my horses would wander in there and get stuck."

"The point is, ma'am," Rawlings said, narrowing a look at Tamara that suggested he thought she'd lost her mind. "Sheriff and I have been all up and down the passages of the tunnel, and there's no body in there."

All three men turned toward her. She bristled. "I saw the body myself! I touched it, not more than four hours ago!"

She shuddered at the memory.

The sheriff looked skeptical. "Did you hit your head when you went down?"

"There *was* a body, Jericho!" Nausea swirled in her gut. Did they think she was lying? Or hallucinating?

"I'm sure you were in shock," Jericho said. "Maybe—"

"No maybes, Jericho." His shoulders squared and stiff, Clay took a step closer to her side. "If Tamara says there was a body, there was a body."

Her protest stuck in her throat. She turned to Clay, wide-eyed, her mind reeling, her heart full. They'd been on opposite sides of so many issues in the final months of their marriage, she'd grown used to butting heads with this stubborn man. Having him back up her story, believe her on something as important as this, touched her deeply, warmed her soul.

Suspicion furrowed tiny creases at the corner of Clay's eyes. "The only real questions here are who moved the body…and why."

# *Chapter 5*

Tamara limped across Clay's family room and eased her throbbing body onto one of the leather sofas. Fatigue bore to her bones. The painkiller dulled the ache, but her muscles were stiff and sudden movement sliced rippling pain through her abdomen. As the prescription kicked in, her body begged for rest and her eyes screamed for sleep. But restless thoughts zinged through her brain.

Where was the dead man she'd found in the tunnel? Was it possible she'd imagined the body, as Rawlings had suggested?

She shook her head to clear the medicated haze. *No!* Her hands had touched cloth. She had smelled decaying flesh. She had seen the partially buried corpse.

Someone had moved the dead man. But who?

Her CSI team would vindicate her. Even now they were searching the tunnel, looking for hairs, blood or tissue to substantiate her claim and try to identify the victim. With luck they'd also find footprints or drag marks showing the body had been moved.

Clay carried two glasses from the large farm-style kitchen and set one on the wagon-wheel coffee table in front of her. "Marie says she made a fruit salad to go with dinner, but you can have some now if you're hungry."

"No, thanks." Tamara sipped her drink. Sweet tea with lemon, just the way she liked it. Clay had remembered.

She closed her eyes and battled the swell of bittersweet emotion the simple kindness stirred. Though stress and the effect of the painkiller had her on edge, she couldn't allow herself to lose it.

Of course he'd remember her favorite drink. They'd been intimately connected since high school, mind, body and soul. He'd have to be thickheaded to forget such a basic preference. Clay was anything but stupid. His slow gait and laid-back manner belied the razor-sharp mind that clicked behind those dark eyes.

"You should go to bed. You've had a rough day." Clay sat on the opposite couch.

"Not until I hear back from my team." She huffed her frustration. "I should be out there. This was my case."

Clay arched an eyebrow and shot her a skeptical look. "You're in no condition to work."

"I know but—" She balled her fists and sighed, trying find the words to express how the waiting killed her, how she hated starting something she couldn't finish, how the need for answers kept her mind in turmoil.

"But it's hard to rest up here when your heart and mind are down at that tunnel with your team," Clay finished for her matter-of-factly.

She blinked, her stomach flip-flopping. "Yeah. Exactly. How did you know?"

He shrugged and took a long swallow of his iced tea. "It's hard for me to delegate, too. I have to be hands-on with anything that matters."

She curled up her mouth. "I remember. It's called being a control freak."

His brow creased. "I'm not a control freak."

"Are you kidding me?" she sputtered. "Control freak is putting it mildly. You're hyperresponsible and a workaholic, too. You're talking to your ex-wife. I *know* you."

"Maybe. But people can change."

Tamara leaned back against the sofa. "Have you?"

He stared down at his boots for a moment before he spoke. "I see the world differently now. I understand what matters, what doesn't." He glanced at her. "That's what changes. A person's beliefs. And beliefs, convictions are what drive decisions."

So what mattered to Clay now? Where did his convictions lie? The questions begged answers, but they stuck in her throat.

Asking would imply that she still cared, still wanted to know what made this man tick. She couldn't risk putting any more of herself on the line than necessary. Being in these familiar surroundings, around so many people and places that evoked heartbreaking memories was difficult enough.

Instead, she flipped open Clay's cell phone, which he'd given her to babysit until she found or replaced hers. No messages. She closed the phone and sighed.

"They'll call when they know something." Clay pushed away from his couch and crossed to the one where she sat. He took the phone from her. "Go lie down. I'll wake you if there's news."

"I'm too antsy to sleep." A giant yawn escaped, calling her on the lie.

"Tee, you're dead on your feet, all banged up, and under doctor's orders to rest. Don't be stubborn." He took her hand and pulled her gently to her feet.

Her head spun. From Clay's touch or the dizzying effect of her pain medicine? She closed her eyes and held on to Clay's shoulders until the light-headedness passed. When she looked up, she met his concerned gaze.

"Tee, you all right?"

"Yeah, it's just the drugs. I see now why Dr. O'Neal advised me to have someone around. This stuff packs a punch." She blinked her dry, scratchy eyes.

"You can nap upstairs as long as you want. If you need

anything, use the intercom and Marie or I will get it. Don't attempt the stairs on your own while you're still under the influence, so to speak. Okay?"

She heard Clay, but his words seemed to travel through water. Her head felt stuffed with cotton, and her eyelids drooped. "Yeah, I promise. No stairs. I…" She stifled another yawn. "I could just sleep on the couch here. I don't need—"

"Don't be silly. You can have my bed."

"Your—" Clay swept her into his arms before she could protest, before her dulled reflexes could respond.

"There's junk piled on the guest bed. Mine's the only one made up right now." Clay's strong arms anchored her close as he started for the stairs in the main hallway.

Clay's bed? Her heart pattered, and a spurt of adrenaline briefly cleared the haze muddling her mind. *Their* bed, he meant. The one they'd bought with the proceeds of his first horse auction. The bed where they'd slept for three years, nursed illnesses, and made love countless times.

Was he trying to make this convalescence harder on her?

She struggled to organize her thoughts as the painkiller numbed her mind. "Clay, wait. I don't think this is a good idea."

"Marie changed the sheets this morning." He climbed the stairs smoothly, without breaking his pace or sounding even a tad winded, despite her added weight.

"No, that's not what—"

He ducked into the first room on the right and lowered her onto the handmade quilt that covered the mattress.

Stretching out on the soft bed, Tamara almost groaned in pleasure. Encroaching sleep suddenly seemed more appealing. The effort to lift her leaden arms seemed daunting, but she was still wearing the dirt-, sweat- and blood-smeared clothes she'd had on when she fell in the sinkhole. No, not a sinkhole. A tunnel.

There was a body. Wasn't there? Her muzzy brain tripped over images and tangled emotions.

"I need to…get out of these…clothes." She plucked awkwardly at the buttons of her blouse. The task seemed almost too taxing as her eyes slid closed.

Clay slid her shoes from her feet and rubbed her tired arches. At the doctor's office… No, he was soothing her feet now. Tamara did moan this time as Clay's strong, talented fingers worked the ache from her heels, her toes…

Bliss.

After stripping off her shoes and socks, Clay massaged Tamara's foot. The bruises on her arms and the scrapes on her face were a chilling reminder of how lucky she'd been not to have been hurt far worse.

He was relieved to see her color returning. When he'd driven her to the doctor's office, her face had been frighteningly pale, evidence of her pain. Pain he'd have gladly endured for her if he could have. Frustration and helplessness haunted him.

A shudder started deep in his bones, working outward until his whole body was shaking. When she fell, she could have broken her neck, could have broken a rib and punctured a lung. He could have lost her.

Clay exhaled a slow sigh. Tamara was already lost to him. He'd given up any claim to her the day he let her walk away from their marriage.

He stroked the side of his ex-wife's face, and she angled her head to rest her cheek against his hand. Her brown eyelashes drifted down and fanned her ivory skin like dark lace on silk.

"Thank you, Clay…for being there today," she murmured sleepily.

"No problem, sweetheart."

So he'd driven her to the clinic. Big deal. But where had he been five years ago when she needed him? Why had she thought she'd be happier without him? The failure of their marriage gnawed at his gut. He couldn't change the past, couldn't change the mistakes he'd made or the hurt he'd caused no matter how much he wanted to.

Her wan complexion, the harsh red scrapes on her chin and the shadows under her eyes made her appear fragile. Vulnerable. His Tee would hate to be called either. But as he watched her drift into a drug-induced sleep, his protective instincts surged.

Drawing a ragged breath, Clay withdrew his hand from her cheek, and she whimpered a protest. He surveyed the stained and torn shirt and jeans she was wearing. The least he could do while she slept was wash the blood from her clothes.

"I'm gonna help you get out of these dirty things, okay, Tee?"

She opened her eyes and nodded.

He slid open the top button of her blouse, while she fumbled to unfasten the bottom one. Working his way down, careful not to bump her bruised ribs, he parted her shirt, and the stark white tape binding her ribs came into view. Clay frowned. He'd had injured ribs before when he was thrown from a horse at a rodeo in high school. Hurt like fire.

He'd do everything possible to make Tamara comfortable and her recovery easier. Knowing she was wounded on his property chafed at his sense of duty all the more. The law might say he was no longer her husband, but he couldn't so easily dismiss his obligation to take care of her.

Tamara tugged on her blouse then winced.

"Careful," he whispered. He eased her elbows from the sleeves, admiring the muscle tone in her slim arms. After discarding the soiled shirt, he turned his attention to her bra. The scrappy lace didn't keep many secrets about what lay beneath. Not that he didn't have images of Tamara's rose-tipped breasts burned in his memory.

Still, Clay hesitated. Heat prickled his skin as erotic memories flashed in his mind.

He'd undressed this woman hundreds of times. He knew every inch of her skin, the exact curve of her waist and hips, the feel of her legs wrapped around him.

But he wasn't her husband anymore.

"Now the jeans." Clay unfastened the fly and tugged on the legs to slide them over her hips while she pushed from the waist.

An enticing hum of pleasure rumbled from her throat as the restrictive denim glided from her legs, and Clay had to bite back his own moan. Tamara's legs were every bit as long and shapely as he remembered.

Blood pulsed south as his gaze skimmed up those sexy legs and paused at the pale pink bikini panties. Panties that matched her lacy bra.

"This, too," she mumbled, sliding the bra's straps from her shoulders. "The underwire is poking me. It hurts."

Air snagged in Clay's lungs as he wedged a hand behind her back to unhook her lingerie, drawing him dangerously close to the nearly naked woman on the bed. Desire vibrated in every muscle and heated his blood. When she pulled the unhooked bra away and dropped it at his feet, he almost choked on the groan that rose in his throat.

Her nipples beaded when bared to the cool, air-conditioned bedroom, tempting him to draw them into his mouth and bathe them with his tongue.

Tamara draped an arm around his neck and nuzzled his cheek. "You smell good. Like sunshine."

Clay swallowed hard, keeping a tight rein on his self-control by reminding himself that she was injured and under the influence of medications. He had too much respect for her to take advantage of her condition.

Her fingers tangled in the hair at his nape, and she pressed a warm kiss to his jawline. "You need a haircut," she murmured. "Maybe I could do it later."

Clay gritted his teeth and pulled away from her tantalizing touch. He thought about past trims—Tamara's fingers combing through his hair and massaging his scalp, the glide of cool steel scissors against his neck, and his wife's long legs straddling him as she snipped his bangs. By the time she'd finished, his every nerve ending would be lit like a firecracker and he'd be ready to explode.

No way in hell could he endure that exquisite torture now and keep his sanity.

When she moved her lips to the shell of his ear, he sucked in a sharp breath and backed out of her reach. His self-control was hanging by a thread, ready to snap.

"I'll get you a T-shirt," he rasped and rose from the bed, his own jeans uncomfortably tight. Clay rummaged through his dresser and pulled out a blue cotton shirt for her to sleep in. With the back of his hand, he wiped a cold sweat from his brow and turned back toward the bed.

If he were a gentleman, he supposed, he'd avert his gaze or close his eyes.

But he wasn't feeling especially gentlemanly at the moment. Besides, this was Tamara. His Tee.

Even five years after their divorce he still felt territorial toward her. She'd given her virginity to *him*. Since high school, *he'd* been her husband, her lover, her protector.

So as he walked back to the bed, he drank in the sight of her. Her golden hair spread across his pillow, and he knew tonight it would still hold her honeysuckle scent. He drank in the expanse of silky skin and the graceful curves of her legs. He gazed hungrily at the hollow of her throat, where she loved to get gentle nips.

In his mind, he raked his hands over the swell of her breasts and teased the budded tips with his thumbs. He remembered how kisses at the small of her back would make her sigh and had to grit his teeth to squelch the need that pumped through his veins to hear that breathy moan again. He let his imagination linger at the *V* of her legs where the pink bikini panties hid a place he'd explored well with his hands and his mouth before claiming her in the most intimate way.

Tamara stirred, her hand stroking down her arm as goose bumps prickled her skin.

Clay shook himself from his erotic daydreams. Wary not to hurt her ribs, he helped pull the T-shirt over her head and smooth it into place. Then, taking an afghan from a chair in the corner of the room, he covered her and stepped back.

A bittersweet ache blossomed in his chest. At the same time, she looked both delicate and strong. Innocent and sexy. Familiar and changed. She looked beautiful.

He didn't question the impulse to kiss her forehead before he left her to nap. It felt right. Just as having Tamara in his home, in his bed, in his life again felt right somehow.

Clay chided himself as he closed the door to his room.

*You're being a sentimental fool. She left you once, and when she's healed, she'll leave again.*

Believing anything else would only set himself up for heartache.

Tamara woke when a quiet rap sounded on the bedroom door.

She opened her eyes a slit and needed a second or two to remember where she was. Clay's bedroom.

When she glanced down to check her watch, she noticed her dishabille. Her eyebrows snapped together. She didn't remember changing clothes. She didn't remember much, in fact, after Clay picked her up and carried her.

Clay?

Adrenaline spiked through her as the possibilities unfolded in her brain. Snapshot images of holding him, kissing him, making love to him flashed in her brain. But were they real memories or wisps of a steamy dream?

"Tamara?" The door opened a crack, and Clay moved halfway into the room.

She bolted upright, and a shattering pain streaked through her chest.

"Oh!" Sinking back to the bed, she clutched her ribs and grimaced as the throbbing made black spots swim before her eyes.

Clay hurried to the side of the bed. "Whoa! Take it easy. The doc said to stay still, move slowly until those muscles heal."

"I know," she wheezed. "I just— You startled me."

"Sorry." Clay pushed hair back from her face, and the light brush of his fingers against her cheek made her forget her pain.

"How long was I asleep? And more important, who…undressed me?"

One black eyebrow lifted, and the corner of his mouth twitched. "You don't remember?"

His amusement didn't bode well for her. She closed her eyes. "Oh, no. What'd I do? What'd I say? And remember, I was under the influence of painkillers. You can't hold me to anything."

His hand squeezed hers. "Don't panic. I helped you change, but…nothing happened."

She peeked up at him and saw heat flickering in his eyes.

"Not that I wasn't mighty tempted." His wicked grin made her toes curl.

While she calmed the jangling inside her, she glanced down at the soft T-shirt she was wearing and fingered the hem. Clay's T-shirts had always been her favorite sleepwear. She inhaled the clean, outdoorsy scent that clung to the shirt and smiled. "And my clothes?"

"In the dryer. Not quite good as new, but at least clean again. You're welcome to wear any of my shirts you want, too."

Tamara nodded. "Thanks."

Clay rubbed his hands down the legs of his jeans. "So…I would have let you finish your nap, but…I promised I'd wake you when I had news."

She perked up. "Did my team find something in the tunnel?"

Lips tight, he gave her a jerky nod. "Blood. No report yet on whether it matches the blood from the Taurus."

"No, there wouldn't be so soon. The analysis takes hours at best. Days sometimes." She chewed her bottom lip as she let this information sink in. "So there was a body. I didn't imagine it."

When Clay frowned, she held up her hand to forestall his comment.

"I only mean this vindicates me. That Rawlings guy, Jericho's new deputy, wasn't convinced I hadn't hallucinated the whole thing. Jericho seemed skeptical, too."

*If Tamara says there was a body, there was a body.*

Clay's voluntary and definitive support spun through her again, warming her.

She cleared the sudden thickness from her throat. "Did they find anything else? Anything that might tell us who took the body?"

"Like a signed confession?" He flashed a crooked grin.

She chortled. "If only it were that easy."

Clay shook his head. "Jericho didn't mention anything else… Oh, yeah—except your cell. They found your phone in the hole. Still works. Needs a good cleaning but you should be able to salvage it. Meantime, you can use mine to call your team, if you want."

"Yeah, I think I will."

When Clay rose from the edge of the bed, she paused and caught his gaze. "Wait, I… I wanted to thank you."

He cocked his head. "For?"

"Standing by me today, believing me when the evidence didn't support me. Your faith in me…meant a lot." The piercing quality of his dark stare stole her breath, held her captive for a few staggering beats of her heart.

He said nothing for several seconds, and she tried to interpret the flicker of emotion that sparked in his eyes. When he wanted, Clay could play his feelings so close to his chest, even she had a hard time reading him.

"You had no reason to lie," he said finally and turned for the door.

She knew this tactic of his well. Minimizing an issue that could stir deeper emotions. Glossing over anything that might delve into his softer side. Heaven forbid the tough cowboy, the born leader, Mr. Responsibility-of-the-world-on-his-shoulders let his guard down.

As Clay left the room and closed the door, disappointment plucked at Tamara, and a years-old ache snuck out of hiding to nip at her again. He hadn't dismissed her gratitude…exactly. But he had avoided the meaning behind what he'd done, the importance of it to her. How many times in their marriage had Clay done much the same thing? When she'd raised a concern, Clay had all but patted her on the head and told her not to worry.

Over the years, in subtle ways, she'd gotten a message that had ultimately undermined her happiness and broken her marriage: she wasn't important. Her opinions hadn't mattered. Her wishes had been ignored. Her feelings had been minimized. She'd never felt an equal partner in their marriage, much less in the running of the Bar None.

Of course, Clay was far too kind and considerate to have done any of it on purpose. In fact, when she'd called him on it once, he'd been truly stunned by the suggestion that he was dismissing or undervaluing her. But intentional or not, the distance between them grew until she even doubted whether Clay really loved her.

The night her pleas to try to save Lone Star rather than put him down were ignored, she'd had enough. She'd left Clay to pursue her dreams, build a life for herself where what she wanted mattered.

Clay hadn't changed. She'd be crazy to make the same mistakes again and to lose herself once more in Clay's overpowering shadow.

The soft pad of footsteps on the stairs pulled Clay from his perusal of the Bar None's business records. He looked up from his desk just as Tamara walked into the office.

"What are you doing up?" he said with a mock severity. "You're under doctor's orders to get bed rest, young lady."

Tamara wrapped a lock of her long hair around her finger and sent him a coy grin. He felt his gut somersault like a schoolboy's.

"I'm supposed to rest, but Dr. O'Neal never said it had to be in a bed. I can rest downstairs. Maybe on a sofa in the family room? I was bored up there by myself."

He quirked a grin and pushed back from his desk. "All right. Can I get you anything?"

"I'll take you up on the offer to use your phone. I want to call my lab."

He unclipped his cell from his belt and handed it to her.

Keeping her back straight and a hand on her sore ribs, Tamara sat on the edge of a chair by his desk and punched in a number.

"CSI lab," a male voice answered, loud enough for Clay to hear.

Wincing, Tamara held the phone away from her ear. "Eric? It's me. What'd you come up with in that tunnel? Clay heard you found blood?"

"Geez, Tamara, are you all right? Sheriff Yates said you'd fallen through the ceiling of the tunnel, got banged up pretty bad." Her boss's voice carried so well, she might as well have had him on speaker.

"Yeah, I fell, but I'll be fine in a couple days. Bruised a few ribs. Nothing major."

"Bruised ribs is nothing major?"

She rolled her eyes, even as she shifted stiffly on the chair. "Don't worry. I'll be back to work in a day or two."

Clay rocked forward in his seat, prepared to interrupt with his protest, when her boss steamed, "Oooh, no, you won't! You're injured. As of right now you are on medical leave for a minimum of one week."

"What?" Tamara gasped, and her gaze darted to Clay's as if seeking confirmation she'd heard correctly.

He crossed his arms over his chest and leaned back in his chair, a satisfied smile on his lips.

"Don't let me see you in here until you are able to give me one hundred percent. I need you healed and in top form. At least one week. Paid leave, of course, but I don't want you to push yourself. If you need more time to get well, take it. Understood?"

"Yes," she groused. A crease lined her brow as she exhaled. "Can you at least tell me where the case stands? What did you find at the tunnel?"

Clay perked his ears. The investigation of what happened out on the south pasture might not involve him directly, but if something illegal, something tragic had happened on his land, he wanted to know about it. This case had already gotten Tamara injured, and he needed facts if he was going to protect her from any further harm.

"Look, you don't…" Her boss hesitated.

"Eric, talk to me." Tamara lowered her head to her fingertips and massaged her temple. "This is my case. I did the initial investigation. I have a right to know."

A heavy sigh rattled from the phone. "Well, we don't have any final results back, of course, but…initial tests show the samples from the car door and the tunnel are the same blood type. The body you saw was most likely the source of the blood in the car. We'll know for sure when the DNA report comes back on the blood and hair."

Tamara's head came up. "Hair?"

"We recovered a few hairs with roots from the scene today."

"What else?" Excitement filled her voice.

"Not much. There were impressions where footprints might have been but they'd been obliterated. Deliberately. Someone is literally covering his tracks."

"Interesting." Tamara chewed her bottom lip as she thought. Passion for her job shined in her blue eyes. He could almost see the wheels of her analytical mind clicking, and pride swelled in his chest. Along with regret. No wonder she hadn't been happy in their marriage. Clearly she was in her element on the crime scene team, dissecting evidence and putting the pieces of scientific data together to see a bigger picture.

"If someone moved the body, could be because they know we're onto them," Tamara said.

Clay sat forward in his chair as his pulse kicked into high gear. He didn't like the new twist on this case.

"Yeah. Could be. And cornered animals are always the most dangerous, so be careful," Eric replied, echoing Clay's thoughts.

As Tamara finished her conversation with her boss, Clay curled his fingers into his palm and stewed over whether news of the investigation could have traveled so fast or if someone could have been watching the crime scene when Tamara had been out there, alone. An uneasy chill slithered down his spine.

The possibility that someone could know of Tamara's involvement in the investigation and could be looking to silence her shook him to the core. Clay gritted his teeth and balled his fists even tighter. Anyone looking to hurt his ex-wife would have to come through him first.

# Chapter 6

The next evening after dinner, Clay found Tamara in the family room, stretched out on one of the long leather couches with multiple pillows stacked behind her. She'd found a pair of his drawstring running shorts and put them on, cinched to fit her slim waist, with another one of his old T-shirts.

As she was reading one of his magazines, she stroked one bare foot down her opposite leg, calling his attention to the sleek curve of her calf and her trim ankle. The action struck him as so provocative, his body tightened in a heartbeat. Of course, since he'd helped her change out of her bloody clothes yesterday, visions of her nude body and her lacy undergarments had taunted him to the point that she could sneeze and he'd find it arousing.

While he stood at the entry to the family room, his body humming, Tamara laid the magazine on her lap and reached down to rub her heel. With a hiss of pain, she sank back into the pillows and grimaced. "Dang it."

Shoving away from the door frame where he'd propped his shoulder, Clay strode forward. "You need another pill for the pain?"

She raised a startled gaze to him. "Considering how the last one knocked me out, I'm not going to take more until I'm ready for bed." She tipped her head. "You're back early. Are you done in the stables already?"

Nodding, he moved around the antique wagon-wheel coffee table and lifted her feet into his lap as he joined her on the couch. "Many hands make light work and all that jazz. I really don't need as many guys as I have working for me now, but I can't bring myself to let anyone go. They have families to feed."

She raised her eyebrows. "And you can afford all those salaries?"

He shrugged. "The past couple years have been good. My new stallions are bringing in top stud fees, and last year I sold some property I wasn't using, which brought in some extra cash. So, yeah. I can afford the salaries for now."

"Good. I'm really happy for you. I'm thrilled to see the Bar None doing well. No one deserves it more than you." She grinned, and the warmth of her smile soaked all the way to his bones.

He wasn't the sort of man who needed anyone's approval to feed his self-esteem, but Tamara's opinion was different. She'd been there from the beginning, when he'd learned ranching during high school. She'd labored beside him from the day he'd inked the deed to the day she walked out of their marriage. She knew how long he'd dreamed of building his own ranch, knew how hard he'd worked to achieve his success. And shared in the pain of what his success had cost him.

Guilt plucked at him, and he quickly shoved the reminders of his failed marriage aside.

Wrapping his fingers around her bare foot, he squeezed her toes and rubbed her heel between his palms. "Your feet are freezing. You want a pair of socks?"

"Mmm, no. Just keep doing that. It feels great." She tipped her head back, arching her neck. A purr of satisfaction rumbled from her throat and ricocheted through him. Heat blasted through his veins, and the tight coil of sexual tension he'd fought all day vibrated, ready to spring.

"You have magic hands, Clay Colton," she said, her tone husky. "I've missed your foot massages." She met his gaze through her fringe of brown lashes, and he recognized the spark of desire that warmed her eyes.

In the past, his foot massages had often been foreplay to more tantalizing moments, and the sights, sounds and sensations of those encounters washed over him in living color. With a breathy sigh, his ex shifted on the couch and offered him her other foot, the movement nudging the already straining fly of his jeans. His gaze traveled up her long legs and stopped at her chest, where his T-shirt clung to her breasts and delineated her peaked nipples. She wasn't wearing a bra. Understandable, in light of her sore ribs. Yet knowing that tidbit made a shudder ripple through him. More fodder for his overactive fantasy life concerning his former wife.

Clay swallowed a moan. He'd known full well what he was doing when he sat down on the couch with her and initiated the foot rub. He'd been playing with fire, testing Tamara. Would she welcome his touch or push him away?

"You know what I'd like?" Tamara wound a wisp of her long gold hair around a finger, a look of pure satisfaction on her face.

"What's that, Tee?" Forcing aside his sensual thoughts, he focused his attention on her request. From the moment he'd first laid eyes on her in junior high, he'd do anything in his power to give Tamara whatever she wanted, whatever made her happy. Even if it meant sacrificing his own happiness. Their divorce was proof of that.

"I was thinking…maybe tomorrow—"

The trill of the house phone interrupted her.

Clay shook his head. "Ignore it. Finish your sentence."

"No. It'll keep." She pulled her feet from his lap. "Answer it. That could be Jericho with important information."

Sighing, Clay shoved off the sofa and retrieved the cordless phone from the kitchen counter. "H'lo?"

"Hi, Clay. It's Jewel."

Guilt kicked him in the shin, and he cringed internally. He'd been meaning for days to call and check up on Jewel Mayfair, the manager at Hopechest Ranch, a home for troubled teens.

Months ago, following the tragic death of her fiancé and unborn child in a car accident, Jewel had moved to Esperanza. His aunt Meredith had been concerned about her niece and asked Clay to keep tabs on Jewel, whom she knew was still hurting and vulnerable. Clay had dutifully taken his distant relative under his wing, but the chaos of the past few days had sidetracked him.

"Hi, Jewel. Is everything all right?" He cradled the phone on his shoulder as he strolled back into the family room. This time he sat on the couch opposite Tamara. A guy could only withstand temptation for so long.

"Oh, we're fine," Jewel said. "I just wanted to bring some of the girls over tomorrow to ride the horses again…if it was okay for you."

Clay raked a hand through his hair, mentally reviewing his agenda for the next day. "I don't see why not. About ten? Before it gets too hot?"

"Sounds great. Thanks, Clay. You're a dear."

As he disconnected and set the phone on the wagon-wheel coffee table, Tamara's expression was curious.

Clay propped his elbows on his thighs and steepled his fingers. "You remember meeting my uncle Joe and aunt Meredith out in California?"

Tamara nodded. "The senator and his wife."

"Right."

"His campaign for the White House has been big news lately."

Clay arched an eyebrow, surprised that Tamara had been keeping up with his family, even if Joe's political career was national news. Nodding toward the phone, he added, "That was Meredith's niece, Jewel. I don't think you ever met her."

Tamara scrunched her nose in thought. "Doesn't ring a bell."

"Well, Jewel recently opened a branch of the Hopechest Ranch here in Esperanza, and she brings the kids over now and then to ride the horses."

"And they're coming tomorrow, I take it?"

He grinned. "That's one of the reasons I fell for you, darlin'. You're sharp."

She smirked. "I can eavesdrop with the best of them."

Clay sat back on the couch, and for a moment, a comfortable quiet fell between them. Tamara was the first to break the silence. "Tell me about the rest of your family. Is Georgie still on the rodeo circuit?"

"For now, although I think she'd like to settle down, give Emmie a more permanent home."

Tamara frowned. "Emmie?"

Clay exhaled slowly and rubbed a hand over the day's growth of stubble on his jaw. "Oh, man. That's right. Georgie didn't tell us she was pregnant until after you left."

Tamara's eyes widened. "Georgie has a daughter?"

Unable to hide his pride when he thought of his niece, Clay smiled broadly. "She's four and a half and is the spitting image of her mother. Precocious. A tomboy like Georgie. And she'll talk your ear off."

"And she has her uncle Clay wrapped around her little finger?" Tamara flashed him a knowing grin.

He spread his hands. "Guilty as charged."

"So then…is Georgie married?"

Clay's gut roiled thinking of the city slicker who'd gotten his sister pregnant then abandoned her. "Naw. The guy left her. But Georgie's a great mom and has a new guy in her life."

Tamara smiled. "A cowboy from the rodeo circuit, no doubt."

"Actually, no." Clay chuckled and dropped his bomb. "A Secret Service agent."

"What?" Tamara sat up too fast and pressed a hand to her ribs. Wincing, she settled back against the pillows. "How did she meet a Secret Service agent?"

Clay summarized the events of the past few weeks, including the break-in at Georgie's house, her brush with identity theft and being framed for threatening Joe Colton and his campaign. He explained the danger Georgie had been in, and how Agent Nick Sheffield had helped clear her name.

Tamara gave a low whistle. "Thank God she's all right. So do I get to meet this hero agent and Georgie's daughter while I'm in town?"

He turned up a palm. "I don't see why not. I'm sure Georgie'd love to catch up with you."

"I'd like that." Tamara's smile faded, and she hesitated. "And Ryder? What do you hear from him?"

Mention of his incarcerated brother sent a jolt of self-censure through Clay. He surged to his feet and stalked toward the fire-place. Keeping his gaze fixed on the Texas flag over his mantel so Tamara couldn't read the guilt in his expression, he said, "I haven't had any contact with Ryder in years."

"Wh-why not?"

Tamara's incredulous tone only deepened Clay's remorse. His broken relationship with his younger brother was difficult enough without Tamara judging him for his decision.

Clay clenched his teeth, and every muscle tensed. "Ryder left me no choice. He wouldn't listen to me, refused to turn his life around. I did *everything* to get through to him and nothing worked. You know how Ryder was in high school. All the trouble he got into, the scrapes with the law. Defacing public property. Stealing cars to joyride with his friends."

"But he was a good kid deep down. He was just rebellious and—"

Clay slapped a hand on the mantel in frustration. "And his re-bellion finally landed him in jail!"

Tamara gasped.

Clay hazarded a glance over his shoulder and met Tamara's stricken expression. Turning away, Clay shoved his hands in his pockets, though the roil of emotions in his gut made him restless.

"He was caught transporting illegals over the border from Mexico. He's serving time."

"Oh, no! Oh, Ryder. How awful."

Acid swirled in Clay's stomach, crept up his throat with the sour taste of failure. "I tried to talk to him at his sentencing, but it was like talking to a stone wall. He wouldn't even look at me. I told him then that I'd had enough."

"Enough?" Tamara repeated hoarsely. "What are you saying? It was your choice to break ties with him?"

Memories of that last day scrolled through Clay's mind. His brother's pale, stony expression. The nauseating scent of floor cleaner that hung in the courtroom. The cold bite of the over-air-conditioned room.

A chill washed over Clay, sending a tremor though him.

When a warm hand touched his arm, he jolted. He turned with a jerk to find Tamara standing behind him, her face wan and confused.

"Clay, tell me you didn't abandon Ryder when he went to jail."

Her stricken expression and strangled tone knotted his chest with grief and frustration. "I'd done everything I knew to do! Ryder wouldn't listen. He was bent on self-destruction, and damn everyone and everything else. He left me no choice! For his own good—and for mine—I had to wash my hands of him."

Tamara's eyes grew round in dismay. "He's still your brother! Doesn't that count for anything?"

"Apparently not." Clay fisted his hands in his pockets, trying to rein in his runaway emotions. "Georgie tried writing to him, but he never replied. He's never responded to any attempt to communicate with him."

Tamara spread her arms. Her blue eyes blazed with condemnation. "So that's it? You just cut him out of your life like some cancer?"

Clay swiped a hand through his hair and clenched his teeth, struggling to keep his temper in check. "What do you want me to say, Tamara? This isn't the way I wanted things to turn out. God knows I tried to save my brother, but I—"

"Gave up." Her clipped tone sliced through him.

He narrowed a sharp gaze on her, stunned by her bitterness. Denials formed on his tongue then died when a nagging voice in his head echoed her accusation.

She stepped closer, one arm holding her ribs, her piercing blue gaze locked on his. "Shouldn't surprise me you'd walk away from your brother. It wouldn't be the first time you threw in the towel."

He stiffened. "What does that mean?"

"You gave up on Lone Star, too."

Clay groaned. "Good God, Tamara, that was completely different! He was incurably sick and hurting. And *contagious*. He'd never recover enough to breed again, so he'd lost his value as a stud."

"So his life was nothing more than a ledger balance to you?"

Clay huffed and rubbed the back of his neck. "Money was a factor, but not the only consideration. If you'd listened to Quinn that night instead of becoming irrational and—"

"Irrational?" Her voice leaped an octave higher. She poked Clay in the chest with a finger, her face flaming. "Just what is so *rational* about cutting someone you love out of your life because they become inconvenient? I loved that horse, but you wouldn't even consider trying to save him. Strangles is easily curable. I asked around. You gave up on him too soon!"

"Tamara, listen to me—"

"No, *you* listen. Growing up, my family had no money. My family was all I had to count on. Family is important. Sure, life can be hard. Relationships are hard, but you don't give up on the people you love without a fight!"

Clay grew still, staring at the color in his ex-wife's cheeks, the tears blooming in her eyes. "Are we still talking about the horse? Or even about Ryder?"

Tamara drew a shaky breath. "What if we aren't?"

He inhaled slowly, struggling to calm the riot jangling inside him. "You're the one who walked away, Tamara. I didn't cut you out of my life."

"But you didn't do anything to stop me. You didn't say a word. You didn't so much as flinch when you signed the divorce papers. I could only assume that meant you didn't care." She motioned to the Texas flag on the wall and the antique lanterns on his mantel. "And where are the lithographs and dried flower arrangements I bought for the mantel? The curtains I made for the kitchen? Don't think I haven't noticed that you removed every trace that I ever lived here or helped decorate this house. The evidence says you *did* cut me out of your life." She ducked her head and swiped a tear that dripped from her lashes.

"Tamara…" He sighed, afraid if he spoke his voice would betray the heartache that had a stranglehold on his throat.

"Over the years," she whispered, her voice cracking, "I told myself you were just in shock. Maybe you did care, but you didn't know what to do or say. That our divorce hurt you as much as it hurt me."

The pain in her voice flayed Clay's heart. A bone-deep tremor wrenched him. "Tee, don't do this…"

"But after hearing how you walked away from Ryder when he needed his big brother the most, maybe I was wrong."

Her words landed a sucker punch. He couldn't breathe. Couldn't think. His body and brain buzzed numbly. He shuffled back a step then turned. "I… I have things to tend to in the stable."

His gait stiff, he stalked toward the back door.

One hand on the doorknob, he paused and jammed his Stetson on his head. Glancing back at her, he rasped, "I know that I failed Ryder, failed you, failed in our marriage. I have to live with that truth every day. But don't for a minute think that I didn't care."

With that, he stepped outside and closed the door.

Tamara fought to calm the ragged breaths that triggered waves of pain in her chest. But the ache in her soul cut far deeper than the injury to her ribs. Clay's parting shot reverberated through her, rattling the defenses around her heart.

His words echoed with a guilt and pain she'd never imagined Clay harbored. The idea that Clay bore the same scars she did from their divorce shook her to the core.

Had it just been easier to leave the ranch, believing Clay hadn't cared? Had her own heartache blinded her to signs he wanted her to stay, wanted to make the marriage work? Signs that he had loved her?

In a criminal investigation, her team had to consider *all* the data. Especially the pieces not immediately visible to the naked eye. Looking at the big picture was essential in order to see where each bit of evidence fit in the greater whole. That she could have been so tunnel-visioned concerning something as important as her marriage galled her. Further proof that emotions skewed her judgment.

At work she appreciated the clinical nature of her scientific analyses and regimen. She considered the elimination of an emotional factor a blessing. Facts were safe. Science didn't break your heart or steal your hope. But data and analysis couldn't fill the empty spaces in your soul on lonely winter nights and didn't bring the joy of sharing life's simple pleasures.

Tamara dashed moisture from her cheek with her hand then, finding a napkin on the kitchen table, she blew her nose.

Her job might be safe, but did she want to be as cold and clinical in her personal life as she had to be on the job? Wasn't that exactly what she found so unfathomable about Clay's dealings with Ryder, with his sick stallions, with their divorce? Life wasn't a crime lab where emotions could be taken out of the equation. Relationships weren't sterile bits of evidence to be dispassionately dissected.

*I know that I failed Ryder, failed you, failed in our marriage. I have to live with that truth every day.*

Her heart gave a painful throb. She should have known her world-on-his-shoulders ex would assume full responsibility for the dissolution of their marriage, that he'd take the blame for his brother's poor choices.

Gathering her composure, Tamara jammed her feet into the shoes she'd left beside the couch and headed outside to find Clay. She regretted losing her temper with him and the hurtful things she'd said. She couldn't let Clay go on thinking their divorce, or Ryder's incarceration, was his fault.

When she stepped out on the back stoop, the sweet scent of alfalfa hay from the stables greeted her, and a chorus of crickets and frogs sang their nighttime melody. The sounds and smells of the countryside in summer carved a hollow ache in her soul.

As a teenager, she'd dreamed of leaving Esperanza as quickly as possible. The confines and isolation of her hometown had felt claustrophobic and limiting. After living in San Antonio for five years, she found that she missed much about small-town life. If she'd been so wrong about Esperanza, what else had she misjudged in her youth?

She strolled slowly to the main stable, careful not to jar her ribs and giving Clay an extra moment or two to himself. They both needed a few minutes to cool off and think.

In the yellow glow of the stable's bare lightbulb, she spotted Clay, leaning against the gate to one of the stalls. Still, quiet, his head bowed, he was the image of a man in pain. Her heart broke and bled for him.

How had they come to this? Clay had been her whole world at one time, her knight on a white horse—or rather her cowboy in a white Stetson. Knowing how they'd grown apart, let petty grievances come between them, left a stark, cold emptiness deep inside her.

As she approached the stable, Hobo, the beagle mix, trotted out to meet her with a wagging tail and a baying bark. Hobo had been Clay's dog when they married, but the mutt's cold nose and sloppy dog kisses had burrowed deep into her affections from the day she'd met the friendly beagle. Leaving Hobo behind when they divorced had been almost as hard as leaving Clay.

Tamara smiled as Hobo wiggled and yipped at her feet. "Hi, boy. How are you?"

Her voice alerted Clay to her arrival. Jerking up his head, he grabbed a curry comb from the nearest shelf and started grooming his gelding, Crockett. Tamara pretended not to notice his haste to cover his pensive brooding.

Hobo planted his paws on Tamara's leg and nuzzled her hand, lapping at her with his warm tongue. The enthusiastic greeting from her old friend, as if five years hadn't elapsed since he'd last seen her, touched something already raw and vulnerable inside her. The tears she'd just gotten under control pricked her eyes again.

"Good boy, Hobo." She bent at the waist to pat the dog, but her ribs protested the movement with a sharp stab. "Ooo!"

Clay glanced over just as she grabbed her side and winced. He crossed the stable in quick strides and pulled the dog away. "Settle down, Hobo. You're going to hurt her."

"No, he's okay. I just tried to pat him and bending down didn't work."

"Oh." Clay met her gaze with a tender warmth that arrowed to her heart. He stooped to scoop Hobo into his arms. "How 'bout this?"

While Clay held the squirming beagle, Tamara leaned in to get canine kisses and rub his floppy ears. As she hugged Hobo, the emotion that tightened her throat came as much from Clay's sweet gesture as her reunion with her old pet. His thoughtfulness didn't surprise her. His consideration and kindness had been at the core of why she'd fallen in love with him.

So how could a man with such a magnanimous spirit *not* have understood that his take-charge manner and solo decision making in their marriage had left her feeling trivialized and unimportant?

"I think the mutt missed you," he said as Hobo wiggled and licked her hands.

"I missed him, too," she replied around the lump in her throat. She swallowed hard and tried to shove down the tears that burned her sinuses. Being so weepy wasn't like her. But, heck, she'd had a couple of highly stressful days, and the pain meds had weakened her defenses. Coupled with the barrage of bittersweet memories that had surrounded her since returning to the Bar None, no wonder she'd become a leaky faucet. With a fortifying breath, she gave the beagle a final pat and stepped back. "Thank you, Clay."

He lowered the dog to the ground and shrugged. "No problem."

When Clay turned to go back into the stable, Tamara caught his arm. "Wait. I came out to say…I'm sorry."

His brow creased, and warm, dark eyes bore into hers. "Don't be. Most of what you said was right. I've made a lot of mistakes." He faced her more fully and nudged his Stetson back. "But I… I'm not as coldhearted as you seem to think. I feel the loss of my brother every day, and I regret my failure with him more than you could know."

"Clay." She pressed a hand to his cheek and moved closer. "Stop blaming yourself for the way Ryder turned out. He made his own choices and has to live with the consequences. You did your best in an untenable position and can't be held liable for your brother's mistakes."

Clay shook his head. "I didn't do enough to save him from the path he was on when I could. If I'd been harsher with him or kept closer tabs on what he was doing—"

"He'd only have rebelled more. Ryder had to learn from his own mistakes, find his own path. You and your mom gave him solid roots, and someday, when he's ready to turn his life around, that foundation will still be there."

He sighed and glanced away. "Maybe."

Frustration clawed at her, but she wouldn't argue the point with him anymore. Not tonight. She had more important things on her mind he needed to hear.

"You can't assume all the fault for our divorce either, Clay. I can't stand the thought that you've blamed yourself for five years."

A muscle in his jaw twitched as he clenched his teeth and

narrowed a trouble gaze on her. "If I'd been the husband you needed, you wouldn't have left."

Her breath snagged in her lungs. "Don't you ever get tired of carrying the weight of the world on your shoulders? A marriage takes two people." She hesitated, knowing she needed to say more. "And…I was wrong to accuse you of cutting me out of your life. You had every right to get rid of my décor from the house. It's your home, and if you didn't like the things I chose—"

"Tee…" Clay sank his fingers into her hair and cradled the base of her skull. Light from the stable glinted in his midnight eyes. "I liked what you added to the house just fine. But after a while, I couldn't take seeing reminders of you, reminders of how I'd let you down. It hurt less to erase you from the house…just as I had to make a clean break from Ryder."

His thumb stroked the sensitive spot behind her ear, and Tamara's head swam dizzily. "You never said anything, never let me know how you felt. During our divorce, you always seemed so distant, so stoic. Why didn't you tell me how you felt?"

His gaze dipped to her lips, and he pitched his voice soft and low. "Would it have made a difference?"

She scowled. "Of course it would have."

He shook his head. "My feelings for you couldn't have solved any of our differences. You had a dream that didn't include ranching. I knew that even when we got married, but I'd convinced myself I could make you happy anyway. Problem was, getting the Bar None up and running filled every hour of my day. That didn't leave much time for you, for your needs. When you were ready to pursue your dream, it would have been selfish of me to hold you back."

She caught her bottom lip with her teeth and sighed. "I just wish—"

"Shh." He pressed a finger to her mouth, and his touch sparked a shimmering heat that spun through her. "No more regrets tonight, okay?"

Tamara threaded her fingers through the raven hair curling at his collar and studied the play of moonlight across his stubble-dusted jaw. The truths she'd learned about Clay tonight, her new insights regarding the pain he'd hidden from her tangled around her heart. "Forgive me, Clay. I never wanted to hurt you. I never meant—"

He silenced her with the soft crush of his lips. His kiss wiped all thoughts of past mistakes and old hurts from her mind. The world shrank to her and Clay. She forgot that she no longer belonged in Clay's arms. All that mattered was the gentle persuasion of his mouth, the sweet sensations that made her head swim and her knees weak. He brushed a callused palm down her cheek, and she leaned into his caress.

*You're home.*

The words filtered through her mind, but some spoilsport part of her brain rejected the idea with a cold dash of reality. The biting chill of truth washed through her and seeped to the bone.

Inhaling sharply, she backed from his grasp and turned away.

"Is it your ribs? Did I hurt you?" Concern softened his tone and added sting to her sobering awareness.

A sinking feeling settled in her gut.

*My feelings for you couldn't have solved any of our differences.*

Clay was right. The problems that had ended their marriage still stood between them. Nothing had changed. No amount of wishful thinking could erase the past five years.

Clay swept her hair from her face and brushed his knuckles along her cheek. "Tee, what's wrong?"

"I can't… We can't…let that happen again." She cast a sorrowful glance to him. "I'll be leaving in a couple of days and…" She dropped her gaze and stepped away. "Let's not complicate things. This is hard enough for me without…" Her voice cracked, and she hurried into the stable without finishing the thought.

Kissing Clay might be paradise, but Clay wasn't her home anymore. She'd signed away the right to hold him, to kiss him, the day they divorced.

## Chapter 7

Clay followed Tamara as she moved from one stall to the next, visiting each horse, asking about every one and stroking the animals' necks.

She had always had a soft spot for the animals on the ranch, a trait that could be a mixed blessing. The night Lone Star had been put down, Tamara's tender heart had been a curse. She'd been deaf to his and Quinn's attempts to explain why euthanasia had been the kindest thing they could do for the suffering stallion. The normally treatable strangles had become systemic, progressed to fatal bastard strangles. Antibiotics wouldn't have saved him.

He thought he'd explained this to Tamara, but her lingering bitterness made him wonder how much of the truth she really understood. That night, she'd been inconsolable. Her reaction made doing the right thing so much harder. He'd hated to see Tamara's pain. With the loss of his best stud, the livelihood of his ranch at stake and his wife an emotional wreck, Clay had held on to his composure the only way he knew how.

Distance. Denial. Corralling his emotions.

When Tamara had walked out and he'd been left alone in the echoing silence of the house, he'd wallowed for one miserable night in pain, tears and drinking. But by the light of day, he'd had to put on a brave face and soldier through for the ranch hands who depended on him for jobs and the animals who had to be cared for—no matter how rotten his life became.

In the weeks that followed, even when he'd thought bankruptcy was inevitable, he'd learned what really mattered to him.

*Tamara.*

Only the realization had come too late. Her leaving had sucked the soul from his life, and all his efforts to save his ranch seemed pointless if he couldn't share it with the woman he loved.

But failure in one area of his life didn't excuse failure in another. Clay had survived Tamara's leaving by burying himself in the business of ranching. He'd been determined that his ranch would not only survive but would thrive. He poured every ounce of his energy into the Bar None, and the ranch's current success bore witness to endless hours of hard work, innovative cost-cutting measures, and his bullheaded pride.

"She looks ready to pop, poor girl. When is she due?"

Tamara's question yanked him from his musing. He replayed the question in his head, mentally catching up. He glanced at the mare in question and scratched his chin. "Um, a matter of days. We're keeping a close eye on her. There were problems with her last delivery."

Concern flickered in Tamara's eyes.

He waved off her worries. "Nothing serious. We're just being cautious."

Tamara nodded and turned back to the mare. "So what's her name?"

"Doesn't have one. You're the one who insisted on naming all the animals. The men and I just call her the roan mare."

Tamara rolled her eyes then tipped her head. "She looks like a Lucy to me."

Clay chuckled and shook his head. "Then Lucy it is."

Judging by her reaction to Hobo and the horses tonight, her tenderheartedness hadn't changed.

Neither had his response to Tamara's kiss. Clay's gaze drifted to his ex's lush mouth, and a renewed kick of desire flashed through him.

She still had the power to set his whole body on fire with the simple touch of her lips. Clay's blood heated thinking about the kiss they'd shared.

*Let's not complicate things.*

Weren't things already complicated? A dead body and stolen car had been found on his property. His ex-wife was recovering in his home from a nasty fall. And after just two days with Tamara, his feelings about his brother, his divorce, his plans for the ranch were all tangled and turned upside down. He was questioning everything he thought he knew about his life and what he wanted for the future.

Not complicate things? He grunted.

That particular horse had already escaped the barn.

Tamara's initial response to their kiss indicated that she still had feelings for him. She had been as deeply affected as he had. Of course, sex had never been their problem. They'd always had a fiery passion for each other and a magical rapport in bed.

Tamara gave the mare's nose another pat. "Hang in there, Lucy. You're in good hands." She turned from the last stall and cast her gaze around the stable as if checking for any horse she'd missed.

He propped an arm on the door of an empty stall. "I think that's everybody."

"Where's Trouble? Do you still have her?"

"Trouble?"

"The kitten I rescued from the Handleys' dog."

"Oh, the barn cat." He chuckled. "I didn't realize you'd named her. I call her Cat."

"Cat? How imaginative." His ex wrinkled her nose and looked

so adorable he wished he could pull her into his arms for a bear hug. But even if her ribs had been in any condition to endure such affection, Tamara had made her wishes clear.

*Let's not complicate things.*

Clay pushed away from the stall with a shrug. "Come on. She's probably out by the truck. I've been finding paw prints on my windshield every morning."

Sure enough, they found the calico curled in the bed of his truck on a horse blanket. While Tamara cooed over the cat, Clay studied the shimmer of pale moonlight in her hay-colored hair, the dusting of freckles that danced across her nose. He'd kissed every one of those freckles when they'd been married and…

With a huff, he kicked the gravel at his toe. Enough living in the past. Tamara's presence at the ranch was an anomaly. The minute her ribs healed, she'd be gone again. Reviving old memories would only prolong the ache when she left.

Trouble stood and stretched, butting her head against Tamara's hand. She laughed and obliged the cat, scratching her behind the ear and stroking her glossy coat while murmuring sweet nothings to the purring feline.

Clay watched, fascinated. "She never begs for attention like that from me."

Tamara glanced at him. "Do you ever give her unsolicited pats?"

*No.* He opened his mouth to answer, but Tamara's knowing expression stopped him in his tracks.

"Maybe she knows not to expect anything from you," Tamara said softly.

So he didn't lavish the barn cat with affection. So what? That didn't mean he was cold and unfeeling as she'd accused him earlier that evening. He simply knew better than to grow attached to ranch animals. Ranching was a business, and emotions played no part in sound business decisions.

Yet as Tamara stared at him this muggy June evening, a hurt he'd seen often toward the end of their marriage shadowed her eyes. His pulse stumbled.

*I don't feel like I matter to you anymore—if I ever really did.
I feel you pulling away and don't understand why. What changed?*

Echoes of their last argument rang in his head, and remorse
bit him hard. Had his wife left because she felt unloved? He'd
always questioned how she could accuse him of not caring about
her.

He looked at Trouble, eating up the loving attention Tamara
offered, and frowned. The cat's affection for him or lack thereof
had never mattered to Clay. The cat merely served a function on
the ranch—catching mice in the barn. Period. But did Trouble's
dismissal of him serve as an allegory for a bigger picture?

Like the cat, had Tamara sensed something lacking from him
in the final weeks of their marriage? Had he given her a message
he hadn't intended, something that told her he didn't care?

Tamara clicked her tongue then laughed when Trouble
flopped on her side and batted at Tamara's long hair.

Watching his ex-wife play with the barn cat, Clay dusted off
the defensive assurances he'd used after the divorce to soothe his
conscience. She was the one who'd broadcasted her unhappiness
like a beacon. She'd made clear her wish to follow her dream of
a career in criminal investigation. Her restlessness had been
obvious in every way. Yet she'd accused him of pulling away. The
irony and unfairness of her accusations had chafed. Now her
claims gave him pause.

Sensing her disquiet and longing for her own career, had he
anticipated her leaving him and withdrawn, held back his heart
in self-defense? Had he unwittingly set in motion a self-fulfill-
ing prophecy that led to his divorce?

The possibilities took root in his brain and grew. Clay's hands
became sweaty, and his heart beat double time. He raked his hand
through his hair, knocking off his hat. He sank down on the
tailgate of his truck while his thoughts roiled and his gut pitched.

He'd always had a nagging sense that he was to blame for
Tamara's unhappiness. But he'd never been able to pinpoint
where he'd gone astray or exactly how he'd let her down.

"Clay, what's wrong?" Tamara moved up beside him and placed a hand on his forearm. Her brow puckered in concern.

"I… Nothing. I just…" He scooped up his Stetson and absently fingered the rim.

Trouble followed Tamara over to the tailgate and rubbed against Clay. He lifted a shaky hand and stroked the cat from head to tail. Encouraged by the attention, Trouble climbed into his lap and butted his hand again.

"See?" Tamara said. "She was just waiting for you to show a little interest."

The good-natured jibe reverberated through Clay, and he held his breath.

Looking back at the events five years ago, he couldn't shake the notion that he'd set in motion a vicious circle. The more he'd withdrawn from Tamara to protect his heart from her inevitable leaving, the unhappier and more unloved she'd felt, precipitating her departure and their divorce.

He expelled his pent-up breath in a whoosh and braced an arm on the truck bed.

Lifting a stunned gaze to Tamara, he rasped, "Did I really withdraw from you in those last months of our marriage? Did I make you think you weren't loved?"

Tamara's face paled. "What makes you say that?"

"That's what you told me the night you left. You said you thought I'd been pulling away, that you felt like you didn't matter."

Tamara shook her head and turned away. "Let's not rehash that argument and stir up hard feelings again tonight. I said I was sorry for what I said earlier and—"

He placed a hand on each shoulder and gently turned her around. "Forget what we said earlier this evening. I'm asking about what I did in the months before you left that made you think I didn't care."

Tamara ducked her head and sighed. "Please, Clay. I don't want to open old wounds again. Can't we just let bygones be bygones?"

"Not if I did something to hurt you." He put a finger under

her chin and made her look at him. Tears filled her blue eyes and clawed at his heart. "Tee, you have to know I'd never consciously do anything to cause you pain. I didn't contest the divorce, because I didn't want to hold you back from following your dream, having the career you wanted."

"I know that. Now. But back then…I was confused." She pulled away, rubbing her arms as if chilled. "I was trying to figure out how to balance my need for a career with my marriage, and all I really knew was the longer I stayed at the ranch, the more I felt I was losing myself in your shadow."

"Tamara, I'm sorry if I—"

She spun back toward him and pressed a hand to his lips. "Don't. There's enough blame for both of us."

He captured her hand and kissed the fingers she held over his mouth. Her eyes darkened to the color of the sky at the first daylight. Finally she slipped her hand from his and stepped back.

"We were so young when we got married, Clay. Maybe if we'd waited…" She shook her head. "Well, we'll never really know. Speculation and second-guessing solve nothing." She took another step back. "Good night, Clay."

With that, she turned and hurried toward the house. He watched her retreat until she disappeared inside the back door, then he tipped his head back to stare at the moon.

Trouble meowed and wound through his legs, purring.

With a grunt, Clay crouched to scratch the cat's head. Second-guessing might not solve anything, but Clay knew tonight there'd be no escaping the regrets and doubt-demons his new insights had created.

## Chapter 8

The next morning, Tamara, with the help of her pain medication, slept in for the first time in many months. After a bite of breakfast, she returned to the guest bedroom Marie had prepared for her to read an action-adventure novel she found on Clay's bookshelf. After a few chapters, she heard a car horn toot, followed by slamming doors and the chattering of young voices. Parting the window's miniblinds, she peered down at the driveway where an SUV had parked. Clay greeted the blond-haired woman who climbed from the driver's side with a hug and a peck on the cheek.

Stepping back from the window, she scowled. She hadn't even considered the possibility that Clay could have a new woman in his life. Did she really think Clay would spend the rest of his life alone? He had so much to offer a woman, so many warm and wonderful traits.

But last night, he'd kissed *her*.

Kiss or not, what claim did she have on him now? She'd chosen to leave Clay years ago, and she refused to second-guess that decision. As she'd told Clay last night, regret served no purpose.

Still, curiosity got the better of her, and she headed downstairs to meet the ranch's guests. With the good night's sleep under her belt and a couple of Advil in her system, she felt considerably better. Her general aches were all but gone, and her rib pain was manageable as long as she didn't move too fast or jar her midriff.

Tamara stepped out on the wide front porch. The day's heat and humidity slammed into her like walking into a brick wall. And it was only ten-thirty. Welcome to summer in Texas.

Clay looked over as she crossed the yard, and his sexy grin made her insides quiver.

"Speak of the devil." Clay slid an arm loosely around Tamara's waist and motioned to the woman with him. "Tamara, this is Aunt Meredith's niece, Jewel Mayfair. She runs the new Esperanza branch of Hopechest Ranch."

As she shook hands with Jewel, Tamara remembered the call Clay had taken last night regarding the plan to bring several girls from Hopechest Ranch over to ride horses. The bubble of jealousy popped. Jewel was family. A distant connection through marriage, but family nonetheless and no competition for Clay's affections.

*Get real. In order to be jealous, you'd have to still consider yourself in a relationship with your ex.*

Admitting she still had feelings for Clay would start her down a slippery slope. Definitely not where she needed to go if she wanted to survive the next few days of recuperation with her heart intact.

While they exchanged the customary courtesies, Tamara took stock of Clay's relative. Jewel was lovely, with short, wavy hair and beautiful brown eyes. Tall for a woman, especially in her fashionable cowboy boots, Jewel Mayfair had enviable curves in her slim figure. Yet for all her elegant beauty, dark smudges under her eyes and fine lines of fatigue in her face hinted that she hadn't slept well or was under a great deal of stress.

Understandable. Running Hopechest Ranch and acting as

mother to numerous teenage girls had to have more than its share of pressures and long nights.

Clay lowered his voice and whispered to Tamara. "You sure you feel up to being on your feet?"

The tickle of his breath in her ear sent a delicious and distracting shiver down her spine.

She met the dark concern in his eyes and smiled. "I'm much better this morning. Thanks."

His gaze lingered as if he deciding whether to chide her and send her back into the house.

"Really," she said, stroking a hand down his recently shaved cheek.

*Mistake.*

Touching him stirred all those old memories of greeting him in the morning with a kiss and savoring the scent of fresh hay that clung to him following his morning chores. A crackling energy zinged through her and made her knees weak.

The fire that danced in his eyes told her he sensed the same electricity humming between them.

She caught her breath. She was treading into dangerous territory. The kiss they'd shared last night was proof of how easily she could slide back into her role as Clay's lover, forgetting the obstacles and hurt between them. Still, all the sexual heat in the world couldn't save their marriage five years ago. Indulging that physical attraction now could only cause more pain in the long run.

Because she couldn't give her body over to Clay without involving her heart.

Jewel cleared her throat, jerking Tamara and Clay from whatever spell had held them the past several seconds. When Tamara glanced back at their visitor, Jewel wore a knowing grin.

Clay shifted his feet awkwardly. "Well, I'll, uh…" He rubbed his hands down the seat of his jeans and stepped back. "I'll leave you two ladies to talk. I gotta finish saddling up a few horses for the girls. I know they're eager to start their ride."

"Thanks, Clay." Jewel gave him a little wave as he strode back toward the barn. Turning to Tamara, she said, "Care to join me at the riding ring? I love to see the girls' faces when they get up on a horse for the first time. They're always so excited."

"Sure." She fell in step with Jewel.

"I was sorry to hear about your fall." Jewel gave her a worried glance. "You seem to be getting around pretty well considering…"

"A full night's sleep did me wonders. I can't remember the last time I had more than five hours."

"Me either." Jewel gave her a forced grin, but her eyes seemed troubled.

Sensing she'd touched on a sore subject, Tamara shifted gears. "So how long have you been bringing kids out to the Bar None?"

Brightening a bit, Jewel shrugged. "Pretty much since we opened a few months ago. Clay's been a godsend with all his support. I can call him night or day if I need something, and he's always willing to lend a hand. And there wouldn't be a Hopechest Ranch in Esperanza if Clay hadn't sold us a piece of the Bar None to build on."

Tamara snapped a glance toward Jewel. "He did?"

"He didn't tell you?"

Tamara shook her head. "Not that he had any reason to tell me. Since our divorce, we don't discuss Bar None business. In fact, before a couple days ago, I hadn't seen Clay in five years."

That news seemed to surprise Jewel. "I'm sorry. I thought… well, I assumed really that…because of the way you two looked at each other just now that…"

Heat climbed Tamara's throat and stung her cheeks. "That what?"

"That maybe you were getting back together…or at least were still close," Jewel ventured hesitantly. "It's just you two seemed so…" she waved a hand as she searched for the right word "…connected."

Tamara opened her mouth to deny Jewel's assumption, but her voice stuck in her throat. What *was* going on between her and Clay? And if his friends were picking up on a shared undercurrent, what signal was Clay receiving from her that she didn't intend?

Already disconcerted by that thought, Tamara glanced toward the riding ring in time to see Clay shake hands with a tall man in his early forties. The man's thick brown hair fell in his eyes and shone with auburn highlights in the morning sun. Her steps faltered. Quinn Logan.

Jewel stopped and gave Tamara a frown. "I'm sorry. Have I said too much?"

Tamara forced a grin and shook her head. "No. It's not you. I just…well, I've sorta seen a ghost from my past."

Jewel turned and scanned the riding corral. "You mean the guy talking to Clay?"

"Yeah." She inhaled as deeply as her sore ribs would allow and blew it out slowly.

"I remember seeing him out here before when I brought the girls, but I was never introduced. Who is he?"

"Clay's good friend, Quinn Logan. He's Clay's veterinarian."

Tipping her head, Jewel arched an eyebrow and gave Quinn an appraising scrutiny. "And quite the good-looking vet at that, huh?"

Tamara wrinkled her nose and resumed walking toward the corral. "I suppose…"

"I hear a *but* at the end of that sentence. Why? Is he married?"

"Widowed. His wife died right before I moved away from Esperanza. I don't think he's remarried. Although I guess *I* wouldn't have heard if he had."

Jewel frowned. "Why not? You said he was a good friend."

"Of Clay's. More like my old nemesis."

Jewel's puzzled look spoke for her.

Scowling, Tamara shook her head. "Sorry. That sounded melodramatic. It's not as bad as that, but Quinn was a major factor in the events that finally killed my marriage."

Jewel gave Tamara a look that said Tamara's comment intrigued her but she was too polite to press for details. They'd reached the split-rail fence that circled the corral, and Jewel walked over to a young Mexican woman who was watching the activity in the ring. "Let me know if you get too hot, Ana. I brought plenty of bottled water, and I'm sure Clay wouldn't mind you going inside if you needed to get out of the sun."

Tamara noticed the young woman's rounded belly when she turned to smile at Jewel. "I'm fine. Stop worrying, Miss Jewel. Baby and I love the sunshine and fresh air."

Jewel laughed. "If you can call the smell of horse manure fresh air…"

Tamara joined Jewel at the rail and propped her arms on the top beam. "If you spend much time around horses, eventually you don't notice the smell."

"Tamara, this is Ana Morales. She's staying with us at Hopechest Ranch until her baby is born."

Tamara greeted the young mother who'd been blessed with all the best features of her Mexican heritage. Her black hair was thick and glossy, and her olive complexion and dark eyes had a healthy glow.

"When are you due?" Tamara asked.

Ana flashed a shy smile. "Three months." She glanced away and slid a protective hand over her stomach. "If you don't mind, Miss Jewel, think I'll go see the other horses."

Tamara gave Jewel a puzzled look as Ana headed toward the stables. "Was it something I said?"

Jewel shook her head and placed a hand lightly on Tamara's arm. "No, no. It's not you. Ana's a sweet young lady, really bright and well-spoken, but she's also very private. She doesn't like to talk about herself."

"So I scared her off by asking about her due date," Tamara said.

Jewel opened her mouth as if to deny it, then shrugged. "Maybe. Please, don't take it personally. She's going through a rough patch, being away from her family, and feels the need to keep to herself more than the younger girls." Jewel paused and gave a self-conscious grin. "Although I've been keeping to myself out at the Hopechest Ranch myself, so I don't have room to talk. I've been in town for several months, and I still haven't met many folks."

Tamara noticed Jewel's gaze stray back to Quinn but kept her own focus on Clay as he tightened the stirrups for one of the girls. "If you want to meet people in Esperanza, you need to go to Miss Sue's diner. Not only do they have the best food in town, it's where everyone who is anyone goes to see and be seen."

Jewel's face warmed, and she nodded. "Oh, yes. I've been to Miss Sue's. I was told as soon as I got to Esperanza that her pecan pie was heaven on a plate."

"Heaven on a plate. That's about right!" Tamara laughed then grabbed her ribs. "Oh, ow! Note to self—laughing hurts."

Jewel winced and muffled a chuckle. When her new friend's attention fixed on Quinn again, something inside Tamara nudged her to explain her cool attitude toward the vet. "I don't want to leave you with the wrong impression about Quinn. I—" Dropping her gaze, Tamara kicked a clod of dirt with the toe of her shoe. "Right before we divorced, we had to put one of Clay's best stallions to sleep." Her heart ached as the memories stirred again. She explained to Jewel in general terms how she and Clay had argued over the best course of action and how Quinn had influenced Clay's decision for euthanasia, despite viable treatment options. "I didn't like the way Quinn handled the whole situation, and I let him know it. When I questioned him about his recommendation, all he'd say was euthanasia was 'for the best.' His evasiveness made me think he was hiding something."

Jewel furrowed her brow. "Like what?"

Tamara sent Quinn a dark look. "I don't know. Maybe he missed signs of the disease in earlier examinations and was afraid we'd sue for malpractice. Or…there's a vaccine for strangles, the disease that Lone Star contracted. So maybe he'd been negligent about vaccinating Clay's horses."

She faced Jewel and shook her head in consternation. Maybe she shouldn't be unloading her frustrations on someone she'd just met, but Jewel held her gaze with an earnest interest and caring. Tamara had felt an immediate connection with Clay's relative, and when Jewel nodded her head for her to continue,

Tamara continued venting. "And why couldn't they have treated Lone Star with antibiotics? Everyone I talked to in town said most horses recover from strangles with the right treatment. Anyway, the whole incident just seemed fishy. And I'm not the only one who thought so. I had people calling me for weeks afterward asking what had happened and second-guessing Quinn's actions."

Jewel's gaze moved to something behind Tamara, and she schooled her expression. With her eyes, she signaled Tamara to brace herself and turn around.

Tamara's gut clenched. She pivoted on her heel.

"Hello, Tamara." Quinn stood behind her with his thumbs hooked in his pockets. He gave her a quick smile that was polite but lacking any warmth. Beneath the scar that ran down his cheek, courtesy of a feisty stallion, his jaw was tense.

"Quinn." Tamara twitched the corner of her mouth, the best smile she could manage with the swirl of resentment and painful memories that churned through her. She dutifully made the introductions between Jewel and the veterinarian without any flourish, and they shook hands.

"What brings you out to the Bar None today?" Jewel asked, picking up the conversation when Tamara and Quinn lapsed into an awkward silence. "None of Clay's horses are sick, I hope."

"No, ma'am. Nothing like that." Quinn's mood brightened when he answered Jewel. "I stable my stallion here." He hitched his head toward a black horse still waiting to be saddled. "That's Noches. I come by a lot to check on him and visit with Clay."

Jewel flashed a smile and nodded. "He's a beautiful animal."

"Before I leave, I plan to check on one of Clay's mares that's about to foal. But first, I promised Clay I'd help him with all those pretty young ladies you brought. Not that we expect trouble." He raised a hand to reassure Jewel. "But it's best to have plenty of hands around when you're dealing with inexperienced riders."

"Well, I appreciate your donating your time to the girls. They love coming out here to see the horses."

"My pleasure." Quinn smiled at Jewel then shifted his attention back to Tamara. His grin faded. "Well, I better be getting back to work. Good to see you, Tamara."

"You, too," she lied, the civility sour in her throat.

As Quinn strode away, Jewel gave a low whistle. "Wow. For June, it sure feels frosty out here."

A twist of compunction tightened Tamara's chest. "I know it's petty of me. I don't like the bad blood between us. But that night was so painful for me…for all of us. There were lots of hard feelings, and bitter words and accusations that can never be erased. I'm as much to blame as he is for the rift in our friendship—and we did used to be friends, just like he and Clay still are. But some things are hard to get past."

"I understand." The sadness that flickered in Jewel's eyes echoed her words, and for the second time, Tamara wondered about the troubled shadows in Jewel's gaze. "Have you talked to Clay recently about what happened that night, why he went with Quinn's recommendation? Maybe now, with some distance from the situation, he could better explain his perspective."

Tamara grunted and cast Jewel a quick side glance. "As a matter of fact, the topic came up last night in a…" she searched for the right word "…heated, no…*emotional* discussion we had. It was the first time Clay and I had talked about some of the issues that led to our divorce and…well, it was a painful conversation with lots of hot buttons."

Tucking a wisp of hair behind her ear, Jewel faced Tamara and leaned against the fence. "I guess I was thinking that with the time you two have had since the divorce, that now might be a good chance to resolve some of those touchy issues. It's obvious you still care about each other."

"I don't know." Tamara's lungs constricted at the thought of hashing out all the old grievances with Clay. He'd tried to discuss some of their problems last night, and she'd bolted like a skittish colt. She wasn't prepared to face those resurrected memories.

Jewel's warm smile encouraged confidences, and again

Tamara felt a kinship and connection to her new friend. "What good would it do to open old wounds?"

"You might find the peace you need to have closure. Or you might be able to put the hurt and resentment aside and repair an old friendship." Jewel sent a meaningful glance toward Quinn.

Tamara stared into the riding ring without really seeing. Rather than Jewel's charges on horseback circling the corral, her vision was filled with reruns of last night's emotional exchange with Clay. He'd given her an opening to explain why she'd left, and she'd dodged the issue like a coward.

"Or…I could just be horning in where my advice isn't wanted." Jewel's comment pulled Tamara back to the present.

With a contrite grin, Jewel shrugged. "Sorry. Hazard of the profession. I spend most of every day counseling and advising the girls at Hopechest Ranch. Sometimes it's hard to turn the psychological training off and mind my own business."

"No, don't apologize. You're right, and you've given me a lot to think about."

As if she weren't already spending every waking hour thinking about Clay—the mistakes they'd made in their marriage, the passion they'd shared in bed, and the cherished traditions they'd created on holidays and special occasions.

The missed opportunities to save their relationship.

She watched Clay lead a younger girl's horse around the perimeter of the corral, coaxing the first-time rider with warm encouragement and sunny smiles, and Tamara's heart split open. She wanted to reclaim all the things she and Clay had once shared. She wanted a second chance to make their relationship work.

But could they overcome the obstacles that had torn them apart the first time? They'd both changed. Their lives were on divergent paths. How could they possibly make it work? And more important, was a second chance even what Clay wanted?

# Chapter 9

Later that morning, as Jewel and the girls from Hopechest Ranch loaded back into their SUV to leave, a blue pickup rolled up Clay's driveway, kicking up a plume of dust.

"Well, we sure are popular today," Clay said under his breath to Tamara, who stood beside him on the front porch, waving goodbye to Jewel and her charges.

"It's Dr. O'Neal. Since when do doctors make house calls?" Tamara cast Clay a curious glance. "Did you call him?"

He shook his head and walked down the steps to greet the doctor.

"So how's the patient doing?" Dr. O'Neal gave Tamara a measuring scrutiny. "I take it you're feeling better if you're on your feet."

She bobbed her head. "Much." Tipping her head, she asked, "Did we miss an appointment or is this a courtesy call?"

"I was passing right by here on the way into the office, so I thought I'd save you a trip into town for a follow-up exam."

"That was thoughtful. But…" Tamara turned her attention to

Clay. "I was just about to talk my ex into taking me to Miss Sue's for lunch."

Clay cocked an eyebrow. First he'd heard. Not that he wouldn't make the time if lunch at Miss Sue's was what Tamara wanted. He conducted a mental inventory of his to-do list. With a bit of rescheduling and delegating, he could free up the afternoon.

"We could have stopped by the clinic after we ate." Tamara's gaze returned to the doctor. "Assuming a follow-up is really necessary. I feel much stronger. My ribs don't hurt nearly as much. Well…unless I cough or laugh or move suddenly."

Dr. O'Neal nodded. "That's good." He paused then angled his head in query. "Are you still taking the painkillers I gave you? Used as directed the drug is perfectly safe but…" His face grew somber. "They can become addictive if you rely on them too long."

Tamara smiled politely. "I've switched to the over-the-counter stuff to control what aches and pains remain."

The doctor raised a palm and grinned. "Then it seems my work here is done." He offered his hand to Clay.

"Any word from Doc Mason?" Clay asked as they shook hands.

The doctor's smile faded, his brow puckering, and he seemed at a loss for words for a moment. "Last I heard, Doc had decided to extend his vacation. He's really taken by the Arizona climate and scenery. In fact, he mentioned retiring there."

Clay exchanged a startled glance with Tamara.

"He's talking about retiring? That doesn't sound like the Doc Mason I know." Clay scratched his jaw. "The man's a ball of energy, and his medical practice, his patients are his life. Why would he leave his friends and home to retire in Arizona?"

Dr. O'Neal scrubbed a hand over the thinning patch of his short-cropped hair and cleared his throat. "I don't have an answer for that, but that's what the Doc's message said." He backed toward his truck. "Well, good to see you're feeling better, Ms. Brown. I'd better be off."

Clay frowned and sent Tamara another curious look as the fill-in doctor beat a hasty retreat. As Dr. O'Neal's pickup crunched down the gravel driveway, Clay climbed the porch steps and tipped his head. "Miss Sue's, huh?"

She grinned. "Please? If you can afford the time away. I've got a powerful hankering for pecan pie. And I'd love to see Becky French and the folks in town."

He slid a hand down her cheek and tweaked her chin. "All right. Anything for you, love. Just let me get my keys, and I'll meet you at my truck."

Clay strolled inside, and as he passed the hall mirror he noticed the sappy grin he wore. He sighed and snatched his keys from the kitchen counter. In the two days Tamara had been with him, he'd gotten lulled into a sense that her presence meant a return to a familiar status quo. Falling back into old habits had been far too easy, and seeing her in his home made five years of her absence melt like snow in Austin.

If she was feeling well enough go into town, if she only needed over-the-counter medicine for the ache in her ribs, she'd be leaving the Bar None again. Soon.

He pressed his hat farther down on his head and strode out to his truck, trying not to dwell on the unrest that swirled in him at the thought of Tamara's imminent departure.

He'd known her stay at the ranch was temporary. He just hadn't been prepared for the mixed emotions she'd awakened in him.

When she'd left five years ago, he'd managed to suppress his pain and shut down his feelings by pouring his energies into the ranch. This time he wasn't sure any amount of avoidance or diversions could heal the inevitable heartache. He now recognized what he'd denied before. For all their differences and difficulties, Tamara meant more to him than anyone or anything—including his ranch.

Tamara gazed out the window of Clay's truck as they rolled down Main Street into Esperanza. Details she had understandably missed on their trip to Doc Mason's clinic, now caught her eye and raised endless questions.

"Is June Yardly still the librarian?" she asked Clay as they passed the small library.

"Nope. She retired a couple years back."

"Yates Feed and Supply is still in business." She smiled. "When did that mini-mart open? Has it hurt business for the local merchants?"

Clay shrugged. "Not that I've heard. Town folk are loyal to their own."

He found an empty parking spot in front of the sheriff's office and cut the engine.

When she'd called her lab in San Antonio earlier that morning, Eric had been evasive, saying that while she was on medical leave, she needn't worry about the current cases. Tamara considered stopping in the sheriff's office to see what new information Jericho had on the investigation. But she caught a whiff of the inviting aromas that spilled out of Miss Sue's across the street, and her stomach growled. The visit to Jericho's office would wait.

Clay escorted her across the street with a proprietary hand at the small of her back. Just as he had on numerous occasions in the past. But those days were gone. And by this afternoon, she needed to be gone from Esperanza as well. She had no excuse for prolonging her departure. A wistful longing pricked Tamara. How was it that in high school she couldn't wait to get out of this small town? Now being in Esperanza and seeing all the familiar faces felt like a homecoming.

When Clay opened the door for Tamara, the clank of an old cow bell heralded their arrival. She preceded him into the diner, redolent with tempting aromas of fresh-brewed coffee and home-baked bread and bustling with lunchtime traffic. She sat at the only free table. After shaking hands with an elderly man she didn't recognize, Clay folded his long legs under the wooden table and set his Stetson on the chair beside him.

Tamara glanced at the other diners, many of whom sent curious stares her way. "I think I know who will be the center of the gossip in town this afternoon." She grinned and leaned closer to Clay as if sharing a juicy secret. "Did you hear about Clay Colton? He was at Miss Sue's today with his ex-wife. Bold as brass. I hear she's been staying out at his place since Thursday! What do you suppose that means?"

She flashed him a playful smile that elicited a lopsided grin in return. He wrapped his hand around hers, and heat curled inside her.

"We could really get the rumor mill buzzing if you were to kiss me right now." He tipped his head, and a challenging glint sparked in his eyes.

A flutter of longing flapped in her chest. Kissing Clay again had immense appeal, but she didn't dare confound things between them. Her emotions were already tangled.

Becky French's arrival at their table with glasses of ice water spared Tamara from responding. "Why, Clay Colton. What are you doing in here in the middle of the day? Don't normally see you in here until supper time."

A resident of Esperanza for all of her sixty-plus years, Becky French had always reminded Tamara of Mrs. Santa Claus. Short, plump and gray-haired, Becky had a bubbly personality and lively blue eyes that cinched the comparison. Seeing the dear older woman was as much a treat for Tamara as the long-anticipated pie.

Clay smiled at the diner's owner and shrugged. "Tamara had a craving for your pecan pie. Who am I to deny a beautiful woman such a basic request?"

Becky's head swiveled toward Tamara, and recognition lit her eyes. "My goodness, Tamara! I'd heard you were in town."

As Becky stepped around the corner of the scarred wooden table to wrap her in a hug, Tamara braced for the painful squeeze. But Becky hesitated then frowned. "Wait a minute, Billy Akers said somethin' about you breaking your ribs? Are you all right?"

"Just bruised, not broken. But I'll take a rain check on that hug today. Okay?"

Becky nodded and stepped back with a smile. "My gracious, it's good to see you!"

Tamara felt more than saw the gazes of other customers turn toward her and Clay. By nightfall, every citizen of Esperanza would know the divorced Coltons were having lunch together at Miss Sue's.

Becky took their lunch order, promising to save Tamara a large serving of pecan pie, and hustled off to the kitchen. Tamara studied the familiar décor. Little had changed since the days when Clay's mother had run the diner. Even the curtain across the front plate-glass window was the same. Mismatched wooden tables filled the tile floor, and framed bits of the town's memorabilia hung on the walls. Though old, the diner had passed from one set of loving hands to another through the years and remained tidily kept and filled with homey charm. Nostalgia tugged her heart as she remembered evenings she'd spent at Miss Sue's, first with her own family and later with Clay during high school.

"Uncle Clay!" The delighted squeal from a little girl at the front door cut into Tamara's memories. The red-headed pixie hurtled herself into Clay's arms and hugged his neck. "I didn't know you'd be here!"

Clay's face lit with a warm grin. "Hey, pipsqueak. How's my favorite cowgirl?"

"Fine as frog's hair!" The little girl's green eyes danced with joy and mischief.

Clay laughed. "Where did you hear that expression?"

She shrugged. "One of Mama's rodeo friends."

The spitfire glanced at Tamara and blinked curiously. Tamara didn't need to see the child's mother entering the diner to recognize Georgie Colton's daughter. The girl was, as Clay'd told her, the image of Clay's sister.

"You must be Emmie," Tamara said with a broad smile.

Dressed in a Western snap-front shirt, jeans and boots, the girl nodded. "How'd you know?"

"Because you look just like your mom."

Emmie rolled her eyes. "Everybody says that!"

Clay tweaked the girl's nose. "Because it's true."

Georgie reached the table with a handsome black-haired man at her side. "Emmie, I've asked you not to—" She stopped abruptly and gasped. "Tamara?"

"Georgie!" Tamara pushed to her feet and ignored the pain as she hugged her former sister-in-law. After a round of introductions, during which Tamara met Nick Sheffield, the new man in Georgie's life, and Clay summarized the events that had brought Tamara back to town, Georgie pulled extra chairs up to their table so she, Nick and Emmie could join her brother for lunch.

"How long will you be in town?" Nick asked Tamara.

"Not long. I'm feeling stronger already, and I really need to get back to work."

Clay grunted. "Your boss put you on medical leave. Remember?"

"But I—" Tamara snapped her mouth shut and swallowed her protest. Nick and Georgie exchanged a look, and in deference to their audience, she changed the topic. "Clay tells me you ran into a little trouble recently yourself."

Georgie shivered. "Yeah. I'm so glad that nightmare is over."

Nick wrapped a protective arm around Georgie. "The important thing is you and Emmie are safe now, and the woman responsible was stopped."

"Amen to that." Clay raised his ice water in salute.

"Have you seen any old friends since you got in town?" Georgie asked and flipped her long red braid to her back. "I mean besides Jericho." She flicked her hand in dismissal. "That was business and doesn't count."

Tamara propped her elbows on the table and knit her brow in thought. "Well, Quinn was out at the ranch earlier, although we didn't say much more than hello." She met Clay's gaze across the table, and his expression said he knew the grudge Tamara still carried toward his good friend.

"Logan? The vet?" Nick asked.

Remembering that the former Secret Service man was new to Esperanza, Tamara nodded confirmation.

"Quinn Logan," Georgie said and clucked her tongue. "I just don't understand why he is still single. Maybe I could introduce him to—"

"Little sister, the last thing Quinn needs is another well-meaning woman trying to fix him up. Give it a rest, okay?"

"I just—"

Clay made a slashing motion across his throat to forestall Georgie's protest.

"Oh, I saw Billy Akers when I was at Doc Mason's clinic to get checked after my fall." Tamara chuckled. "Man-oh-man, my brother and Billy used to give me such a hard time when I'd beg to tag along with them."

Georgie grinned then her smile dimmed. "I heard his mom was real sick. Did he say how she was doing?"

Tamara sobered and nodded. "He said it's ALS. She's not doing well." She glanced at Clay. "Before I leave town, I want to stop by and give Mrs. Akers my best. She's such a dear lady, like a second mother to me. It's been far too long since I visited her."

Clay nodded. "Just say when. I'll take you."

"Wait, I thought Doc Mason was out of town." Georgie tipped her head. "Who treated you when you went to the clinic?"

"His fill-in, Dr O'Neal."

Becky French arrived at the table with Tamara and Clay's orders. "Frank O'Neal? Nice fella. Needs a little more meat on his bones if you ask me. He came in here for lunch a few days ago and ate a salad and unsweetened tea." Becky harrumphed. "No wonder he's skin and bones." She slid Clay's hamburger and Tamara's tuna melt onto the table. "I think he's planning to buy into Doc Mason's practice when the good doctor retires."

Georgie chuckled. "*If* he retires. Doc Mason loves his work more than anyone I've ever met!"

Clay frowned. "Which is why this sudden vacation he's on seems odd to me. Dr. O'Neal stopped by the Bar None this morning to check on Tamara and said Doc Mason has extended his trip. He likes Arizona so much he's thinking of retiring there."

"I've been to Arizona! Haven't I, Mom?" Emmie chirped. "With the rodeo."

"Righty-o, honey."

The diner owner shook her head. "Staying in Arizona? That's crazy. The people in Esperanza are family to Doc. Why would he retire someplace he doesn't know anyone?"

Clay shrugged, and Tamara recognized the worry that darkened his eyes. The old doctor's absence really bothered Clay, and she was itching to discuss his suspicions when they had more privacy.

"Speaking of family—" A smile lit Becky's face, and she pulled a white envelope from her apron pocket. "You haven't seen my sweet grandbabies! I just got a new set of pictures from my youngest son, Tamara. Have a look."

Tamara took the stack of photos the diner's owner handed her and, while Becky took Georgie, Nick and Emmie's orders, she flipped through the series of smiling-baby shots. Maternal longing tugged deep inside Tamara as she studied the photos.

If she and Clay hadn't divorced, would they have a child by now? Would their baby have had Clay's brown eyes or her blue ones? She shook her head and set the fruitless thoughts aside.

"Can I have a milkshake?" Emmie asked. "I promise to eat my whole lunch."

Georgie ruffled her daughter's short hair. "All right. But for dessert. Deal?"

Emmie beamed. "Deal!"

Becky laughed. "Enjoy this age. They're not always so agreeable. When they become teenagers…" The older woman threw up her hands and rolled her eyes. "Take T. J. Ward, for example. Macy's got her hands full with that one. Jericho got called outta here the other night because T.J. was stopped out on the county highway driving eighty miles per hour. Drag racing the Horner boy, I think. Macy, the poor dear, has had such trouble with him. The boy's been so rebellious lately, and it just keeps getting worse."

Shaking her head in dismay, Becky headed back to the

kitchen with Georgie, Nick and Emmie's orders. Clay traced the grain of the wood in their table with the handle of his fork and shook his head. "I know what Macy's going through. Ryder was the same way after Mom died. Let's hope she figures out how to get through to T.J." He heaved a sigh and stabbed at his hash browns. "My lack of parenting skills landed Ryder in prison."

"Clay—" Tamara began before Georgie sputtered.

"What! Back up there, big brother. Your lack of parenting skills? It was Ryder's lack of self-discipline and good judgment that landed him in jail. You did all you could."

"And it wasn't enough or our brother wouldn't be in prison." He waved his fork in dismissal. "Forget I said anything. Let's not ruin our lunch by discussing my failures."

Georgie leaned across the table and grabbed her brother's wrist as he tried to eat a pickle spear. "I'll drop it if you get one thing straight. You gave Ryder and me the best foundation you could after Mom died. No one worked harder or coulda been more dedicated. I turned out okay thanks to your guidance, so keep that in mind before you start calling your efforts a failure."

Tamara held her breath while Clay locked silent stares with his sister. When he dropped his gaze, he said calmly, "Your sleeve is in my ketchup."

Georgie jerked her arm back with a gasp, checking the damage.

"Oh, well. It'll wash," Emmie said, patting her mother's back. Tamara hid a grin behind her napkin as she wiped her mouth.

"Did you tell Clay about Meredith's trip out here yet?" Nick asked.

Clay cocked his head. "Aunt Meredith's coming to town?"

Georgie nodded and swiped one of Clay's pickles. "On Friday. Mostly she's coming to check up on Jewel, I think, but I was hoping we could all get together for a meal. You have plans for this weekend?"

Clay glanced to Tamara and raised his eyebrows in query, as if consulting her.

She waved a hand. "Don't look at me. I'll be back in San Antonio by then."

"Aww," Emmie whined.

"Why the rush to get back?" Clay asked. "Your boss has you on medical leave, and I know Meredith would love to see you." He cocked his head toward Emmie. "You wouldn't want to disappoint my niece, would you?" Emmie beamed and gave a smug nod. To Georgie, Clay said, "Why don't y'all come out to the Bar None. I'll smoke some brisket and ask Marie to make a big bowl of potato salad. Y'all can bring a dish, and we'll have a family barbecue."

"Yeah!" Emmie's eyes danced, and she squirmed on her chair. "Can we, Mom?"

Georgie cast an inquiring glance to Nick, who gave a nod. "Sounds like a plan. Tamara, please stay for the barbecue. It's only a couple extra days, and it's been too long since we had a chance to catch up."

Her gaze moved from Georgie's expectant look to Emmie's eager face, before meeting Clay's piercing dark eyes. "I…guess so."

While Emmie cheered, Tamara's lunch did somersaults in her stomach. As much as she appreciated the invitation to join the Coltons' barbecue, she was no longer a part of the family and pretending only made it harder to leave.

Clay leaned close to his niece and whispered something that made the girl giggle and his own eyes light with affection. His love for Georgie's daughter was heartrending.

A wistful longing gripped Tamara by the throat. Why couldn't Clay have loved her with the same devotion and obvious joy that he had for his family and his ranch? If she had another chance to make her marriage work, if she tried harder to show Clay…

Tamara cut the thought off, unfinished.

She had a new life, a new career, a new appreciation of who she was and what she could accomplish when she dedicated herself to a goal. She'd worked hard to get where she was in the CSI department. How could she give that up to come back to the Bar None? Her dreams had taken her away from Esperanza, but had her dreams changed? She'd taken for granted her home, friends, family when she lived here, and she wanted those things again. But did she have the same courage to follow *that* dream as she'd had when she pursued her career years ago? Was it worth the risk of getting hurt again?

Tamara sighed and mentally chided herself. An invitation to a barbecue hardly translated to Clay wanting a second chance or meant that his feelings for her had changed.

Becky French returned to the table with food for Georgie's family and a large slice of pecan pie for Tamara. She gave Becky an appreciative smile then stared at the sumptuous dessert with a heavy heart.

Her return to the Bar None, this treasured glimpse at how the Colton family was doing since she'd last seen them, the precious moments she'd spent with Clay were drawing to a close. Suddenly Miss Sue's pecan pie didn't seem nearly as sweet or satisfying as spending time alone with Clay.

# Chapter 10

As they left Miss Sue's diner after lunch, Clay's thoughts returned to the startling news of Doc Mason's plans to retire out of state. Clay had known the man his whole life and had never heard the doctor mention living anywhere besides Esperanza. Doc Mason loved the small town and its citizens. This new twist on his vacation sounded odd.

As he cranked his truck's engine, he glanced across the front seat where Tamara was leaning her head against the headrest and had closed her eyes. "Tee, are you all right?"

"Mm. Just sleepy. My full stomach plus the warm truck are a double whammy." She yawned to punctuate the sentiment.

He lifted a lopsided grin and tucked a wisp of her hair behind her ear.

Her eyes flew open at his touch, and she turned a bright gaze to him.

"Do you feel up to making a stop on the way home?"

She shrugged. "What'd you have in mind?"

He shifted gears but didn't back out of the parking spot yet. "I'd like to stop by Doc Mason's clinic and talk to his nurse. Maybe Mrs. Hamilton knows something more about the reasons behind his changed plans."

Her brow furrowed. "This thing with Doc Mason really bothers you, doesn't it?"

He gritted his teeth and glanced away for a moment. Opening up about the depths of his concern and his disappointment that Doc Mason could be leaving town for good needled him awkwardly.

But this was Tamara. Sharing his worries with her felt natural, felt right. Despite the five intervening years since their divorce.

"I've told you how Doc Mason used to take me fishing as a kid, right?" He glanced at her, and she nodded. "Well, he did other stuff for us, too. Maybe because we didn't have a dad around, maybe just because he's a nice man. But I… I always looked to him as something of a father figure—even now that I know Graham Colton is my real dad."

Tamara's eyes softened, and her expression warmed. "I suspected as much."

Encouraged by her response, Clay added, "In fact, Doc Mason has always been more like a father to me than Graham Colton ever could be. Doc was there when we needed him as kids, and he's still a good friend. What I'm hearing about his retirement plans just doesn't add up."

His ex-wife sent him a poignant smile. "So let's go see what his nurse knows."

Clay turned the truck engine off, and they walked the short distance to Doc Mason's clinic.

Ellen Hamilton was behind the reception desk when they entered the waiting room, and she greeted them with a cheery smile. "What brings you two in today? I thought Dr. O'Neal checked on Ms. Brown this morning."

"He did," Tamara said, "and I appreciate the personal attention."

Clay slid his hands in his pockets and rocked back on the heels of his boots. "We're here on another matter. I have some questions about Doc Mason's vacation and his new retirement plans."

The welcome in Ellen Hamilton's face morphed into wariness. "What questions?"

"Well, for starters, exactly what did he say when he called?"

Ellen picked up a pen and tapped it on the appointment pad. "I wouldn't know. I didn't take the call."

"Who did?" Tamara asked.

Ellen divided a nervous glance between them as she hesitated. "Our…answering service."

"Someone in town?" Clay studied Ellen's telltale fidgeting. Why did their questions make the nurse so edgy?

"No. We use a professional answering service based out of San Antonio. The message was included in a morning e-mail with a report on all calls taken."

Clay removed his Stetson and raked his hair back from his eyes before replacing his hat. "What exactly did the e-mail say?"

Scowling, Ellen stood and stepped away from the reception desk. "Perhaps I should get Dr. O'Neal if you have more questions."

Clay narrowed a curious gaze on the nurse as she backed toward the patient rooms. "Is there a problem?"

"Wait here." Ellen disappeared down the hall for a moment during which Clay exchanged a puzzled glance with Tamara.

"What do you think?"

She twisted her lips in thought. "I smell a rat. She seems awfully nervous."

"You think they're lying?"

"Not necessarily. But maybe we aren't getting the whole truth either."

A frowning Dr. O'Neal appeared from the hallway. "What's going on here, Colton? Why are you giving my nurse a hard time?"

Clay lifted his eyebrows, startled by the doctor's assessment. He cast a quick glance to Ellen as she returned to the front desk. "We're just looking for a few answers about Doc Mason's sudden change of plans."

"How do you know the change is sudden?" Dr. O'Neal crossed his arms over his chest and glared back at Clay. "Maybe he's been considering retirement privately for some time. What business is it of yours what he does anyway?"

The doctor's combative attitude set off warning bells, but Clay kept his reply calm. "He's my friend and has been for years. I'm worried about him."

"No need to be. The man's on vacation. No harm in that, is there?"

From the corner of his eye, Clay noticed Tamara shift her body to a more defensive position as the conversation took a decidedly hostile tone. But Clay kept his gaze narrowed on Dr. O'Neal.

"Where did he go? Did he leave the name of the hotel where he'd be staying or a number where he could be reached?"

"Of course." Ellen pulled a sheet of paper from the top drawer and waved it. She smiled smugly as if she'd just won a point in an argument. "Right here."

As she stashed the sheet back into the drawer, Clay moved forward and stuck a hand on the edge of the drawer to keep her from closing it. "Mind if I have a look?" He snatched up the paper before she could answer and quickly scanned it. The sheet was a blank piece of stationery from a resort called the Desert Palms, Inc.

Ellen snatched the sheet back. "You can't do that! If Doc Mason had wanted you to know where he was, he'd have told you!"

Dr. O'Neal stepped closer. The thin, balding man puffed up as if ready for battle. "I have to ask you to go now. We're quite busy and don't have time for any more of your questions."

Clay sent a meaningful glance to the empty waiting room but didn't comment. "Fine. But if Doc Mason calls again, please let him know I want to speak with him. He knows both my cell and home number."

Dr. O'Neal shifted his feet and jerked a nod. "I will."

Clay touched the brim of his hat and gave Ellen a tight smile. "Ma'am."

Tamara preceded him out of the office and sighed as the clinic door swooshed closed behind them. "Wow. They sure were acting weird. I have to wonder why they would be antsy about us asking such basic questions. We weren't accusing them of anything."

"I'm wondering the same thing. Hey, you have a pen with you?"

"Uh, probably." Tamara dug in her purse and came up with a ballpoint pen.

"Thanks." He uncapped the pen with his teeth and scribbled a number on his hand.

Tamara tipped her head, and her inquiring expression asking what he'd written.

He turned his hand to show her. "The number for the resort where Doc Mason is staying. I plan to call him myself and see what's going on."

She nodded and gave him a coy smile. "Good thinking. I was wondering if you got a long enough peek at that paper to get any valuable information."

They headed down the sidewalk toward his car in companionable silence. Clay started to drape a possessive arm around Tamara's shoulders as they walked but stopped himself.

Tamara wasn't his anymore.

The past several days had felt so comfortably familiar, so natural, he had to remind himself the divorce wasn't some terrible nightmare he'd woken up from three days ago when Tamara returned. Her presence was temporary.

*We can't let that happen again. I'll be leaving in a couple of days....*

A pang of disappointment shot through him, and he tucked his hands in his pockets with a sigh. He both treasured and damned the circumstances that had brought Tamara back into his life. For the past five years, he'd managed some semblance of a normal life by numbing himself against the pain of his failures, locking away reminders of what he'd lost. But having Tamara back at the ranch these past few days had brightened his life like sunrise after a dark night, refreshed his spirits like a cool breeze on a stifling day. He'd begun to *feel* again. Joy and pain. Hope and regret. A whole tangle of emotions he'd shoved down and denied for the past five years.

*Let's not complicate things.*

Clay curled his fingers around the keys in his pocket and squeezed his fist until the metal bit into his palm.

"If they'd been at a crime scene I was working," Tamara said, her nose scrunched in thought, "and I'd gotten answers like that, coupled with the jittery, defensive behavior they exhibited, I'd have them at the top of my suspect list."

"But they're not suspects in a crime. So why so touchy?"

"Beats me." She bit her bottom lip and sent him a side glance as they strolled past storefronts on Main Street. "My lab should have some results back on the blood sample they found in the tunnel. I'd like to stop at the sheriff's office long enough to see if Jericho has any new information."

He nodded. "Good idea."

When Clay and Tamara walked into the sheriff's office, Jericho's deputy, Adam Rawlings, looked up from a large sandwich. Mouth full of the bite he'd just taken, he mumbled, "Can I help you?"

Before Clay could answer, Tamara stepped forward and took the lead. "Is Jericho in? We were hoping he had the results back from my lab on the blood found at the tunnel."

Clay cocked his head and studied the taut, all-business stance Tamara had assumed. A measure of pride tickled inside him at seeing his ex-wife in professional mode. She'd always been competent and unintimidated in business matters, but he detected a new level of self-assurance and assertiveness that he'd never known her to have before. His teenage bride had grown up a lot in the five years they'd been apart.

Deputy Rawlings bobbed his head as he chewed. "He's in. And I think he just took a call from the CSI lab this morning."

The scuff of shoes heralded Jericho's arrival from a back

room. When he noticed his visitors, the sheriff's face brightened. "Hey there. What brings you two to town?"

Clay shook his friend's hand. "The quest for pecan pie originally."

Tamara quirked a smile and gave Jericho a peck on the cheek. "Now that Miss Sue's has satisfied my pie craving, I wanted to check with you about the results of the blood analysis my lab ran. Do you have that data?"

Jericho's expression grew more somber, and he hitched his head toward his desk. "Came in earlier. I've got it over here." As he crossed the floor to his desk, he gave Tamara a measuring glance. "You appear to be feeling better. Those ribs all healed up?"

"Not entirely, but I'm making progress." Tamara lowered herself carefully into a chair in front of Jericho's desk. She sat on the edge of the seat, keeping her back straight, and pressed a hand to her side when Jericho ducked his head to dig out a file from his desk drawer.

Clay frowned. Was the long trip out wearing on her? If so, why hadn't she said anything?

"You can look over the specifics if you want, but the long and short of it is, we got a match. The blood in the tunnel, presumably from the body you saw, is an exact match to the blood from the door of the stolen Taurus." Jericho slid the file folder across his desk to Tamara.

"And what have you learned about the car?"

Jericho stroked a hand over his mustache and sighed. "Dead end there. The surveillance camera at the rental agency has been on the fritz for about three weeks. There is no security tape of the night the Taurus was stolen."

"What about the money? Any leads on where it came from?" Clay asked.

"Nope," Rawlings called across the room from his desk. Clay turned on his heel to face the new deputy, who wiped his mouth on a napkin before continuing. "I called every bank within a hundred miles. No one withdrew a lump sum of one hundred thousand dollars in the past two months. A few random large withdrawals—" He waved a hand in dismissal. "Fifty K here, thirty-five K there, but recent history on those accounts didn't show the withdrawals to be unusual. Big business accounts. Nothing that'd send up a red flag anyway. Same with deposits. Nothing suspicious happening. I've sent word out on a broader scope around the country, but nothing's come back yet."

"So another dead end?" Tamara pressed her mouth in a hard line of discontent.

Jericho's frustration etched creases around his mouth and eyes. He rocked back in his chair, and the springs squeaked. "That's about the size of it right now. Wish I could tell you more. I don't like the idea of an unsolved car theft and a possible murder—with a missing body—any more than you do."

Clay's gut pitched as the words *missing body* struck a raw nerve. The body had turned up shortly after Doc Mason left on his vacation. The idea sifted through his brain and chilled him to the marrow.

Clay folded his arms over his chest and lowered his brow. "Jericho, are you aware that Doc Mason is out of town?"

"Yeah, I heard something about that at Miss Sue's earlier this week. Why?"

"Tamara and I were just at the clinic, and they've had a message that Doc Mason is extending his vacation and may retire in Arizona. But no one has actually talked to Doc and…well, something about his absence just doesn't sit right with me. He's not the sort to leave town for long periods. This town is his life, his home. He never wanted to leave. So why now? What changed?"

Jericho rocked forward again and propped his arms on his desk. "I have to admit, I hadn't given Doc Mason's trip any real thought, what with everything else that's been on my plate, but…now that you mention it, it does seem out of character."

"Honestly, the timing of his absence, what with this body

being found…" Clay blew out a breath through pursed lips, not even wanting to vocalize the rest of that horrible thought.

Tamara gasped. "Oh, God, you don't think…?"

"Rawlings," Jericho interrupted, "get out to Doc Mason's house and have a look around. I want to know if there's any sign of foul play or clues where he might be."

"Yes, sir." Rawlings shoved back from his desk and headed out.

Clay glanced at the number written on his hand. One way to put his mind at rest.

He stepped forward and placed a hand on the receiver of Jericho's phone. "Can I make a toll-free call? We might be able to settle at least one question with a call to the resort where Doc's supposed to be staying."

Jericho nodded. "Be my guest."

Clay dialed the number, and when the line at the other end rang, he punched the speaker button on Jericho's phone.

"Desert Palms Rehabilitation Center. How may I direct your call?"

Clay frowned. "I was under the impression Desert Palms was a vacation resort. I'm looking for someone, last name Mason, who said he'd be there."

"A patient?"

"Well, I…don't know." Clay rubbed his jaw, unsettled by this new twist regarding Doc's whereabouts. "He's supposed to be on vacation. But he's a doctor so maybe he was there for a seminar or something?"

"No, sir. We don't have seminars, and there is no doctor on staff named Mason. Privacy laws prevent me from giving out patient information."

"Ma'am," Jericho said, leaning toward the phone to be heard better, "this is Sheriff Jericho Yates in Esperanza, Texas. We can issue a subpoena for patient records if needed, but right now we just need to confirm that Doc Mason is, in fact, at Desert Palms. He's the subject of a missing persons search and possibly connected to a murder investigation."

"Murder?" the operator gasped.

"I can verify my credentials with your supervisor and local authorities if you wish, but if you'd just check your records to see if Doc Mason is there, you could clear up a lot of issues in our investigation without digging into the red tape."

"Sir, I—" The woman hesitated. Sighed. "We had a Dr. John Mason scheduled to check in here a couple weeks ago, but…he never arrived."

Ice streaked through Clay's veins. "Did he call to cancel the reservation?"

"No, sir. He just never showed up. We never heard from him, and no request was made for a return on the deposit for the room. That's all I can tell you."

Tamara's and Jericho's faces reflected the same worry that was churning through Clay.

"Thank you for your cooperation, ma'am." Jericho gave the woman his contact information and badge number to file regarding the inquiry and disconnected the call.

A pregnant silence filled the room. No one moved until Bea Hooper stormed through the office door from outside.

"Sheriff, if you don't do something about Walter Sims's dogs, I swear I will! They got into my garbage again last night, and they bark at all hours! How many times do I have to complain before somebody does something?"

Jericho's shoulders drooped, and he rubbed the back of his neck. "Clay, Tamara, I'll keep you posted if I hear anything new. For now, let's keep this between us. Agreed?"

Clay nodded. "Got it." He spared Mrs. Hooper a quick glance before sending Jericho a last sympathetic look. "Good luck."

The corner of Jericho's mouth twitched, but he composed himself as the irate woman stomped up to his desk. Clay led Tamara outside, and they strolled in silence back to the truck. Once inside with the doors closed and the air-conditioning cranked full blast, Tamara voiced what Clay was thinking. "We need some of Doc's DNA to determine whether the body I found was his. Should we call Jericho back and ask him to have Rawlings collect a sample from Doc's house?"

"No need," he replied. "I know where we might get a sample of his blood."

# Chapter 11

Tamara frowned as she gaped at Clay. "You know where to get Doc Mason's blood?"

He nodded. "Doc and I went fishing Memorial Day weekend, and while he was cleaning a fish with my knife, his grip slipped, and he cut his hand."

"And you didn't clean the blood off the knife?" she asked in a tone that said she was more surprised by the possibility that he'd neglected to clean up than she was asking about the viability of a sample.

"We wiped it off some, but it's a fishing knife, Tee. A little more dirt wasn't going to make a difference. We were more concerned about disinfecting Doc's cut and finding a clean wrap for it until he could get to his office to sew up the gash. I hadn't given the knife any more thought until just now. But there's probably still enough of his blood on the blade for your tests."

She nodded. "Okay. We can take it to my lab today and get tests started."

Clay squeezed the steering wheel, reluctant to consider that his friend could be dead. "Tamara, you saw that body. Do you think it could have been Doc? Could you tell anything about the person's age or hair color or anything?"

With an apologetic glance, she shook her head. "Not really. I was so stunned to realize what I was looking at, what I had touched… It was too dark to see any detail, and the body was mostly covered by dirt from the cave-in. I didn't look closely. I know I should have, but I was shaken up, hurting… I wasn't thinking professionally at the time."

"Understandable, considering the circumstances." Clay tipped his head from side to side, stretching the kinks knotting his neck.

"Clay?" Tamara paused, her gaze steady on him and concern dimpling her forehead. "Did you know… Did you even suspect that Doc Mason had a drug addiction?"

"We don't *know* that he does." Clay took a slow breath and reined the defensiveness in his tone before continuing. "Let's not jump to any conclusions until we get all the facts."

"He made a reservation and paid a deposit to go to a drug rehab center in Arizona. That's not a vacation. He was trying to break an addiction. What other reasonable explanation could there be?"

Frustration balled inside Clay's chest. He smacked the steering wheel with his palm. "I should have known, should have seen it."

Tamara gave an incredulous laugh. "Don't you go assuming the blame for this, too! Why would you know? How often did you see Doc?"

"Not all that often. But I just went fishing with him a few weeks ago."

"How did he seem then?"

He sighed. "I got the feeling he wasn't himself, wasn't feeling well that day, but…I didn't say anything." Clay thought back, remembering details about the last time he'd seen Doc. "His hands were shaking when he cleaned that fish. That's probably why he cut himself. But a drug addiction? Doc Mason?" He shook his head. "It doesn't make sense. Doc would never—"

He exhaled a sharp breath. Denials didn't change the fact that Doc *had* made that reservation at the drug rehabilitation center.

Tamara turned toward the window and leaned her head back on the seat. The outing had taken a toll on her. She needed to get off her feet, needed rest.

"Do you know if Doc has any enemies? Anyone who would want to ruin his reputation or…hurt him?" She angled her head to look at him again.

"Enemies? Doc Mason is one of the kindest men I know. He never met a stranger, would never hurt a fly. He was a healer, and he loved people. All people." He cut a side glance to Tamara. "So, no. I can't imagine anyone wanting to hurt Doc in any way."

"I know you love him like a father, Clay, but I need you to think about the question as objectively as possible. Did he mention trouble with any of his patients the day you went fishing?"

Clay pinched the bridge of his nose, trying to recall what he'd talked to Doc about on their fishing trip. "No. The man doesn't have any enemies that I know of."

Clay slowed the truck to make the turn at the Bar None. As he bounced down the gravel driveway, he noticed Tamara clutching her side and squeezing her eyes shut.

"How easily…can you find…that knife?" she asked between pothole jolts.

"Real easy. It's in my tackle box."

"Get it, put it in a plastic zip-top bag, and let's take it to my lab. The sooner we know if the body I saw was Doc, the sooner you can put your mind at ease."

Clay's need for answers about Doc Mason battled his concern for Tamara. As eager as he was to get the DNA tests started, his ex-wife needed rest more than she needed to make a trip to San Antonio. "Why don't you come in and take a nap first. We can bring the knife to your lab tonight or first thing tomorrow."

Tamara blinked her surprise. "Tomorrow? I thought you were chomping at the bit to get answers."

"I am. But you need to rest. I saw you holding your side. I know you're hurting."

Her expression softened. "Maybe a little, but the case is more important. I'll have another Advil and be fine."

When he shook his head, she pressed a hand to his cheek and smiled. The cool touch of her hand sent a cascade of sensation over his skin. His breath snagged.

"I'll be fine, Clay. Right now, what we need is answers. Get the knife. Okay?"

The gentle request in Tamara's cerulean gaze burrowed to his heart. How could she not know he'd always been eager to do her bidding? The few times he'd had to tell her *no* had devastated him. Especially the night Quinn had put Lone Star to sleep. Clay could still see Tamara's tears, hear her pleas, feel the anguish that had rolled off her like a smothering flood.

Shoving those memories down, he wrapped his hand around hers. "All right. But if I get any hint you're taxing yourself, we come straight back here so you can rest. Deal?"

"Deal. You're sweet for worrying about me." She brought his fingers to her lips, and the soft caress of her mouth, her breath, slammed into him like a fist to the gut.

He gritted his teeth and fought down the urge to grab her and kiss her the way his body and his heart wanted. Deep, hot, soulful embraces. The way he had kissed her, here in this truck, so many times before. Knowing she wasn't his to kiss anymore ripped through him with a gnawing ache.

He swallowed hard to clear the bitter disappointment from his throat. His muscles taut with frustration, he backed away and opened the truck door. "I'll be right back."

As he stalked to the barn to find his tackle box, the sultry summer day seemed to mimic the need humming in his body. Thick humidity clogged the air in the same way heated desire made his blood run heavy in his veins. A dragonfly buzzed past him, its wings fluttering in the rapid tempo of his runaway pulse.

Clay took off his Stetson and, with his forearm, swiped the

perspiration beading on his brow. Sex, as good as it had been with Tamara, hadn't been enough to save his marriage. Sex with his ex-wife would only cause complications and mixed emotions neither of them were prepared to deal with right now.

Doc Mason was missing, possibly dead.

He had to put thoughts of Tamara's sweet touch and sensual body out of his head and concentrate on finding out what had happened to Doc.

Taking his fishing gear from a shelf in the barn, Clay found the knife and carefully held the grip with two fingers. Smears of blood still stained the blade near the handle.

His gut twisted. Who could have known the bloody knife had been a harbinger of the blood that would later be spilled on his property? Had Doc been murdered less than a mile from Clay's house?

Clay sighed and headed for the kitchen to find a plastic bag. He didn't know what had happened to Esperanza's doctor, but he owed it to his lifelong friend to find out.

The chill from the over-air-conditioned forensics lab nipped Tamara's bare arms as she meticulously swabbed a sample of blood from the fishing knife's jagged blade. Having a personal stake in the results made her job feel strangely different. The emotions she typically locked away in the lab crowded around her and set her on edge.

Or maybe it was just having Clay hovering behind her, watching her work, that made her hands shake. She sensed his gaze on her, had the image of his dark, bedroom eyes in her head as she transferred the blood onto a slide.

Earlier in his truck when she'd kissed his fingers, the fire in his eyes had scorched a path through her. His desire to devour her on the spot had been all too clear. A rebellious part of her soul had wanted the same. Desperately.

Yet something had stopped Clay. He'd walked away without

so much as a kiss. The voice of reason or memories of old hurts had cooled the heat of the moment and doused his passion.

While the wild part of her that wanted to make love to Clay with careless abandon stung from the rejection, her practical side sighed with relief. Making love to Clay could only lead to more pain, reviving more memories of what could have been. She'd wallowed in enough regrets the past few days. Being back in her lab, in the environment where she had to be clinically detached, helped her steel her nerves and push away the maudlin moment.

After she'd prepped the blood sample, she stripped off her latex gloves and rubbed the chill bumps on her arms. She usually wore a lab coat, but had left hers in her apartment the morning she'd gone to the Bar None to make a second search of the area where the stolen car had been found. She hadn't been back to her apartment since.

She jotted a few notes in the case file and rubbed her temple.

As long as she was back in San Antonio, maybe she should stay at her own place. For good. When she remembered the barbecue Clay was planning for his family on Saturday, her heart sank. She didn't want to miss the opportunity to visit with the rest of the Colton clan. But was that wise?

Spending any more time with Clay, renewing attachments to him and his family, the animals at the Bar None and her friends in Esperanza taunted her like a carrot dangling just out of reach. That wasn't her life anymore. She'd made her choice five years ago, and she wouldn't look back.

She had a satisfying job and… Tamara frowned. What else? She had her job and…nothing. No boyfriend. No family nearby. Few friends outside of the forensics department. Not even a pet.

She'd left Clay to pursue her dream of a career in forensic science, and since then she'd buried herself in her job. Her work *was* her whole life.

Her lungs seized. Her ears buzzed. Her pen clattered to the table. Knees shaking, she eased onto the stool beside her.

She'd sacrificed her marriage for her career because she'd felt incomplete, she'd felt lost and smothered at the ranch. She'd pursued one dream, but sacrificed the home and family and love that nourished her soul.

No wonder the time she'd spent at the ranch was such a welcome change. No wonder seeing the animals and smelling the hay and breathing the country air brought such a rush of relief and pleasure.

"Now what do you do?"

Clay's question cut into her whirling thoughts, and it took a moment for her to realize he meant the next step in the DNA analysis, not what she wanted to do about her lonely life.

Flustered, she smoothed an unsteady hand over her hair and tightened her ponytail. "I, uh… I'll be right back."

"Tee, what's wrong?"

With Clay's worried gaze following her, Tamara scurried out of the lab and down the hall to the ladies' room. Bending over the sink, she splashed cool water on her flushed cheeks. She sucked in a calming breath and dried her face with a wad of paper towels.

Raising her eyes to the cracked mirror above the sink, she stared at the pale woman reflected there.

Her life was still out of balance. She'd been living a clinical, emotionless life, centered around her career. She'd neglected her empty ache because acknowledging what was missing brought back memories of the man she'd loved and given up.

With a humorless laugh, she shook her head. "Now what do you do?"

She had no answer. She couldn't change the past, and now she and Clay had too much hurt, too many barriers, too much distance between them to move forward. Didn't they? Her head gave a painful throb, the first sign of a potential migraine. She shoved her troubling new revelations aside, hoping to forestall a stress-induced headache.

Upon returning to the lab, she finished the notes she'd been making in the case file and mustered the courage to face Clay's curious scrutiny. "The analysis takes a while and can be pretty tedious. You could…go out for coffee or a snack, find someplace more comfortable than our lab to wait. I'll call your cell when I'm finished."

Clay crossed his arms over his chest. Angling his head, he studied her with a narrowed gaze before answering. "Am I in your way?"

Tamara blinked. "Well…no."

He glanced to Jan Howard, one of the technicians working near them. "Ma'am, am I interfering with your job?"

The female tech gave Clay a lustful grin. "Heck, no. I've enjoyed having such handsome company this afternoon. Your presence has made comparing fingerprints way less boring. Besides, I'm off in ten minutes, and then I'll be out of *your* way." With a wiggle of her eyebrows, she continued working.

He jerked a nod to Tamara. "In that case, I'll stay and wait with you."

Tamara drew her brow into a *V*, making a mental note to kill her coworker. Working with Clay watching her every move—especially after her upsetting revelation and with a burgeoning migraine—was nerve-racking to say the least. "But wouldn't you rather find a coffee shop or browse through a bookstore?"

His gaze was unflinching. "No. I want to be here."

Covering a sigh, she shrugged. "Okay. Have it your way." Tamara rolled her shoulders to loosen the kinks and moved to the next step in the analysis.

Her stomach flip-flopped. After Jan left for the day, she would be spending several hours in her lab—alone with Clay.

"So now we wait for the computer to do its thing before we go on to the next step." Tamara rolled her chair back from the desk where she'd been working for an hour and rubbed her eyes. Whatever had upset her before, she'd shaken it off and dived into her work with dedicated professionalism.

Clay had watched in fascination as Tamara proficiently manipulated the blood sample, mixed chemical solutions and operated high-tech equipment with finesse. She seemed so at home in the lab, so energized and skilled, that Clay could only marvel at how far she'd come from the early days when she'd learned the ropes at the ranch. The crime lab was where she belonged, not mucking horse stalls.

His chest squeezed with regret. Any doubt he'd had about whether he'd made the right choice by standing aside to let her follow her dream vanished. Any faint hope he'd had that spending a few days with him at the ranch might make Tamara consider reconciling flickered out.

Clay frowned. At what point had *he* begun thinking in terms of a reconciliation? False expectations were dangerous, and he'd do well to keep his wishes in check. The raw ache gnawing at him as he watched her now proved that point.

After what seemed like endless waiting, Clay stood and stretched his sore back. If his muscles were this stiff, he could only imagine how badly Tamara's ribs must hurt. For the past hour she'd kept one arm curled around her abdomen, and he'd seen her wince several times when she likely thought he wasn't looking.

Concern for her well-being frayed his patience with the tedious process. The clock in the corner of the computer screen read 10:04 p.m., so she'd been on her feet or hunched over a computer better than half a day. And that was after spending the morning about town in Esperanza.

Something had to give. She was driving herself to exhaustion, and his private thoughts were making him stir-crazy.

Clay cracked a knuckle and looked around for an excuse to convince her to take a break. "Can I get you anything from the vending machine? I'm ready for some midnight munchies."

She shook her head. "No food in the lab. Sorry. Our break room is down the hall and around the corner. Be warned—the coffee is toxic," she said without looking up from the computer monitor. "Stick to a soda from the machine."

"You're not coming? I thought you said we had to wait on the computer."

She tipped her head from side to side and massaged her neck.

"I'm going to catch up on some backlogged work while I wait. You can go on without me."

Clay braced a hands on his hips and gritted his teeth. "Like hell."

His profanity caught her attention. She glanced up with a bleary-eyed gaze. Lines of fatigue and pain creased the corners of her eyes and mouth. "What?"

He stepped over to her chair and wrapped his hand around her upper arm. "You're done for the day. I'm taking you home."

"I'm not finished." Tamara tried to shrug away from his grip but he held fast, careful not to hurt her in the process.

"Someone else from your lab can take over and call us with the results."

"If we're going to expedite the results, I need to—"

"Then we won't expedite the results. Your health is more important than getting some tests back a few hours faster. Hand this off, so you can get off your feet. You look ready to drop."

She hesitated, holding his gaze, clearly weighing her options and taking stock of her fatigue. "Let me finish one more thing, and I'll leave the rest for Eric to pick up in the morning."

He narrowed a skeptical gaze on her. "How much longer?"

She turned up a hand. "Twenty minutes. Half hour max."

He huffed his resignation and released her arm. "Twenty minutes. No more."

Tamara opened a file and scribbled notes as she clicked through several computer screens, documenting her progress. Clay reclaimed his seat on the stool behind her, watching the clock. Twenty minutes to the second, and they'd be outta there.

After a few minutes on the computer, Tamara called her boss to brief him. Eric promised to pick up the analysis first thing in the morning, then he read her the riot act for disobeying his order to stay away from the lab until she'd fully recovered.

Clay lifted a corner of his mouth. He liked Eric more all the time.

Tamara groaned as she hung up the phone. Then, scrubbing her hands over her face, she turned her chair to face him. "Okay, I'm ready to go."

Gathering his Stetson from the worktable behind him, Clay handed Tamara her purse and hustled her out of the lab. In the elevator, Tamara slumped against the wall and closed her eyes. "We missed dinner."

"I offered to take you out to get something," Clay countered.

She peeked up at him. "I know. Thanks. But I couldn't leave in the middle of things." Eyes drooping, she said through a yawn, "You could have gone without me."

"Where's the fun in that?"

She smiled and laid a hand on his cheek. "You must be starved."

"I'll live. Drive-throughs are still open."

The elevator opened, and he followed her outside into the humid night air.

"You have a preference where we stop?" he asked as they started down the concrete steps. He realized that she was lagging behind and turned to find her.

"Anything you want is—"

She stumbled down a step. Her hand flailed for something to grab.

His heart lurched, and he rushed forward. As she pitched off balance, he caught her around the waist. Tamara landed against him with enough force to knock the breath from him. She gave a small cry of pain that wrenched his gut.

He dragged air back into his lungs. "Tamara, are you okay?"

She clutched his arms, steadying herself and catching her breath. The scampering beat of her heart against his chest matched the galloping thud of his own.

Tipping her head back, she peered up at him with wide eyes. "Yeah, I—I don't know what happened. I just got so dizzy for a minute, and—"

"Because you've pushed too hard today."

She ducked her chin to rest her forehead against his shoulder. "I am awfully tired."

Clay scowled in self-censure. "I should have insisted on taking you home at the first sign you were wearing out."

"Stop blaming yourself. You're not my keeper." She sighed. "Maybe I should skip dinner and go straight home. Will you take me to my apartment?"

Her request plucked a twinge of disappointment in him. He shouldn't be surprised that she'd call her apartment *home* or that she'd want to go to her own place instead of back to the ranch. But hearing her call someplace besides the Bar None *home* stung.

Clay pushed aside his hurt in order to concentrate on what was best for Tamara. Tonight, however, what she needed was the Bar None.

He cradled her face and tipped her head back to meet her gaze. "I'll take you back to the ranch with me. You're exhausted, and I want to make sure you rest like you're supposed to tomorrow."

"Clay..." Her expression reflected her disagreement but also her reluctance to argue the point. She pushed against his chest, but he wasn't ready to let her go.

Instead he raked a hand through her hair, freeing the soft strands from the cloth band she'd worn as she worked. He finger-combed the silky tresses to fan over her shoulders and frame her face. The golden highlights shimmered in the Texas moonlight, and her eyes were sparkling sapphires.

His heart swelled to overflowing. Why had he ever let her go? Only after she'd disappeared from his life did he realize how much she meant to him. And now it was too late. She had a new life, a new career that made her happier than he ever had.

He rubbed his knuckles along her jaw and sighed. "You were amazing today. Criminal investigation suits you, and you're good at what you do. I'm glad you were able to make your dream a reality."

She blinked, apparently startled by his compliment. "I— Thank you, Clay."

"It's all the more obvious to me today after watching you work that this is where you belong. I guess things do have a way of working out for the best, huh?"

Moisture filled her eyes, and her expression darkened. If he hadn't known better, he'd have said his assessment had disappointed her.

Or was that just wishful thinking on his part? He'd give anything to hear her disagree, to hear her say she wanted to come back to the ranch—back to him—for good. But he couldn't ask her to give up her dreams for him. Her head bobbed in a small nod. "I guess they do."

One second stretched into the next and still he held her close, already hating the emptiness to come when he let her out of his arms. His Tee was so strong, so lovely, even with fatigue shadowing her eyes. She'd become even more confident, more poised, more beautiful as a woman than she'd been when she first captured his attention in high school.

Remorse twisted a knot in his chest. He couldn't undermine her newfound independence. This time around *he* had to be strong enough to walk away from *her.* But he would take one last memory. He may have seen the truth about her new life, but at that moment, nothing in heaven or earth could stop him from kissing the woman who still owned his heart.

With a gentle hand at her nape, he drew her close and lowered his mouth to hers. Her startled gasp melted into a contented sigh as she relaxed against him. The brush of her lips on his fired every nerve ending and shot sparks through his blood. He teased the seam of her mouth with his tongue, and she opened to him willingly.

She tasted as sweet as the honeysuckle nectar he'd sipped as a kid. As sweet as he remembered. Clay angled his head to deepen the kiss and savor her more fully.

Her hands slid to his back and curled into his shirt. When a raspy moan rose in his throat, she answered with her own mewl of pleasure. The seductive purr reverberated inside him until his whole body vibrated with desire, coiled tight and ready to spring.

Clay surrendered to the ebb and flow of her kiss. The bittersweet memories that raced through his mind of other times that he'd held Tee, kissed her, made love to her rocked him to his marrow. But none compared to the power and depth of the sensations and emotions Tamara's kiss stirred in him tonight.

The combination of sensual heat and his cold regrets made a strange cocktail. For the moment, Clay tried to ignore the acid bite in his gut that knowing he'd lost Tamara stirred. He focused instead on the caress of her fingers as she kneaded his shoulders then ran her hands through his hair, knocking his hat onto the steps.

She gasped unsteady breaths as he trailed kisses along her jaw to nuzzle the place behind her ear that always sent her over the edge. She whimpered her pleasure when he flicked his tongue over that sensitive spot, and he nearly came undone himself.

A car horn blasted down the block, and Clay tensed. He yanked himself back from the brink. This wasn't the right time. Wasn't the right place.

With a few more tender kisses to his cheek and chin, Tamara also backed away. She buried her face in his chest, trembling despite the warm evening air. "We should go."

"Yeah." Clay gritted his teeth and struggled to regain his composure. This small taste of Tamara wasn't nearly enough.

But already he'd taken more than he should.

*Let's not complicate things.*

Too late. His feelings for his ex-wife were nothing if not complicated. He was torn, aching inside. As desperately as he wanted her, he wasn't what she needed. The ranch wasn't where she belonged. He'd never put his desires ahead of what was best for Tamara. Just as he hadn't when they divorced. Now, after seeing Tamara in the forensics lab, he knew with a greater certainty that their divorce, however painful, had been the best gift he could give her. He pressed a kiss to the top of her head, inhaling the delicate floral scent of her shampoo. "I can bring the truck around for you if you—"

"No." She laced their fingers and squeezed his hand. "I'm okay now. I'll walk."

Keeping his hand in hers, ready to steady her if needed, Clay led her down the stairs toward the parking lot. His own legs felt a tad rubbery still, thanks to her potent kiss, but he'd be damned if he'd show her any sign of weakness. His failure today had already cost her too much. No matter what she said, he'd been wrong to let her stay in the lab so long when he knew she was hurting and exhausted.

As they neared his truck, his thoughts returned to the reason they'd been in the lab to start with. Doc Mason's disappearance. The possibility his friend had been murdered.

"So how far in the DNA analysis did you get? How soon will we hear whether the blood in the tunnel is a match with Doc's?"

She squeezed his hand and shrugged. "Not far enough to make me happy. When we hear results is gonna depend on Eric. He said he'd try to expedite it, but we also have a local caseload."

Clay nodded. "I know. I appreciate your department pushing this through. It's just not knowing what might have happened to Doc…"

Tamara stopped and clasped his hand between hers. "Clay…"

He met the dark look in her eyes with a tremor of apprehension. "What?"

"I know what Doc Mason means to you, but my gut tells me you should prepare for the worst."

## Chapter 12

Thanks to a full day of ranch duties, Clay didn't see Tamara the next day until after he'd given the horses an early dinner and finished his evening rounds, securing the stables. He checked on Lucy, the pregnant mare, before heading in for his own supper, but she still showed no evidence that she was ready to foal.

He rubbed the stubble on his jaw and scowled. Quinn had told him if the foal didn't come by the weekend, they'd need to induce labor or consider a C-section.

As he entered the house, the enticing aroma of popcorn greeted him. Following his nose, he found Tamara curled on one of the couches in the family room with a large bowl on her lap. As welcoming as the scent of food was, having Tamara waiting for him gave him greater pleasure.

"That sure smells good. I'm famished." He hung his hat by the door and sauntered closer to snitch a piece of the buttery treat. His gaze drank in the warm glow in Tamara's cheeks and the sparkle in her eyes. More than food, he was hungry for her.

She patted the sofa cushion beside her. "Join me. Marie brought a DVD with her she thought I'd like. I was just about to start watching."

Clay tugged at his sweaty shirt. "I need a shower. Can you wait about ten minutes?"

"Sure. While you clean up, I'll reheat the stew Marie left." Tamara pushed carefully off the couch and padded barefooted into the kitchen. "Marie is great. Where did you find her?"

Desire flared hotter as he appreciated the way the running shorts she wore hugged her fanny and left her long legs bare. He schooled his thoughts. What had she asked?

"Oh, uh…her husband is one of my hands. Their only son just left for college so between empty-nest syndrome and tuition bills to pay, she was thrilled to have someone new to look after. Her cooking alone is worth every penny."

Clay's stomach growled, and he grabbed another handful of popcorn before taking the steps two at a time. Upstairs, he hurriedly stripped out of his dirty work clothes, eager not to waste a single moment that he could spend cuddling with Tamara. Chick flick. Thriller. Horror. The movie didn't matter to him as long as he could hold Tamara the way he used to, feel her smooth legs stroke his, smell her shampoo as she tucked her head under his chin, savor the warmth of her body. He might not get another chance to hold her, and he intended to enjoy every moment tonight.

In the shower, as the steam and pounding spray massaged his tired muscles, he conjured images from past showers. Memories of Tamara's sleek body, glistening with soapy bubbles as she rose on her toes to kiss him, pumped heated need through his blood.

Since their kiss on the steps outside the CSI lab, Clay's thoughts had lingered dangerously close to various scintillating memories involving his ex. Even the grueling manual labor he'd done today, hoping to push the erotic images from his head, had been no use. His body hummed like a live wire, and no amount of hammering or shoveling had helped.

In record time, he was showered, shaved and loping down the stairs to join the beautiful woman sharing his home.

Tamara glanced up when she heard Clay bound down the stairs. So did the cat on her lap. She stroked Trouble's back, enjoying the soothing purr that rumbled from the cat's throat.

Clay stopped in the entry to the family room, and his contented smile morphed into a confused frown when he spotted Trouble. "What's the cat doing in the house?"

Tamara ignored the gruffness of the question and lifted a sassy grin. "Getting a good head pat, right now, I'd say."

Clay arched an eyebrow, silently calling Tamara a wiseacre. "Okay, *why* is the *barn cat* in the house? She's bound to have fleas."

Tamara continued scratching Trouble behind the ear. "Maybe. But I got lonely after Marie left and…well, I guess I should have asked first, but I didn't think you'd mind."

Clay opened his mouth then shut it again. He crossed the room and sat on the edge of the sofa next to Tamara. He gave Trouble a perfunctory stroke. "I don't mind in principle, but she should be treated for fleas before you make this a habit."

Tamara met Clay's eyes and held her breath. *A habit* implied she'd be at the ranch enough in the future to establish a routine. Did he mean he wanted her to stay?

As if sensing she'd read something into his statement, Clay backpedaled. "I mean, if you were going to be here or if you wanted to—" He sighed. "Hell, Tee. We need to quit dancing around what's on both of our minds."

Tamara's curled her fingers into the cat's fur, her pulse keeping time with the old railroad clock on Clay's mantel.

He turned to face her more fully. "Having you here has been great. And I think it's pretty plain we still have feelings for each other, but…"

He shook his head. *But.*

The one word was a pinprick to any fantasy she'd harbored concerning the future.

"But we're still divorced, still haven't settled the issues that led to our breakup, still have separate lives, different goals, demanding jobs?" she finished for him.

His eyes darkened to the color of midnight, and a muscle in his jaw ticked. "Pretty much."

His agreement snuffed her last glimmer of hope that this time, with hindsight to guide them, they could make a fresh start, have a second chance. Disappointment and grief even deeper than she'd known when she'd first left him years ago sliced through her.

Forcing a note of cheer into her voice, she gave him a tight smile. "Well, at least we've had a chance to clear up a couple misconceptions and renew our friendship. Maybe this time we could keep in touch?"

He took a while to answer, but finally shrugged. "Yeah, maybe. For tonight, let's just enjoy each other's company and not let regrets or recriminations spoil this chance to just…*be*."

*Just be?* He made it sound so easy. As if she could turn off the rush of bittersweet memories that surrounded her, stem the tide of affection and desire that washed over her whenever he was near.

But one thing was clear. Her feelings for Clay and her nagging questions about whether they could have a second chance to make their marriage work didn't matter. Just as he'd been able to dismiss her and what she wanted when they were married, with his declaration that their time together was almost up and reconciliation was off the table, he'd shut out her opinion once again.

*Nothing had changed.* She'd been telling herself that since she arrived, but she'd let a few kisses and tender moments fool her into thinking she mattered to Clay, that they had a chance…

She scooted the cat from her lap and dusted Trouble's hair from her shirt and shorts. "I'll fix your stew, if you'll start the movie."

*Oh, Lord…* She prayed Clay hadn't heard the wobble in her voice. She had to be strong, not let him know how badly the idea of leaving the ranch again hurt.

She drew on the detachment she'd learned in the CSI lab and shoved the tears in her throat back down. *Just be.* For tonight she'd do her damnedest to simply savor Clay's company and accept the evening as a gift. A stolen moment with a man whose part in her life she cherished but who'd moved on.

On her way back from the kitchen with Clay's dinner, she gave Trouble one last pat then let her out the back door.

Clay ate his stew from a tray as the movie, an action-adventure with a romantic subplot, started. Tamara tried to lose herself in the storyline, but the scent of soap from Clay's shower and the clink of his spoon as he ate kept her hyperaware of his presence. Of every move he made. And if she weren't already more attracted to her sexy cowboy than her heart could stand, Clay's nothing-will-come-of-this stance taunted her like a penniless kid in a candy store. The kisses they'd shared had had her secretly dreaming of making love to her ex. At times, when Clay looked at her with desire blazing in his eyes, she'd hoped their mutual attraction was the first step to a reconciliation. Likewise, their compatibility as they searched for answers concerning Doc Mason's disappearance had her believing they could work through their personal differences with the same cooperation.

She'd deluded herself.

With the remote, Clay paused the movie long enough to take his dish to the sink. When he returned, he sat on the sofa where Tamara had her feet tucked under her and a throw around her shoulders. Stretching his legs out on the couch, he nudged her shoulder, guiding her to lean back against his chest.

Her heart pounded, and the emotions she'd barely managed to quash resurfaced.

What was he doing? Cuddling on the couch was his idea of just being?

"Clay…" A thousand questions and protests tangled with the part of her that wanted to burrow against his body and shut the rest of the world out.

"Hmm?" He rearranged the throw to cover them both.

She hesitated.

"Did you get enough to eat?" she said instead of the words of longing on her tongue.

*How can you say we have no future one minute then hold me like this the next?*

"Yeah. Thanks." He kissed her temple then used the remote to restart the movie.

As he gently wrapped his arms around her, nestling her head under his chin, Tamara relaxed against him. Safe. Warm. Wishing she could stay there forever.

Again two words filtered through her head. *You're home.*

Tears pricked her eyes. If only Clay felt the same way.

## Chapter 13

The next morning Tamara woke to the early stages of a migraine headache. Though she didn't get them often, when her migraines struck, they were debilitating. By noon she was curled up in bed, the room dark, and one of the painkillers Dr. O'Neal prescribed in her system, lulling her into a restless sleep. Marie and Clay checked on her a few times, but she had no appetite and even soft voices hammered her head.

The day was a wash. Wasted.

The morning after that, feeling significantly better but a bit like she had a hangover, she mourned the precious time with Clay she'd lost. Eager to make up for the day she'd spent in bed, Tamara rose early and met Clay downstairs as he came in from feeding the horses and making his morning rounds.

Concern shadowed his eyes when he spotted her at the kitchen table sipping her coffee. "Headache gone?"

"Mostly. Tylenol should be enough to handle the last dregs today. So what'd I miss while I was wiped out yesterday?"

"Well, Lucy dropped her foal."

She sat straighter in her chair. "Are they okay?"

"They're both fine, thanks to Quinn. Things got hairy for a while when the foal got stuck, but Quinn worked a miracle to bring Linus into the world safely."

She exhaled deeply. "Thank goodness."

Relief that the horses were all right swirled with disappointment that she'd missed the arrival and grudging gratitude that Quinn had been on hand to help. She took another sip of coffee before something Clay said registered. "Linus?"

"You named the mother Lucy, so I figured Linus was appropriate. You know, Peanuts?"

"Yeah, I... You *named* the foal." Her heart swelled, and she gaped at Clay in wonder and joy. What had changed with Mr. The-Animals-Aren't-Pets?

Clay hesitated. "Yeah. Sorry, did you want to do that?"

"No, that's not... Look who's turned over a new leaf!" She chuckled and jabbed him playfully in the arm.

Grinning sheepishly, he ducked his head and rubbed the back of his neck. "Well, since his mom had a name, I figured..." He shrugged, minimizing what he'd done.

But Tamara couldn't write off this change in Clay's attitude so easily. Naming a new foal was a small thing, but it pointed toward a willingness to make changes. The hope that had died two nights before flickered to life again, tumbling her thoughts and perceptions about her ex once again.

Before she could question him more about the birth or other ranch business, the house phone rang, and Clay snatched it up on the second ring. "Bar None. This is Clay."

His eyes flicked to her, his brow creasing. "Yeah, she's right here. Who's calling?"

Worried over Clay's frown, she held out her hand for the phone.

"It's your lab. The results are in on the blood sample from the knife."

Adrenaline spiked her pulse as she raised the receiver to her ear. "Hey, what'd you learn? What do the tests say?"

Clay held her gaze with a dark, uneasy scrutiny. A muscle in his jaw twitched as he gritted his teeth, a sure sign he was as apprehensive about the results as she was.

"Let's see…" Eric cleared his throat, and she heard rustling papers. Her nerves jangled while he scanned the report. "Ah, here we go. Looks like the two blood samples are a match."

Clay obviously read the heart-wrenching truth in her expression.

Doc Mason, a man who'd been like a father to him, was dead.

Covering his mouth with a hand, he squeezed his eyes shut and bit out a curse word. He turned his back to Tamara, and his shoulders slumped.

Tamara fought down her own grief, wanting to stay strong for Clay, needing her professional detachment as her boss continued, "The root hair they found in the tunnel is excluded though. So we may have identified the body, but we still don't know who put the guy in the tunnel. Want me to call this in to the sheriff? What's his name? Yates?"

She drew a slow breath. "No, I'll let him know." Keeping an eye on Clay, who'd braced his arms on the kitchen counter and hung his head, Tamara finished up with Eric then disconnected. Her heart ached for Clay, who'd already lost so many people in his life he cared about. His mother, Ryder…his wife.

Tamara squared her shoulders.

*No.* He hadn't lost her.

They might not be married any longer, but she cared deeply about him. Tamara swore she'd be there for him as he grieved for Doc Mason. Without speaking, she returned the phone to its cradle and wrapped her arms around Clay from behind. She laid her head on his bent back and heard the steady thud of his heart.

A heart she knew was breaking.

He turned to draw her into a tight hug, heaving deep breaths as he battled his emotions. His eyes were dry, but pain ravaged his face. "Who could do this? Why would someone want him dead?"

She rubbed his back, at a loss for words. "I don't know, sweetheart."

"Someone moved his body." Clay's body tensed, and his voice quivered with anger. "Someone faked calls to his answering service, lied about him being in Arizona and retiring."

"It would seem."

He leaned back and narrowed a keen gaze on her. "And that money. That doesn't make any sense. Who would leave that kind of money behind? What was the money for?"

Tamara shook her head. She wished she had answers for Clay. "Jericho is a good lawman. He'll get to the bottom of this."

"Things like this don't happen in Esperanza. Who could have—" Clay stopped, and his gaze shifted away as if a thought had occurred to him.

"What?"

"Dr. O'Neal. He's not from Esperanza. He's taken over Doc Mason's practice and was acting nervous when we were there asking about Doc."

Tamara stiffened as a memory from the day she'd injured her ribs tickled her brain. "Clay, I didn't say anything before because, honestly, I didn't think it meant anything and—"

"Tell me." He dark eyes lasered into her.

"The day you took me to get my ribs X-rayed, I overheard an argument between Dr. O'Neal and his nurse. I was waiting for my prescriptions and, well, I heard raised voices in the corridor behind the exam rooms."

Clay stepped back but kept a hand on each of her elbows. "What did they say?"

She shook her head slowly, trying to remember. "I only heard bits and pieces, but I remember him saying something about accounting for narcotics. I think something was missing. I thought he was fussing at her for sloppy paperwork, because he said something about it being her job." Her gaze snapped to Clay's. "She said Doc Mason always did whatever it was himself. Keep the records of narcotics in the office maybe? I know I heard 'missing' and 'narcotics.'"

Clay's jaw tightened.

"Do you think this was about drugs? Could Doc have caught someone stealing drugs and been murdered for trying to stop them?"

Clay flinched at the word *murder*. The shadow of grief, temporarily pushed aside as they reasoned out the mysteries surrounding Doc's death, returned with vengeance.

"We need to tell Jericho all this," he rasped.

She nodded. "In a minute." Stroking his cheek, she hugged him closer, not caring about the lingering soreness in her ribs. Only Clay mattered.

When he pulled away a moment later, he raked his fingers through his raven hair and grimaced. "We don't even have his body to bury. Doc took care of people his whole life, and we can't give him a decent burial."

"We'll find him, Clay. I swear we will. And we'll find the person responsible for his death, too. I know Jericho won't rest until the culprit is caught." She paused and caught his hand in hers. "And neither will I."

Conviction and tenderness flared in his dark brown eyes. He gave a jerky nod then lifted the phone again. He punched in a number, and when Jericho answered, he put the sheriff on speaker. "Tamara's here with me. She just heard from her lab."

"And?" She heard the squeak of Jericho's chair and pictured him leaning forward, stroking his mustache and bracing for the news she had.

"The DNA from the blood on Clay's fishing knife, Doc Mason's blood, matched the sample my team recovered in the tunnel where I saw the body." She filled him in on the other details Eric had about the unmatched root hair, then waited for Jericho's response.

His sigh whispered over the phone. "Well, damn. Doc was a good man. He'll be missed."

She told him about the argument she'd overheard between Dr. O'Neal and his nurse as well. "I don't know if it has anything to do with Doc's death, but all that money…well, I thought it was an angle you might want to explore."

"You bet. I'll leave no stone unturned," Jericho promised.

"So where do we go from here? How do we catch the bastard who murdered him?" Clay asked.

"Whoa," Jericho said. "Slow down, partner. We don't *know* that he was murdered. We don't have any hard evidence that points to murder."

Clay slammed his palm on the kitchen counter. "Sure as hell looks that way to me!"

"But Jericho and I have to work from the facts," Tamara said. "Not appearances, not speculation or hearsay." She swallowed hard, knowing how difficult all the unknowns had to be for Clay.

"Clay, you know I'm doing everything I can to solve this case. What I need from the two of you is time. As before, I'm asking you not to tell anyone what we know." Jericho's tone made clear the request was more an order. "If word gets around that Doc is dead and his body's missing, we could tip off whoever's responsible and give him more lead time to cover his tracks."

"Or…" Clay crossed his arms over his chest as he leaned a hip against the counter. "Knowledge that we're onto him might make him panic. Flush him out. Make him careless. If he makes a mistake, maybe we'll finally have something to catch him with."

Tamara chewed her bottom lip, deferring to Jericho. This aspect of the investigation was out of her jurisdiction. Esperanza's sheriff had to make the call.

"Clay, I understand your frustration, but we're going to do things my way for now, especially for the next few days until the funeral is over. Rumors spread like wildfire when the whole town's gathered in one place like that."

Tamara knitted her brow. "But we don't have the body and—" She stopped when it clicked that Jericho wasn't talking about Doc's funeral. Icy dread balled in her gut. "Jericho, what funeral do you mean? Who died?"

"You hadn't heard? Geez, I'm sorry. I figured as close as

you'd been to her someone would have called…" He sighed and pitched his voice lower, softer. "Honey, Tess Akers died. The funeral's Thursday."

Tamara gasped, shock and grief kicking her hard. Tears flooded her eyes, and she met Clay's gaze. His arms opened, and without giving it a second thought, she stepped into his embrace. They held each other, leaned on each other, grieved with each other for long silent moments. In a span of minutes, they'd both lost someone near and dear to their hearts.

Sharing the ache of loss with each other seemed as natural as breathing. She couldn't think of anywhere she'd rather be, no one who could understand and comfort her the way Clay did. For years he'd been her lover, her best friend, her confidante. They had a bond no divorce document could sever. That truth didn't escape her.

As she wept quietly in Clay's arms, she grieved for their marriage as well. When she'd left Clay, confused and hurting, lost and alone, she'd walked away from her soul mate.

The entire town of Esperanza turned out for Tess Akers's funeral. The woman who'd taught home economics at the high school and Sunday school at the Baptist church, who'd chaired the town's rodeo festival for years and been a regular at Miss Sue's diner for Saturday lunch, had touched many lives. But none more than Tamara's.

While Clay and Quinn Logan talked with Jack Akers, Tamara strolled through the Akerses' house, telling herself she *wasn't* avoiding Quinn. Nursing her years-old grudge seemed petty in light of Jack and Billy Akers's loss.

Still, she wasn't up to the awkwardness of making idle chatter with Quinn today.

She glanced at pictures of the woman who'd opened her home when Tamara had tagged along with Billy and her older brother after school. Mrs. Akers had been a mentor and friend to her in high school after Tamara's mother died, and she'd encouraged

Tamara to follow her dreams of a career in forensic science after she'd married Clay.

Tamara's chest squeezed. She hated that she'd neglected to come by and visit Mrs. Akers as she'd sworn she would when she heard how ill the woman had become. But she'd been too preoccupied with Doc Mason's disappearance, too wrapped up in her feelings for Clay, too confident that there'd be time later for visiting….

"That one was always my favorite of her."

She hadn't noticed Billy Akers's approach until he spoke. His blond hair was a mess, and his tie was askew. He gestured with a hand that clutched a highball glass to a photo of the family on the wall in the corridor. The smell of alcohol wafting around him told Tamara the drink in his hand wasn't his first.

"She was a beautiful lady. I'm so sorry for your loss, Billy."

Pain filled his eyes, and he took another gulp of his whiskey. "Thanks, Tam'ra," he slurred.

She couldn't blame him for wanting to numb himself to the ache. She hurt for him and his obvious grief. Still, she hated to see her friend get publicly drunk at his mother's funeral. She reached for his glass. "Can I freshen that up for you? Maybe with iced tea this time?"

Billy frowned at his empty glass. "Yeah. Whatever."

He followed her into the kitchen where Jewel Mayfair and Becky French had their heads together murmuring quietly as they arranged finger sandwiches on a tray. They glanced up when Billy and Tamara entered the room.

"Oh, Billy," Becky said, "I was just telling Jewel how much I hate that Doc Mason missed the funeral. I know your mother was a dear friend of his."

Tamara's stomach lurched, and she busied herself pouring Billy some tea. She kept her eyes cast down, hoping her expression gave nothing away.

"From what I hear, though, he's earned this vacation," Jewel added. "You know, he came out to the Hopechest Ranch in the middle of the night a few months ago when one of the girls spiked a high fever. He seems like such a nice man."

"He is. And he truly cares about his town and his patients." Becky bustled past Tamara to take a jar of relish from the refrigerator. "Billy, he's going to be heartbroken about Tess."

Billy grunted acknowledgment and leaned drunkenly against the door frame. "Yeah, I s'pose he would've been. He and Mom went way back."

Tamara looked at the tea she'd poured Billy and wondered if coffee might be a better option.

Becky held the tray of sandwiches out to Billy. "Here, darlin', have one. I haven't seen you eat anything all day."

Billy waved the food off. "Not hungry, thanks. Think I'll go outside for a smoke."

After he left, Becky sighed heavily. "Poor fella. I remember how much it hurt when my mother died a few years ago. He's taking it so hard."

Jewel pulled back the filmy window sheers and cocked her head as she watched Billy outside. "Grief affects us all differently. I'd say as long as he expresses his grief, he'll be all right. It's when a person tries to suppress their emotions that problems can arise. It's unhealthy. If they—" Jewel laughed self-consciously. "Good gracious, listen to me prattling on like Dr. Phil."

Tamara gave her a grin. "It's okay. You're allowed."

"And you're right," Becky chimed in. "This town has always been supportive when one of our own is in need. And Jack and Billy are going to need us in the coming weeks. We'll pull them through this."

Tamara glanced out the window at Billy and decided to give her friend a few moments alone, away from the cloying attention of the people gathered in his house. Instead she went in search of Clay, who was now chatting with Nick and Georgie beside the spread of food on the dining-room table. She gave Georgie a small smile of greeting when Clay's sister hugged her. "Who's watching Emmie while you're here?"

"Jewel suggested we let her stay with the girls at Hopechest for the afternoon." Georgie grinned. "When we left, she was embroiled in a no-holds-barred game of crazy eights with Ana Morales."

Jack Akers approached the table and cast a strained smile to the group. "Eat up, people. Even with Billy's appetite, I don't know how we'll use all this food before it goes bad." He shoved a cookie toward Clay. "Try these, Colton. Macy Ward brought them. They'll melt in your mouth."

Clay flicked a dubious glance to Tamara then took the proffered cookie. "Thanks."

"Georgie, how's that little cowgirl of yours?" Jack asked, his voice unnaturally loud and overly bright.

Though Tamara couldn't see any evidence that the father had been drinking like the son, his forced upbeat conversation was uncomfortable. He seemed strung tight and ready to snap. As if the only thing keeping him going was maintaining the illusion of cheer.

*Grief affects us all differently,* Jewel had said. Perhaps Jack thought he had to keep smiling, convince everyone he was fine, or he'd break down. Whatever his reason, the widower's stilted smiles and cowboy jokes were difficult to bear.

Tamara made eye contact with Clay and hitched her head toward the door.

"Excuse us for a minute," he mumbled and slipped away from the table with her. When they were out of earshot, he gave her shoulder a squeeze. "You ready to go?"

"Not quite yet. I want to check on Billy again." She sighed and tucked her hair behind her ear. "This would be hard enough even without knowing about Doc. But not telling people the truth about Doc feels like we're lying. I hate it."

He nodded and rubbed his knuckles along her chin. "I know. But it's just for a little while. Just buying Jericho a little time."

She glanced outside and studied Billy's slumped shoulders as he leaned against one of the cars parked on the street. "Did I ever tell you that Billy volunteered to be my escort for homecoming when I was a freshman? My date got sick at the last minute, and I didn't have anyone to walk me out on the football field during halftime 'cause my dad was working. Billy heard about it and showed up at the game in a tux." She smiled at the memory. "I told him he was my hero."

Clay gave her a lopsided smile. "Are you trying to make me jealous?"

She lifted one eyebrow. "Did I mention the tux was powder blue and had a ruffled shirt?"

Clay pulled a face and covered a laugh with a cough.

Sobering, Tamara turned back to the storm door. "I only mention it because Billy has been there for me lots of times over the years. And now when he's hurting, I don't know what to do or say."

"I think just being here says a lot." He nudged her back. "Come on. I'll go with you."

Billy looked up when the storm door creaked open. He glanced at the cigarette in his hand then to Tamara as she approached. "I know, I know. B'fore you lecture me on how bad these things are f'r me, let me say, I've been trying to quit."

She lifted her palms and grinned. "Did I say anything?"

"Didn't have to. You had that look in your eye." Billy dropped the half-smoked cigarette on the street and tamped it out with his toe. He gave Clay a nod of greeting, which Clay returned.

Tamara braced her hands on her hips. "What look?"

"The same one Doc Mason always got before he'd lecture me. He hated my smoking."

"Hmm, a doctor who doesn't want his patient to smoke. Unheard of!" Tamara grinned and bumped Billy with her shoulder as she propped next to him. "Sounds to me like you just have a guilty conscience."

Billy scoffed and crossed his arms over his chest as if he didn't know what to do with his hands. "Like he had room to talk. An addiction is an addiction. It's not easy to quit smoking. And

I have cut back. Or I had…" His volume dropped to a mumble. "Before Mom got so sick."

Tamara rubbed his arm, looking for a way to lighten the mood. "Hey, I was just telling Clay about that blue suit you wore to homecoming my freshman year."

Billy raised his head and wrinkled his nose. "Aw, man. Just don't go pulling out any pictures."

Clay flashed a lopsided grin. "There are pictures?"

Billy raised a hand. "Not if I can help it."

Tamara wrapped her hand around Billy's arm. "You were really sweet that night. It meant a lot to me."

He glanced quickly to Clay then away. "Yeah, well, don't let it get around. I have a reputation to maintain. Wouldn't want the guys thinking I'm a softie."

Silence fell among them for a moment before Billy hitched his head toward Clay. "So what's the story? Is a reunion in the future?"

Tamara's heart jumped, and she flicked a glance at Clay to gauge his response.

With a stiff laugh, Clay shrugged. "Well, I heard the cast of *Love Boat* was considering an anniversary show. Personally I think all these 1980s reunions are overrated."

Billy scrunched his mouth sideways and shook his head. Turning his face toward Tamara, he arched an eyebrow. "What do you say, Brat? You getting back with that ole cowboy or what?"

Had he not been drinking, she doubted Billy would have been so cheeky. She fumbled for a way to dodge the question as Clay had.

Forget butterflies. A flock of mallards flapped their wings in her stomach as she looked for an answer under the penetrating gaze of both her ex and her old friend. She prayed neither of them could read her confusion and anguish in her expression. She swallowed, trying to moisten her suddenly dry mouth. "I…well, I…guess time will tell."

Clay met and held her gaze, his expression hard to decipher. Tamara realized she was holding her breath and released it with a slow exhale.

"Time, schmime. Georgie will tell. I bet if I ask your sister, I'd get the real lowdown." Billy pushed away from the car where he'd been leaning and dusted the seat of his suit pants. "Think I'll get myself another shot of my friend Jack Daniel's. Clay?"

Her ex shook his head. "No, thanks. I'm driving."

Billy smiled as he excused himself with a drunken wave of his finger. "But I'm not."

Tamara opened her mouth to dissuade Billy from his drunken binge. Clay's warm hand on her arm stopped her.

"He'll be all right. May have a hell of a hangover tomorrow but don't worry about him."

She watched until Billy disappeared inside, then lifted her eyes toward the bright summer sun. She replayed their conversation with Billy, fretting over an uneasy sense that something wasn't right. She tried to dismiss the unsettled feeling that pricked her as a remnant of his bold question about a reunion between her and Clay. But her disquiet had started before that moment, had started even before they'd come outside. If she were honest, her sense of foreboding was as much what had prodded her to seek Billy out again as her concern for his well-being.

"What am I missing?" she asked aloud.

"Pardon?" Clay lifted his head with a small shake as if roused from deep thoughts.

"Something about Billy seemed…off." She chewed her lip and stared at the ground trying to puzzle through her odd sense.

"You mean besides the fact that he was drunk as a skunk and mourning his mother?" Clay stepped closer and massaged her neck with one strong hand. The warmth of his touch, the relaxing kneading of her muscles and the contradictory tingle of arousal that flashed over her skin detoured the line of thought that beckoned with a nagging urgency. As much as she hated to, she stepped out of Clay's reach so she could think more clearly.

Clay's frown didn't escape her notice.

"I need to concentrate," she said by way of apology, "and you were distracting me." She twitched her lips in a sideways grin.

"Concentrate on what?" His dark eyes queried her from under the brim of his Stetson.

Her mind backtracked through every detail of the funeral and the current gathering of mourners at the Akerses' house. Snippets of conversation, facial expressions, the food…

Her gaze landed on the cigarette Billy had dropped on the street. *What look?*

*The same one Doc Mason always got before he'd lecture me. He hated my smoking.*

The logical part of her brain began to tick as realizations fell in place.

"He used the past tense," she mumbled to herself.

"What?"

She replayed everything Billy had said about Doc Mason, and her stomach twisted. "Every time Billy mentioned Doc Mason, he used the past tense. But you, me and Jericho are the only ones in town who are supposed to know Doc's dead."

Clay's face paled. "Jericho told me once that killers often give themselves away by referring to a missing person in the past tense before their death is officially confirmed."

Tamara raised a hand, even as panic swelled inside. "Slow down, Clay. Remember Billy is drunk, and there has been lots of talk in town lately about Doc Mason leaving town to retire. Maybe that's all he meant." But her CSI experience had already led her to more ominous explanations. Every reasoned conclusion met with heartsick denials. Her pulse thundered in her ears, and nausea roiled in her gut. She paced the street, shaking her head. "Billy's not involved. Doc Mason was his parents' friend since before he was born."

"Tamara."

She faced Clay, tears stinging her sinuses and dread knotting in her chest. Clay pressed his mouth in a firm line, but his eyes were soft with compassion.

"He's my friend," she said, her voice cracking.

"And Doc was mine."

She rubbed her arms as goose bumps rose on her skin, despite the Texas heat.

She had to clear Billy of any involvement. To put *her* mind at rest if nothing else.

She glanced around her, her mind in overdrive, and her gaze landed on the cigarette at her feet. "I need a plastic bag. A clean zip-top bag and…a clean spoon or something."

"Why?"

She locked a determined stare on Clay's dubious frown. "I can get Billy's DNA and fingerprints off this cigarette. You and I both saw him smoke it and drop it there. We have an unmatched root hair at the CSI lab and fingerprints from the trunk of the Taurus on file. With a few tests to that cigarette butt, I can clear Billy."

Her chest contracted. *Or convict him.*

# Chapter 14

After bagging the cigarette butt and paying their last respects to the Akerses, Clay and Tamara left the funeral and headed for San Antonio. In the elevator, as they headed up to the CSI lab on the seventh floor, Clay cast Tamara a stern look.

"We're only dropping off the cigarette for your team. You're still on medical leave, and you aren't staying." Concern prodded him when he recalled how hard she'd pushed herself the last time they'd brought in evidence and how her fatigue had set back her recovery. Despite the progress in her healing, Clay swore not to let her endanger her health that way again.

His ex's returned gaze challenged him with cool blue determination. "Like hell. Billy's my friend, and I owe it to him to run the tests myself. I already feel like a traitor even suspecting him of something so heinous as being involved in Doc's death."

The elevator doors rumbled open, and Tamara brushed past him as she stepped off. Clenching his teeth, Clay followed her into the lab. "I wouldn't have brought you if I'd known you were going to insist on running the tests yourself."

She sent him an annoyed glance and set to work without responding.

Short of throwing her over his shoulder and carrying her from the building, he didn't know how he was supposed to get her to leave the work for her team to finish.

Clay approached the desk where her office phone sat. Several autodial buttons had been labeled with the names of important contacts. He scanned the list. Eric was the third button. Lifting the receiver, Clay punched the speed dial for Tamara's boss.

"Crime Scene Investigation, this is Eric."

"Hey, Eric. Clay Colton here. Tamara's ex."

Tamara gasped and spun around to face him, a murderous expression darkening her eyes and a bottle of chemical solution clutched in her hand.

"We just brought in some new evidence related to the case in Esperanza y'all are helping out with," Clay continued, undaunted.

Still holding the chemical bottle, she marched over to her desk and tried to pry the phone from him.

With a twist of his body and his height advantage, Clay kept her at bay just long enough to reach his desired goal. "Tamara has started the tests, but—"

"She's here? Working?" Eric sighed heavily. "I gave her a direct order to stay out of the lab until her leave was over. If there is evidence to process, we have plenty of capable technicians here who—" He stopped and grunted his frustration. "Tell her I'm on my way down."

Clay flashed Tamara a cocky grin. "Will do, Eric."

She pressed her lips in a grim line. "You rat! Are you trying to get me fired?"

"No, I'm trying to keep you from setting back your recovery by exhausting yourself like last time. Besides, you've got personal stakes in the outcome because of your history with Billy."

She pinned him with a glare. "Are you saying I'd let my

emotions get in the way of doing my job? Feelings don't influence hard scientific data. Tests can't be altered because I want—"

"Tamara, what are you doing here?" Eric demanded as he stormed through the door.

She aimed a finger at Clay's nose. "I'll deal with you later." Squaring her shoulders, she faced her boss. "I'm fine, Eric. I can start these tests and get—"

"No, you won't. You're on medical leave until Monday." Eric plucked the bottle from her hand and crossed the room with it. "You can leave any evidence that needs to be processed, but you aren't staying to do the analysis yourself."

"Eric, these tests are important. An old friend of mine—"

"Every test we run is important, Tamara. Every victim, every criminal, every witness is somebody's child or spouse or dear old friend."

A flicker of contrition flickered across Tamara's face, and Clay's chest contracted. How did Tamara, with her soft heart, do her job day after day, knowing the lives that would be altered when her analyses came to light?

Eric planted a hand on Tamara's back and scooted her toward the door. "Vamoose, Ms. Brown. Don't let me catch you in here again before Monday or else."

Tamara divided a glower between Eric and Clay. "Fine. But you better call me the minute you know anything. If you push them through as a priority—"

"Then we'll be even farther behind on the tests we've already scuttled aside when we expedited the last evidence you brought in." Eric crossed his arms over his chest and angled his chin. "Tamara, we have a mountain of work to catch up on when you get back Monday. So if you promise to go home and get rested up so we can make some progress on the backlog next week, I'll run all the analyses on your new evidence over the weekend."

"The weekend?" Tamara's impatience vibrated in her tone.

"That's the best I can promise. Esperanza isn't the only city with unsolved cases."

She opened her mouth, clearly ready to launch another plea for haste, but Clay took her elbow and nudged her toward the door. "This weekend will be fine. Thanks for helping out. Say good-night, Gracie."

Sighing, Tamara marched out of the lab and gave Clay the silent treatment for the first twenty minutes of the ride back to the Bar None.

As they reached the Esperanza town limit, she snapped a sharp glance across the front seat. "You never change. You're so bossy and controlling sometimes I could scream. You take charge even in things that are not your business."

He rubbed his chin and weighed his response. She seemed to be spoiling for a fight, but the last thing he wanted tonight was to argue with Tamara. "If I overstep my bounds on occasion," he stated calmly, "it's only 'cause I've had to take charge so many other times. As the oldest kid, I had to step up when Mom died or my family would've been split up, sent to foster homes. And the Bar None being my ranch means I'm the boss. I guess it's a habit. It's who I am."

"But a marriage is supposed to be a partnership!" Tamara poked a finger on the bench seat between them to emphasize her point.

"A marriage?" He cast her a startled glance. "This is about our divorce? I thought you were just mad about me calling Eric tonight at the lab."

She drew a deep breath and blew it out slowly. "I am mad about your stunt at the lab, but it's just an example of how you ignored my wishes when we were married. You were so busy being in charge of *everything* that I never got a say in *anything*."

"That's not true!" He squeezed the steering wheel as his blood pressure spiked. So much for avoiding a fight.

"It sure seemed that way to me. When you made decisions without consulting me, I felt like I didn't matter to you, like my opinion didn't count for anything." She pitched her volume down, but the passion in her voice caught him off guard.

"That's ludicrous," he sputtered. "I've always done everything I could to make you happy."

She aimed a finger at him. "You're doing it now! I'm telling you how I felt, and you're calling it ludicrous. But it *was* how I felt, Clay! Why can't you hear what I'm saying? Why can't you understand?"

"I didn't say—" He bit back the angry response on his tongue and searched for his composure. He didn't want this to evolve into a shouting match with his ex. When he met her gaze, the wounded look in her eyes stole his breath.

"When the tractor broke down the summer before I left," Tamara said in a calmer, softer voice that rippled over him like a balmy breeze, "you spent all the money in our savings to fix it. Without consulting me."

"I *did* tell you about it," he countered.

"Yeah, you *told* me about it. After the fact."

"We had to have a working tractor to run the ranch." Clay hated the defensiveness in his tone, hated more the way her shoulders slumped in frustration. He clamped his mouth shut and exhaled deeply. "Sorry. Please finish what you were saying."

They'd reached the Bar None, and he turned up the driveway.

Tamara stared out the passenger window as she continued, her tone more defeated, more tired. "We'd saved the money in that account to buy a new stove for the kitchen. Only one burner worked on the old stove and cooking dinner took forever. I was counting on getting a new one."

When they reached the end of the drive, he cut the engine and leaned his head back on the headrest. Matching her quiet tone, he said, "I'm sorry we didn't have the money to do both, Tee. But I thought the tractor was more important."

"And it probably was. But it was *our* money. I worked hard on the ranch helping save what little we had, and it hurt that you didn't talk to me before you spent it. The stove could have waited, yes. That's what I would've said. But when you didn't give me a voice in the matter…"

Clay's gut tightened as her point drove home. "I hurt you."

She looked at him sadly and nodded. "That's just one example."

He stared out the windshield, making no move to get out as what she'd said rolled about in his brain. "The night you left, when Quinn put Lone Star down…"

When he didn't finish the thought, she said, "I begged you to just hear me out, but you walked away. You said Quinn was the vet, and he knew what he was doing. His was the only opinion you'd listen to."

"The horse was suffering, Tee. Putting him down was the only humane thing to do. The disease had advanced to a point that all Quinn could do was treat the symptoms. Lone Star would never recover and could have spread the disease to the rest of the horses."

"Why wasn't he vaccinated? If Quinn had done his job right to begin with, Lone Star wouldn't have gotten sick!"

"He *was* vaccinated. But the strangles vaccine isn't one hundred percent effective. It was my fault for not recognizing how ill he was until too late. When the bacteria became systemic, there was little Quinn could do. Bastard strangles is nearly always fatal. If you want to blame someone, blame me. But Quinn did his job."

Tamara pulled her brow into a deep *V*. "Bastard strangles?"

"That's what it's called when the bacterial infection becomes systemic. That's what Lone Star had. He wouldn't have survived."

She gaped at him. "Why didn't you tell me this before? I would have understood."

"I tried to, but we were both so upset that night, I don't think either of us really heard what the other was saying. After you left, I figured the particulars were a moot point."

"Except that for years now I've blamed Quinn for something he didn't do." She nibbled her bottom lip, digesting the new information. "When you wouldn't listen to me, didn't give me a chance to be heard, it made me feel like all my contributions to the ranch and our marriage were for nothing. I figured if I didn't matter to you or to the ranch, why was I staying? I wanted to do something with my life that mattered. That's why I left."

Amber rays from the setting sun backlit Tamara and made her hair shine like spun gold. In the fading daylight, her skin glowed with subtle color from her time spent outdoors over the past week. She looked radiant. Beautiful.

Desire coursed through him. The hunger he'd held at bay clamored inside him, fed by a new understanding of the woman he'd once called his wife. He'd always known she was intelligent, but seeing her on the job at her CSI lab had given him a new respect for her sharp mind. The maturity and perspective they'd both gained in the past five years allowed them to finally begin to settle issues that had once torn them apart. And her time at the ranch had reminded him of the friendship and sizzling attraction that had drawn him to Tamara from the beginning. A tender ache swelled inside him along with his restless sexual appetite. Love and lust packed a powerful one-two punch.

Was he falling in love with his ex-wife again? Had he ever fallen out of love?

"Clay, do you suppose it's too late for an apology?"

He cocked his head, trying to remember what they'd been talking about before his mind had wandered, distracted by the play of sunlight that made her shine all the brighter.

"To Quinn," she added.

He shrugged. "I don't think it's ever too late to set things right."

Tamara's eyes widened then, shifting on the seat, she stared down at her hands. She opened her mouth to say something then seemed to reconsider. With a little shake of her head, she reached for the passenger door. "I hope you're right."

That evening as they ate a late dinner, Tamara poked at her food, ruminating on the events of the day. The funeral. The question of Billy's possible involvement in Doc Mason's death. Her spat in the truck with Clay.

No wonder she had no appetite. The day had been an emotional roller coaster.

"You feeling all right?" Clay asked as he stabbed a bite of Marie's glazed ham.

"Hmm, yeah. Just thinking."

"About?"

"Lots of stuff. The Akerses, for instance. I wish I could do something to help them. I know how hard it is to lose a loved one." She scoffed and set her fork down. "But what do I do instead? Cast suspicion on one of my oldest friends."

"No, Billy did that to himself. The facts will speak for themselves, and you shouldn't feel guilty about doing your job." Clay cut himself another bite of meat and furrowed his brow. "Speaking of the Akerses, did Jack's attitude at the funeral seem weird to you?"

"You mean all his false bravado and forced cheer?"

He pointed at her with his fork. "Exactly. His wife had died and yet he was telling jokes and acting like folks were gathered at his house for the Super Bowl instead of a funeral. It was creepy. Pitiful."

"I agree. But Jewel said today that everyone has their own way of grieving. He's from the generation of men who were raised to be tough and strong. The real-men-don't-cry crowd."

"Yeah, maybe so. But if it had been my wife who died—" Clay jerked his gaze to hers, his expression shaken, as if he'd only then realized what he was saying. The blood drained from his face leaving his work-tanned skin ashen. "I— Never mind."

"No, finish. What if it had been me who died?"

Shaking his head, he put his fork down and shoved his plate away. "I don't even want to think about that."

Tamara put herself in Jack's place, imagining how she'd feel if Clay died. The onslaught of gut-wrenching grief brought a flood of tears to her eyes. She choked on a ragged sob. "Oh, Clay...I'd be devastated if anything happened to you."

He raised a startled glance from his plate, a dark scowl hardening his mouth. The shock her assertion brought to his eyes softened to sympathy and compassion. Moisture sparkled in the rich brown depths of his gaze, and the intensity of the stare that clung to hers burrowed into her soul. Fear, grief and desperation reflected in his eyes, mirroring the anguish ripping her apart.

When she tried to speak, emotions squeezed her throat, and her voice was no more than a strangled rasp. "I'd want to die. I can't imagine this world without you. It'd be... I'd be—" Her shoulders heaved as sobs racked her body.

Clay's chair toppled as he bolted from it. In a heartbeat, he'd folded her in his arms and buried his face in hair.

Tamara was crying so hard, her ribs ached. As she gasped for breath between her tears, she tried to shove down the spontaneous tears. But the dam had opened, and all the seesaw emotions of the past week poured from her in a cleansing flood.

She felt safer in Clay's arms than she had in years. Nestling closer, she inhaled the familiar earthy scents that were far sexier than any store-bought cologne. Fresh air, clean straw and mellow leather combined in an aroma that was pure Clay, all male strength and raw appeal.

His grip tightened around her, and he kissed the top of her head. As he murmured comforting words in his low, rumbling bass voice, a quiver started low in her belly. She pressed her ear to his wide chest and heard the steady thump of his heart. On the heels of the horrid notion of Clay's death, the life-affirming sound reverberating in his chest was sweet music, a seductive tango. After admitting how devastating his death would be, all pretenses and excuses were stripped away, and denying the depth of her feelings for this man seemed pointless.

A desperate need clawed at her, a yearning to rediscover the physical bond that they'd once shared. She curled her fingers into his back, wanting more of him, needing to be closer. He moved his soothing kisses to her temple, still whispering words of reassurance, calming her in the same hypnotic timbre he used to quiet a spooked colt. She tipped her chin up, met his eyes. And was lost. His dark bedroom eyes held her spellbound.

As he framed her face with his callused palms, his moist gaze drank her in. "I've missed you, Tee," he rasped, his deep voice stroking her, building the clamoring need inside her.

With a low rumble in his throat, he pressed soft kisses to her eyelids, and she sagged against him. His warm lips skimmed her cheek, the hollow of her throat, her chin. He moved his mouth to hover above hers, his breath fanning her skin as he waited.

"Make love to me, Clay," Tamara whispered, barely able to speak as anticipation tightened her lungs and stole her breath. She rose up on her toes to close the distance to his lips and sealed the invitation with a kiss.

With a growl of approval, Clay angled his head and swept his tongue into her mouth. His fingers twisted loosely in her hair, and he walked her backward until he'd anchored her body against the wall. Tamara raked her fingers down the muscles of his broad shoulders, reveling in the taste of his lips. Her tongue tangled with his, and she strained upward to deepen the kiss. While they were married, she'd kissed Clay thousands of times, yet tonight the sweet pull of his lips on hers held a magical newness, the thrill of rediscovery.

Clay raised his head, his dark eyes gleaming with passion, his breathing a light, staccato rhythm of desire. His hands restlessly stroked her face, her hair. "I don't want to hurt you."

Tamara's pulse missed a beat. Did he mean physically? Was he worried about her ribs?

Or was he worried about the emotional attachments making love would inevitably bring?

Either way, the reward was worth the risk. She needed to feel Clay holding her, needed have his warm skin next to her, needed the spiritual connection she'd always experienced when they joined their bodies. She'd been away from Clay too long, and she needed new memories to tide her through the lonely days to come.

"I'll be fine," she told him, praying she was right. Could she really make love to Clay again, then walk away unscathed when it was over?

Holding her gaze with a dark piercing look smoldering in his eyes, Clay scooped her into his arms and carried her upstairs. Once in his bedroom, he lowered her gently onto his bed and followed her onto the mattress.

"You're beautiful, Tee. Even more lovely now than when we were first married." He traced the line of her jaw with a crooked finger, and a sensual shiver slid through her.

"When you look at me like you are now," she whispered, "I feel beautiful. I feel safe. I feel…" *Loved.*

She swallowed the word that sprang to her tongue. Was it love she saw in Clay's eyes or just her own wishful thinking? Clay had devoured her with his hungry gaze many times when they were married, but she'd had little similar evidence of his feelings outside the bedroom. He still hadn't said anything to indicate he felt more than basic affection.

As he released the buttons on her blouse, Tamara shoved aside the pang of regret that twisted in her chest. Tonight she simply wanted to savor the intimate pleasure of this man who still owned a piece of her heart. She tugged at his shirt, pulling the hem from the waist of his jeans, and smoothed her hands over the warm skin of his back. As his fingers skillfully freed her of her blouse and bra, he captured her lips again for a soul-shaking kiss.

One by one, more articles of clothing were shed, and the fire that had smoldered between them the past week burst into flame. Every touch, every sigh, every heated glance heightened her anticipation. Erotic sensations swamped Tamara's body and left her languid and breathless.

Clay remembered all of her most sensitive and erogenous zones as if five years hadn't come between them. He licked her earlobes, teased her nipples, kissed the back of her knees.

Months of heartache and loneliness melted away.

Tamara returned his tender ministrations, nibbling the curve of his throat, sliding her body along his and stroking every inch of his warm, taut skin. Their limbs tangled, and their mouths explored, renewing the sizzling passion that had been a hallmark of their marriage.

By the time he'd donned a condom and braced on his arms above her, ready to join their bodies, he'd reduced her to a puddle of quivering nerves and tightly coiled desire.

When he nudged her with his erection, she nearly shattered. Lifting her hips, she wrapped her legs around him and dug her fingers into his buttocks, urging him to complete the union her body desperately craved. Finally, with a long, slow stroke, he entered her.

"Clay!" Tamara cried, a maelstrom of sensation washing through her.

He captured her lips and groaned his pleasure. His arms trembled as he braced above her, and she realized that his restraint was in deference to her injured ribs.

"Hold me tighter, Clay. You won't hurt me." She wrapped her arms around his back and clung to him. "Please, hold me tighter."

Nuzzling her ear, he hugged her closer and buried himself deeper. His arms squeezed her body against his, tightly enough that she could feel the pounding of his heart against hers. In the circle of his arms, she savored the completeness, the safety and the heartfelt connection she'd missed the past five years. The sense of destiny and peace she'd known only with Clay.

As he brought her to a shattering climax, tears pricked her eyes. She was falling in love with him again. Maybe she'd never fallen *out* of love with him.

But she could never love him enough to make up for the shortfall in his feelings toward her. She had no doubt he desired her, was sure he had affection for her. But without the unconditional, soul-deep love she needed from him, they were no better off than the day she'd walked away from their marriage. She needed to know, really *know,* that she mattered to him. That she was truly important to him on every level, not just as a sex partner.

Long minutes passed before Clay loosened his grip and eased away from her. His ragged breathing calmed, and he rained gentle kisses on her cheeks and chin. She met his dark eyes and smiled at him. "Well, some things don't change. You still make the earth move for me."

A sexy laugh rumbled from his throat. "Back at ya, darlin'." He tucked a wisp of her hair behind her ear, and his expression sobered. His voice husky and quiet, he said, "No one has ever been as special to me as you are, Tee."

Her heart gave a hard thump.

*Special?* Hardly the declaration of undying love she'd hoped for, yet even the watered-down, vanilla affirmation fed her hungering soul.

A hollow ache she'd known well in the last days of her marriage returned in force. Perhaps *special* was all she was to Clay. The sooner she accepted that fact, the sooner she could move on with her life.

But for tonight, she wanted to treasure the precious moments she had left with Clay. She snuggled under his arm and stroked a toe down his leg. "Stay with me tonight? I want to know you're beside me while I sleep."

He pressed a kiss to her hair. "Wild horses couldn't drag me away."

She sighed and closed her eyes.

Maybe wild horses wouldn't steal him away tonight, but in the morning she would have to face the cold truth. Clay was no more hers now than he had been the day they divorced.

## Chapter 15

Two mornings later, Tamara rose early with Clay and accompanied him to the stable as he did his chores. The routine was so familiar, yet strangely foreign. Perhaps because she and Clay had never done the ranch work *together*. When she tried to help separate the flakes of hay for the mares to eat, Clay stopped her. "You're supposed to be resting."

"I'm tired of resting. Besides, ranch work is cathartic in its own way."

He pulled a frown. "I thought you hated ranch chores."

"I never said that. Being back on the ranch has been good. I missed the Bar None."

He leaned on the pitchfork he'd been mucking stalls with and cocked his head. "Ranching has a way of getting in your blood."

She gave him the raspberry. "You have to say that. It's your business."

His expression grew thoughtful. "Naw, it's more than a business for me. I love it. I love the work, the fresh air, the horses." He propped the pitchfork against the wall and stepped closer to her. "I've been thinking about the conversation we had the other day. About Lone Star."

She raised a hand. "Let's not argue about that again."

He caught her fingers and kissed them. "Not argue. But I want you to understand."

She tipped her head and eyed him warily. "Understand what?"

"If I shut you out that night, it was largely because I didn't know what to do with my own grief. Seeing your pain only made it harder to do what I had to. The horse was suffering. Quinn couldn't save him once the disease went systemic."

She nodded. "I know that now, but—"

"I was hurting, too, Tamara. Losing my best stallion was a tremendous blow to the ranch when we were already struggling financially. I didn't know how we would survive without a breeding stud."

"But you did."

He closed his eyes and nodded. "Yeah. But my point is, I wasn't hurting that night because of the loss to my business. I hurt because I was losing Lone Star. I'd raised him from birth. I'd groomed him and fed him and spent hours working with him. I know I'd told you not to get emotionally attached to the animals, that ranch animals aren't pets. But I wouldn't be in ranching if the horses didn't matter to me. I was grieving for Lone Star the same as you."

Tamara stared at Clay with moist eyes, a tender ache filling her chest. She moved closer, wrapping her arm around his neck. "Thank you for telling me."

"I know it doesn't change what happened that night." He sighed and brushed a kiss across her lips. "But I wanted you to know." Planting his hands on her hips, he levered away from her. "Now quit distracting me, or I'll still be mucking stalls when my family arrives for the barbecue."

"So let me help." She reached for the pitchfork, and he pried it from her hand.

"Uh-uh. You overexerted yourself yesterday doing chores, and it took its toll. I saw the pain you were in, so don't try to deny it."

She arched an eyebrow. "I wasn't too tired to make love to you, and I had several hours' rest last night."

She'd only intended the statement to support her argument, but mention of their lovemaking the past two nights changed the atmosphere in the stable like a flash of lightning from the blue sky. Immediately the air seemed charged, and Clay's body tensed.

A muscle in his jaw twitched, and his eyes darkened with the same heated desire she'd seen in them last night and the one before. The mild abrasions his stubbled cheeks had left on her skin tingled again with anticipation, and a heady sensation spun through her and made her tremble. Clay stepped closer, still holding the pitchfork. With his free hand, he stroked her cheek, and her blood flashed hot.

"You got a big day ahead of you. My family will be here in a couple hours. Don't you want to go back to bed for little while?"

Her mouth went dry. "Depends. Will you be joining me?" Her attempt to add a note of levity to the challenge came out as a husky croak.

Clay drew a deep breath, his nostrils flaring and his eyes zeroing in on her mouth. "Tempting as that offer may be, these chores don't finish themselves." His hand curled around the nape of her neck, and he pressed a kiss to her temple. "Maybe a rain check?"

Tamara opened her mouth to agree then stopped. Her pulse fluttered. A rain check implied there would be a future opportunity for redemption. After the barbecue, what excuse did she have for staying with Clay any longer? The simple fact that she'd felt well enough to make love to him the past two nights proved she'd healed enough to return to work on Monday. To be alone at her apartment. *Alone.*

Her heart gave a painful kick. She hated the idea of her lonely apartment after the past few days in the welcoming comfort of Clay's ranch, surrounded by family and friends from Esperanza. Even the presence of the ranch hands and horses made the Bar None feel more homey, buzzing with life and love.

She smiled wistfully at Clay. "Rain check." She'd keep that promise if only for the chance to store away a few more precious memories with Clay. She gave him a peck on the cheek before backing toward the stable door. "I'll see if Marie needs help in the kitchen."

The ensuing hours were a frenzy of preparation for the Colton barbecue. As time for the rest of the family to arrive neared, Tamara found herself pumped with anticipation and humming.

Jewel and Meredith were the first to arrive. As Clay welcomed his aunt and her niece with hugs, Tamara marveled at how much Jewel resembled her mother's twin sister. Other than age and the fact that Meredith wore her golden hair in a chic bob now, the two favored each other in almost every way, right down to the stately and dignified way they carried themselves.

Tamara smoothed a self-conscious hand over her own casual ponytail before stepping forward to greet Meredith.

"Tamara, honey, it's so good to see you!" The older woman air-kissed her cheeks.

"Wow. To think, I could be hugging the future First Lady," Tamara said with a laugh.

"From your lips to God's ears!" Meredith crossed her fingers and held them up.

Emmie burst through the front door without knocking. "We're heee-re!"

The adults chuckled as the spitfire skipped into the family room.

Clay scooped her up for a hug. "Hey there, squirt. Did you bring your mom and Nick with you or did you drive yourself?"

Emmie rolled her eyes. "I don't have my driver's license yet."

He tweaked her nose. "Then you better not let Sheriff Yates catch you behind the wheel."

Clay's rapport with his niece spread a gooey warmth inside Tamara. How many times in their marriage had she pictured him bouncing a child of their own on his knee?

Giggling, Emmie squirmed out of his arms and greeted Tamara with a hug. "Hi, Aunt Tamara!"

*Aunt.* Tamara's heart turned over. If only…

Georgie and Nick bustled in, giving the front door a perfunctory knock as they entered.

"Did anyone see a little kid come in here? Four years old. Red hair. *No manners.*" Georgie directed the last to Emmie with raised eyebrows. "You didn't knock, and then you left the door wide open. Were you raised in a barn?"

Emmie flashed a sassy grin. "Yes! The rodeo barn."

Clay cocked his head. "She got you there, sis."

"I hear there was a bit of excitement here a couple nights ago? Your foal arrived?" Nick offered his hand to shake Clay's.

"Yep," Clay said with the grin of a proud new father. "And he's a beauty. I was just out to check on them a few minutes ago and mom and baby are doing fine."

"Wonderful," Jewel said.

Her smile seemed genuine, yet Tamara detected a note of sadness in her eyes.

"Mama, can I go see the new foal?" Emmie asked, tugging on Georgie's arm and dancing from foot to foot. "Please?"

"I'll take her," Jewel said then hesitated and glanced to Georgie. "If that's all right?"

"Fine by me." Georgie aimed a finger at her daughter. "Remember, you have to be quiet and calm. Don't stress the baby or her mother, young lady."

Emmie gave a dramatic groan. "I know. I know."

A bittersweet pang twisted in Tamara's chest as Emmie skipped out the back door with Jewel. Clay's niece was as precious and precocious as they come. She wished she could be around to see the girl grow up. But despite all she and Clay had shared in recent days, nothing had been said about her staying. Too many obstacles still stood in the way of making a go of their relationship this time. The past days had been a sweet diversion, an emotional walk down memory lane, but by Monday morning, she would be back in San Antonio, back in her lonely apartment, and burying her heartache in her job.

"Clay," Marie called as she came in from the backyard. "If we're going to use that table outside to eat, we'll need a big table-cloth. You have one big enough to fit?"

He stared at Marie as if she were speaking Greek then shrugged. "I have no idea. Anything I have would be in the closet by the mudroom, though, if you want to check."

"Let me do that," Tamara volunteered, glad for a task to occupy her and get her mind off all she'd miss, not being part of this family in the years to come.

"And a large platter for the meat?" Marie added.

Clay hitched his head toward the back hall. "Same place, if it's anywhere. In the kitchen, anything beyond a cereal bowl and the microwave is out of my domain."

Georgie snorted. "You're not kidding. I remember your attempts to cook before I took over to save us all from starvation." She hooked her arm in Tamara's. "Come on. I'll help you."

They made their way back to the large walk-in storage room at the back of the house, and Tamara pulled a dangling string to turn on the bare lightbulb overhead. "I can remember getting a large checkered tablecloth as a wedding gift. It's bound to be around here somewhere."

Assuming Clay didn't get rid of it when he got rid of everything else from their married life. An arrow of resentment shot through Tamara. The stripped-down, highly masculine version of the Bar None ranch house was a far cry from the warm home that was a blend of their personalities when they were married. One more reminder that Clay had moved on, had eliminated Tamara from his life.

"Holy cow! I'm afraid to move anything," Georgie said with a laugh as she looked around the crowded storage area. "Pull one thing, and the whole closet becomes an avalanche!"

Tamara roused from her dreary thoughts and blinked at the stuffed shelves and clutter-lined floors. "Good grief! How are we supposed to find anything? We never had this much in here when we were married."

"Cripes, when did my brother become a pack rat? He never used to keep so much stuff around."

Tamara appraised the miscellany, wondering where to begin. As her gaze traveled down the top shelf, a familiar pattern caught her eye. She gasped.

"What?" Georgie said, drawing her arms close to her chest. "Is it a spider? A roach?"

"My curtains," Tamara murmured as she reached for the top shelf. Intent on recovering her homemade window dressing, she ignored the pain that streaked through her when she stretched her arms above her head.

Pulling the dusty curtains down, she stroked a hand over them then clutched the folded material to her breast. Her mind buzzed, and her heart thumped a wild cadence. She lifted a stunned gaze to Georgie as tears pricked her eyes. "He kept them."

Georgie tipped her head and pulled at the cotton fabric to see what Tamara had found. "Hey, I remember these. They used to be in the kitchen. Didn't you make those in home economics class with Mrs. Akers or something?"

Tamara nodded, still shaken by her discovery. A more intentional scan of the storage closet revealed more surprises. Propped in the back corner were the lithographs she'd selected for the living room. On the shelf below the curtains, she found various knickknacks that had been conspicuously missing from the family room. And carefully boxed and stored on a bottom shelf were her dried flower arrangements.

Tamara's gaze darted from one item to the next, recognizing wedding gifts, high-school memorabilia and keepsakes from the first years of their marriage.

Clay had kept everything.

Right down to the tattered scrunchies she'd used to keep her hair back when she did her ranching chores. The tears that had threatened all day rose like a flash flood. With a choked sob, Tamara sank to the floor.

Georgie knelt beside her, concern creasing her brow. With a

cool hand, she pushed Tamara's long hair away from her face. "Tamara? What's wrong?"

"He saved it all. Everything. I thought he'd cut me out of his life, but he kept everything of mine." She blinked, clearing the puddle of moisture in her eyes. "Why would he do that?"

Georgie barked a laugh. "I'd think that was obvious. Certainly anyone who has seen the change in Clay these past few days wouldn't have to ask."

Tamara narrowed her gaze. "Changes?"

The redhead chuckled. "Heck, yeah. He's smiling again. Even at the funeral the other day, despite his polite somberness, he just seemed…happier. Whenever he looked at you, I saw a spark in his eyes that hasn't been there for five years. Today his grin is downright contagious."

Tamara frowned skeptically. "Because his family is here. He loves his family."

Georgie's shrug didn't deny Tamara's assertion. "Because you're here. He loves *you*."

Breath backed up in Tamara's throat. She tried twice to speak before any sound would come. "But if that's true…"

Her thoughts spun. As much as she wanted to believe Clay loved her, he hadn't said anything about his feelings for her. Even after they'd made love, the best he could say was that she was *special* to him. "But he hasn't given me any reason to think he wants anything to change. If he wanted me to stay and try again—" She hesitated.

What would she do if Clay asked her to stay, to give their relationship a second chance?

Georgie tugged on the curtains Tamara still held with a white-knuckle grip. "Here's your proof, crime lady. Clay only keeps things that are important to him. Do you really think these curtains matter to him because of the lovely print? No. He kept them because you made them. He kept them because you matter to him."

Hope fired in her soul, tempered by the logical side of her brain that needed hard evidence. Her pulse fluttered an uneven cadence, wavering between joy and denial.

"Just because he kept the things I chose for the ranch, doesn't mean he wants me back. Maybe he's saving them to give to charity. Or to give back to me. I left in a rush that night and never asked for any of the things from our marriage. I wanted a fresh start. It was easier to start over without painful reminders around me of what used to be."

"And why were the reminders painful?" Georgie asked, then plunged on before Tamara could answer. "Because you loved Clay, right?"

After a moment to consider how honest she could afford to be with Clay's sister, Tamara nodded slowly.

"So why would Clay be any different? He moved the reminders of you out of his sight, because he cared so much it hurt."

Georgie's argument made sense, but accepting it as truth meant turning everything she'd ever believed about Clay's attitude toward her on end, smashing every assumption she'd made about his cool reserve during the agonizing days of their divorce.

Georgie pulled a tissue from her pocket and wiped the moisture from Tamara's cheek before handing it to her.

Tamara blew her nose and gathered her thoughts. "So what do I do?"

"I think the only real question is whether you still have feelings for Clay and are willing to give him another chance." Georgie squeezed Tamara's hand and met her gaze with a probing scrutiny. "Do you love my brother? Will you stay, or are you going to leave him again?"

Tamara drew a shaky breath. "It's not that simple. I have a job I love in San Antonio."

"So? Nick loved his job with the Secret Service, but he loved me and Emmie more. He quit and moved to Esperanza to be close to us. But you don't have to quit. I mean, San Antonio is— what?—a half-hour to forty-minute drive? Big-city folks spend that much time in traffic or on a bus each morning. You *could* commute from the Bar None. It's doable."

Tamara blinked as the possibilities she hadn't let herself

consider began percolating, bubbling like champagne and lifting her hopes.

"Georgie? Tamara?" The sound of footsteps accompanied Meredith's call. "Did you get lost? Clay's afraid the closet swallowed you."

"In a way, it did," Tamara said under her breath. She dashed the tears from her eyes and schooled her expression just before Meredith appeared at the storage-closet door.

Clay's aunt wasn't fooled. "Oh, dear! You've been crying. What happened?"

"We're fine." Georgie pushed to her feet. "Just girl talk."

As Tamara blew her nose again, she saw Georgie mouth to Meredith, "Tell you later." Tamara lifted a corner of her mouth. In a big family there were few secrets. She couldn't begrudge them that, though. Families shared each other's travails because of the love they shared. To be included in the Coltons' circle of affection and acceptance after five years by herself...

Fresh tears welled, but Tamara quickly stanched the flow. Tapping the strength she'd developed to face a crime scene objectively, Tamara got herself back under control. She had plenty to think about, thanks to her discovery of the curtains and Georgie's angle on what the contents of the storage room meant.

A second chance with Clay? The idea both thrilled her and scared her silly.

Regardless of her interpretation or Georgie's, what mattered were Clay's feelings for her *now* and whether he wanted another chance to make things work. He still hadn't said that he loved her as Georgie claimed, and Tamara refused to make the mistake of assuming anything this time around. She needed hard evidence, not hearsay.

As she awkwardly climbed to her feet, she spotted the red and white checked tablecloth they'd been sent to retrieve at the back of a lower self. "Here it is. Not sure I would have seen it if I hadn't been at this angle."

Georgie gave her a knowing grin. "Amazing what you discover when you look at things from a new perspective, huh?"

With a long-handled spatula, Clay poked the coals in his barbecue pit and added another handful of mesquite chips to the fire. The woody scent of the smoke curled up around the slab of ribs he'd started slow-roasting a couple hours earlier, and Clay's mouth watered. Texas barbecue, in his opinion, was like nectar of the gods.

"Oh my, that smells great! Joe is going to be so sorry he missed this," Meredith said as she approached from the house. "The girls found the tablecloth." His aunt held the checkered cloth up as proof. She hitched her head toward the table. "Come help me with it, Clay?"

"Sure thing." He wiped soot from his hands on his jeans and strode over to the picnic table he and Tamara had set up that morning. Mention of his uncle Joe reminded Clay how Georgie had recently been falsely accused of threatening Joe Colton's bid for the presidency.

"How is Joe doing? Any more harassing e-mails or threats to his campaign?" Clay asked.

Meredith unfolded the tablecloth and flicked a corner to him. "Joe's in California, working, and no more threats, thank goodness! Maybe that terrifying chapter of this campaign is finally over. I'm so relieved. It was pretty scary to think someone was out to sabotage Joe's campaign—or worse, hurt Joe."

Clay nodded. "Scary for us, too. The fact that the threats have stopped supports the fact that the real culprit was Rebecca Totten, not Georgie. It was plenty nerve-racking at this end knowing Georgie's identity had been stolen to frame her for the campaign threats."

Meredith tsked and sent him a worried frown. "I can imagine. Poor Georgie." Together they shook out the table cover and smoothed out the wrinkles. "While it is great to see you and Georgie—and this barbecue was a wonderful idea—I guess you know the real reason I came to Esperanza."

He cast a quick glance toward the corrals where Jewel and Emmie were watching the horses. "I have a good idea."

"And how is my niece doing?" Meredith flipped her hand in inquiry.

"I've kept an eye on her like I promised."

His aunt smiled. "I knew you would. Is Jewel adjusting to Texas? Does she seem happy?"

Clay scratched his freshly shaved chin and decided how best to be honest without alarming Meredith. "She seems...content. When I ask how she is, she always assures me she is fine. Lately she's been bringing girls over to the Bar None to ride horses. The progress she is making with the girls clearly makes her happy. But..."

Meredith's gaze darkened. "But?"

"Well, I'm concerned she might be working too hard. She looks tired to me most of the time, as if she's not sleeping well or she's pushing too hard and doing too much."

"Have you mentioned it to her?" Meredith asked.

"I didn't feel like it was my place to get too personal, but whenever I've asked if I can do anything else to help her out, she's told me she's fine." He shrugged. "I don't know that she'd confide in me, though."

Shoulders drooping, Meredith replaced the salt and pepper shakers and stack of napkins she'd moved to cover the table. "Well, thanks for looking out for her. I feel better knowing she has you nearby." Her scowl deepened. "The poor girl has been through so much with the loss of her fiancé and baby. I can't help but worry."

Clay's chest constricted, remembering the conversation he'd had with Tamara concerning how devastating it'd be to lose the other. The possibility was too painful to consider.

Yet Jewel had lost the love of her life and her unborn child as well.

He sent another glance toward the corral where Emmie was bouncing excitedly on her toes, and Jewel smiled at the little girl wistfully. He prayed that someday Jewel would find someone to bring her the kind of happiness that Tamara gave him.

His heart stuttered.

Holding his breath, Clay replayed the last thought. Tamara made him happy. She made his life feel complete, meaningful. With an ache in his chest, Clay realized that come morning, Tamara would return to San Antonio, leaving him alone again.

As if mimicking his thoughts, a cloud passed in front of the June sun, casting a long shadow over the ranch.

"Clay, did you hear me?" Meredith touched his arm, jolting him from his melancholy musings.

"Huh, no. Sorry. What did you ask?"

"I said, how is Ryder? Have you heard from him? Written to him?"

His gut tensing with guilt, Clay's mood slipped another notch. He busied himself placing condiments and silverware on the table. "No. I haven't heard from Ryder since he went to prison."

"At all?" Meredith's dismay was clear in her tone.

Unable to meet her gaze, he shook his head. "I gave up trying to get through to him when he was arrested this last time. I had to accept that I'd failed my brother, that there is nothing else I can do for him now that he's in jail."

"Clay Colton!" Meredith's stern tone caught him off guard. He glanced up and met an equally chastising stare from his aunt. "I would have never pegged you for a quitter. Why, you didn't build this ranch from nothing by giving up when it got hard. Making the Bar None a success was a labor of love for you. And sometimes family relationships take the same effort and sacrifice. If you love your brother, he deserves better than for you to turn your back on him."

Clay sat on the end of the picnic table bench seat, stung by the truth of Meredith's rebuke. "I don't know what else to do for him."

"Love him. Let him know you are still there for him." She sighed and sat down across from him. Reaching for his hand, she added, "Don't forget, I had a sister who hurt and disappointed me, too. Now I wish I'd tried harder to reach out to her before it was too late. But it is not too late for you and Ryder. You've only failed when you quit fighting. Isn't your family worth fighting for?"

Meredith's question smacked Clay between the eyes.

He sat straighter, pulling his shoulders back as a tingle of fresh insight washed over his skin. "Of course they are."

No wonder he had such guilt regarding his brother. For a man who hated failure and worked his fingers to the bone making his ranch a success, his decision to walk away from Ryder, to quit fighting for the brother he loved went against everything he espoused.

"It's not too late for you to save your relationship with your brother. Regrets are a miserable companion, Clay." Meredith squeezed his fingers before getting up and heading toward the corral where Jewel and Emmie were patting the mares.

Resolve coalesced inside him. He had to reach out to Ryder again.

Why had he given up on his brother so easily? Did he hate the taste of failure so much that he'd chosen to abandon his brother rather than feel his continued efforts to reach Ryder were in vain? In truth, his real failure had come when he'd given up. His guilt was over his quitting, not his lack of success with Ryder. Clay removed his hat and plowed his fingers through his hair. He blew out a slow cleansing breath.

"You all right?"

He jerked his head up to see Tamara standing a few feet away, holding a bowl of Marie's potato salad. "Yeah, I just had an…enlightening talk with Meredith. She gave me a lot to think about."

Tamara's cheeks drained of some of their color. "About what?"

"Uncle Clay," Emmie called as she charged over and flopped against Clay's lap. "When do we eat? I'm a growin' girl, ya know. I need to eat to get bigger."

Clay ruffled her hair. "Well, by all means, let's eat then. I think everything's ready now. Wanna help me round the crew up?"

Emmie bounced on her toes. "Yeah!"

"We'll talk later," he told Tamara as his niece dragged him by the hand toward the house. She nodded, her eyes burrowing into him with a bright intensity.

"Race you!" Emmie shouted and took off.

As Clay broke into a jog behind the girl, a heart-stopping new thought filtered through his brain.

Had he given up too easily on his marriage and Tamara as well?

The question nagged him as his family gathered around the table and joined hands to say a blessing over the food. When he lifted his head at the end of Meredith's prayer, his gaze collided with Tamara's. Her eyes were red and her skin looked a little blotchy as if she'd been crying. He frowned and mouthed, "Are you all right?"

She twitched an uneasy grin and nodded as Nick tapped his fork on his glass to get everyone's attention. "Since we have all of you, our family and friends, gathered here today, Georgie and I decided this would be an excellent opportunity to make an announcement." Curious eyes turned toward the former Secret Service agent. "A few nights ago when we were discussing our plans for the future, Georgie and I—"

"You're getting married!" Emmie squealed excitedly, bouncing on her seat.

Georgie sent her daughter a wry grin. "Way to steal our thunder, Em."

"Then she's right?" Clay asked, dividing a glance between his sister and Nick.

A glow radiated from Georgie's face as she glanced to the man at her side and wrapped his hand in hers. Nick leaned over and gave her a kiss.

"Yes, we're getting married," Georgie said.

A collective cheer went up around the table, the most boisterous coming from Emmie.

"When? I want to be sure Joe and I are free to attend," Meredith asked.

"July." Nick stared into Georgie's eyes, and the love Clay saw in the man's face filled him with reassurance that his sister was in good hands.

Excited conversation buzzed around the table as dishes were passed and plates filled until Emmie stood up on her chair and waved her hands.

"Wait a minute. Wait a minute!" A look of horror washed over his niece's face.

The adults quieted.

"Emmie, what's wrong?" her mother asked.

"At the wedding," Emmie said, scrunching her nose in disgust, "will I have to wear a...dress?"

Laughter bubbled like champagne around the table.

Georgie shook her head. "Not if you don't want to, honey."

# Chapter 16

On Sunday morning after a late breakfast together, Clay and Tamara went to the small nondenominational church where most of the citizens of Esperanza gathered faithfully each week. The peaceful setting, the inspiring sermon and the familiar hymns usually proved a respite for Tamara from her inner turmoil. That morning, though, she couldn't get out of her head the Akerses, the pending DNA test results on Billy's cigarette or the inevitable end of her stay at the Bar None.

"I want to take some of the extra food from the barbecue over to the Akerses this afternoon," she said on the drive back to the Bar None. "They weren't in church, and I'm worried about how they're doing."

Clay gave her an unreadable glance then nodded. "Sure. Give me a chance to check on the new colt and talk to my foreman about a couple things, and I'll drive you over later."

She smiled her appreciation then dug in her purse for her cell phone. Switching it back on after having it silenced for the service, she checked her messages.

Nothing.

"I'd hoped I'd have heard from Eric by now." She shoved the phone back in her purse and sighed. "I know he said he was busy but…"

"What will you do if the tests show that the hair your team found in the tunnel matches Billy's DNA?"

She turned to stare out the side window. "I hadn't let myself even think that far. I've been so busy praying I was wrong in my assumptions and suspicions." She angled her head to look across the front seat to him. "I'll have to turn him in to Jericho, I guess. What else could I do?"

"Maybe we should have told Jericho about the things Billy said at the funeral and your theorics about his involvement."

She shook her head. "Not until we have proof. I could be totally misconstruing things Billy said, and he was drunk, after all."

Clay reached over and squeezed her shoulder. "Let's hope you're right."

When they got back to the ranch, Tamara gathered up the extra uncut apple pie she'd made for the barbecue, large helpings of smoked chicken, potato salad, baked beans and thick slices of Marie's homemade bread. She wrapped and packed all the food to take to the Akerses then checked her cell for messages again.

Still nothing.

Clay came in from the stables and did a double take when he saw all the food she'd fixed. "Don't you think they'll still have a full refrigerator from the funeral? Every family in town had to have brought a full meal's worth of chow."

"And now it's my turn. Besides, I hate to show up empty-handed."

Clay shrugged. "Whatever. Ready?"

She stowed her phone in her handbag, and he helped her load the food in his truck.

On the way to the Akerses, she checked her cell for messages twice more.

Clay chuckled. "You've heard the saying about a watched pot, haven't you?"

She jammed her phone in her purse again and twisted her mouth in a frown. "I know. I'd just feel better about this visit if I already knew Billy had been cleared."

As they pulled up to the Akerses' driveway, Tamara noticed a *for sale* sign in the front yard. She exchanged a dubious look with Clay. "Did Jack or Billy mention selling the house when you talked to them at the funeral?"

Clay opened the driver's door. "Naw. This is news to me."

They headed up the sidewalk as Billy came out the front door carrying a large box.

"Need a hand?" Clay asked, hurrying up to the porch to hold the door.

"I got it, thanks. What brings you folks by today?" Billy propped the box on the porch railing and wiped his brow with his arm.

"Well, we didn't see you at church this morning and thought we'd stop in to see if you were all right. And we brought food." Tamara lifted the pie toward Billy. "Made it myself. Well, with some help from Clay's housekeeper."

Billy arched an eyebrow. "Say, Brat, that looks good enough to eat. Thanks."

She returned a withering glance. "You're welcome. I think. Where should I put it?"

"Anywhere you find a spot. Go on in. I'll just put this in the car and be right back."

Clay held the door for Tamara, and she headed for the Akerses' kitchen, weaving through the collection of boxes, stacks of books, piles of clothes, and general clutter that had taken over the Akerses' home. Not only were the Akerses selling their house, they were packing their possessions as if their departure was imminent.

An uneasy jitter chased down Tamara's spine. Why were the Akerses leaving so abruptly, and where were they going? She didn't think she'd like the answer. She silently conveyed her concern to Clay with a meaningful glance.

He arched an eyebrow and mouthed, "Suspicious."

She bit her bottom lip and strode into the kitchen.

Jack Akers stood by the sink wrapping glasses in newspaper and packing them in a box. He sent Tamara a startled glance when she breezed in with the pie. "Tamara, uh, hi."

"I hope you like apple pie. And Clay's bringing in plates of barbecue." She forced a note of casual cheer in her voice.

Blinking, Jack set aside the glass he held. "Love apple pie, hon. Thank you."

Clay set the dinner plates on the counter next to the pie and offered his hand to Jack. Mr. Akers glanced at the ink on his fingers and shuffled his feet before shaking Clay's hand.

Tamara gestured around the room. Keeping her tone light and curious, not accusing, she asked, "Mr. Akers, what's all this?"

The man hesitated, blinking rapidly again, then turned his back on them. "It's, uh…Tess's things. We're just giving some of her stuff to charity."

Tamara glanced at Clay who, with a slight nod of his head, directed her attention to the box at her feet. Fishing trophies and hunting gear filled the plastic crate.

"Mrs. Akers didn't hunt, did she?" Tamara picked up a reel and turned it over, examining it.

Jack faced them, a puzzled look on his face. "No, why'd—" His gaze dropped to the fishing items, and color suffused his face. "That's, uh…"

Billy bustled back inside and met the deer-in-the-headlights expression on his father's face. "What's going on? Dad?"

Jack cleared his throat. "I was just telling Tamara and Clay that we're packing up a few of your mother's things to give away."

Billy drew his brow in a frown and narrowed a dubious gaze on Tamara. "That's right. And we're rather busy with it so…"

"Billy, we saw the *for sale* sign in the yard." She stepped closer to her friend and placed a hand on his arm. "Why would you move? You've lived in Esperanza your whole life. This town is your home."

Hands fluttering against his legs, he shrugged. "Maybe with Mom gone, Dad and I decided it was time to move on. See more of the country."

"But why not give it more time? Your mom *just* died. Don't make any rash decisions while you're still staggering from that loss. Wait a couple months and give yourself time to think it over."

Billy jerked his arm from her touch and paced across the room to start slamming his mother's cookbooks into a box. "No need to debate it, Brat. We've done all the thinking we need to. We want to make a fresh start. Now's as good a time as any."

Tamara exchanged a worried look with Clay. Clearly the Akerses meant to be packed and gone in a matter of days, maybe even hours. But why the rush? The obvious conclusion didn't bode well.

"Doc Mason apparently thinks Arizona is real nice. You might consider giving that area a try," Clay said casually.

Tamara tensed.

Billy paused mid-motion as he loaded another book in the box. He frowned and glanced at Clay then his father.

An awkward moment later, Jack scoffed loudly and slapped Clay on the back. "Naw, I'm tired of this heat. I'm ready for cooler summers and maybe a little snow at Christmas. I'm thinking Missouri, maybe Nebraska."

Billy went back to stacking the books, but his motions were stiff and jerky. He kept a wary eye on Clay as he worked.

"We'll miss you. You've been good friends for a lot of years. I hope you'll keep in touch." Tamara rubbed her hands on the seat of her jeans, looking for a way to break the tension in the room. Or was she only imagining the nerve-splitting vibes zinging around the Akerses' kitchen? She prayed the mood she detected was simply remnant grief, more of the odd reaction Jack and Billy had had to Tess's death.

Her phone jangled in the ensuing silence. Startled by the harsh ring, she flinched. Jolted with adrenaline, her hands shook, and her heart thumped. The eyes of the three men flew to her, as she fumbled to dig her phone from her purse.

Already heading for the hallway to take the call, she flicked the phone open quickly to stop the ringing.

"Tamara, I've got the results of those DNA tests on the cigarette you wanted," Eric boomed over the line before she could even say "Hello."

She stifled a groan, praying her boss's voice hadn't carried as much as she'd feared.

"Hi, Eric," she replied in a lower tone, hoping he'd follow suit. "Can I call you b—"

"It's a match. Same DNA as the hair from the tunnel," Eric blurted.

Because she was trying to cover the bad timing of the call, the news took a split second to register. When the significance of the results crashed down on her, she gasped. Instinctively her gaze flew to Billy's.

He stiffened and narrowed his eyes warily. Cast his father a warning look.

Too late she realized how telling her actions had been. In a fraction of a second, the damage had been done. She worked to school her face, hoping she could still smooth over her reaction somehow. Her mind scrambled.

"What's more, the fingerprints we lifted from the cigarette match the partial print that was on the trunk of the Taurus abandoned in your ex's pasture," Eric continued, snapping her attention back to the call.

"Oh, that's a relief!" She faked a smile and divided a quick glance between the men, gauging their reaction. "I'm so glad no one was hurt."

Clay's jaw tightened, and a muscle in his cheek twitched. Billy opened and closed his fists, shifting his weight as he kept a keen watch on her. Jack hung his head, his eyes closed and his shoulders drooping.

"Uh, Tamara? What are you talking about?" Eric asked. "Did you hear what I said about the prints?"

"Right, of course. Sounds like a close call."

"Someone's in the room with you?" Sure. *Now* Eric chose to lower his volume.

"Yeah."

"I've already called Sheriff Yates's office," her boss continued more quietly. "Figured he needed to know ASAP."

"Right. Thanks."

"And I'll see you back here at the lab in the morning, right?"

"Okay." She noted Billy's suspicious expression and Jack's dark look, and she added, "Tell Brenda accidents happen and not to blame herself. Give her my love. 'Bye."

She disconnected the call before Eric could respond and gave the room's occupants a forced grin. "My boss. He and his wife were in a fender bender. No one was hurt, but he needs us to come pick him up."

She met Clay's eyes, needing the reassurance of his steady composure. She drew a deep breath and headed back to retrieve her purse from the countertop where she'd left it. "Sorry we have to run."

Billy took a long step and blocked her path. In a flash, his arm snaked around her waist. Grabbing her wrist, he twisted her around and hauled her up against his chest. "Not so fast, Brat. Who was that on the phone? What did they tell you?"

"Get your hands off her," Clay growled. He took a threatening step toward Billy, his posture vibrating with barely harnessed violence.

With one hand clamped around her wrist, Billy dragged her back a couple steps and snatched open a cabinet drawer.

Black metal flashed in her peripheral vision.

"Stay back!" Billy yelled. "I swear, Colton. I'll pop her if you so much as blink."

Cold steel kissed her temple.

A gun.

Denials flooded her brain even as her knees buckled. Her childhood friend could *not* have a gun to her head. Not Billy. Not—

But the stark terror in Clay's eyes told the truth.

Bile rose in her throat, and she swallowed to shove down the bitter taste of fear.

Clay raised his hands, palms out. "All right. Easy."

"William!" Jack barked. "For God's sake, put that gun down now! You'll only make matters worse for yourself if you hurt the girl."

"No, Dad, I'm not gonna let them take me down. It was an accident!" Billy's grip on her wrist tightened, and pain shot up her arm as he wrenched it to an unnatural angle behind her. "An accident!"

"Wh-what was an accident?" Tamara kept her tone nonconfrontational, warning Clay to back off with her eyes. Her ex's face had blanched to a pasty gray. He wore an expression between rage and panic.

Billy scoffed. "I know you've figured it out, Tamara. I suspected as much as soon as Colton cracked that comment about Doc Mason liking Arizona."

"I didn't—" Clay started.

"Shut up!" The muzzle of Billy's gun jabbed harder.

Tamara's heart jolted, and her mouth dried.

Keeping his eyes fixed on her, Clay reached slowly for his hip and fumbled there. Did he have a weapon hidden under his shirt?

*Please don't let him try something that will get him hurt.*

"I think we all know Doc never made it to Arizona, so quit pretending. I heard your friend on the phone. You have some kinda DNA evidence against me, don't you?"

"Billy, I—" Tamara considered lying, but she didn't want to anger Billy further.

Jericho knew of the new evidence against Billy. Eric said he'd called it in. Surely the sheriff was on his way to arrest the Akerses' son even now. If she could just stall…

"Don't you?" Billy shouted, the gun in his hand poking harder.

"Billy, don't!" Clay gasped, lunging forward another step, desperation written in his dark eyes. "You said it was an accident. I'm sure if you explain that to the cops—"

"I ain't talking to the cops! If she's got proof I did it, they'll send me away for life. Maybe give me the chair." Raw fear rolled off Billy in waves. She heard it in his voice, felt it in the tremble in his hands, smelled it on his skin.

Frightened, trapped criminals reacted much like cornered animals. They could panic. Be unpredictable. Turn deadly in a second.

"Tell me what happened, Billy. Maybe we can find a way out for you." She forced calm into her tone, hoping to defuse the situation.

"It was my fault," Jack said, tears in his voice. "I asked Doc to help Tess. I begged him to end her suffering."

Clay scowled and glanced at the senior Akers. "Assisted suicide."

Jack squeezed his eyes shut, and fat tears rolled down his face. "Yes. I couldn't stand to see my Tess ravaged by that horrid disease."

Shaking his head, Clay glanced back at Billy. "Doc would never—"

"He didn't. He told Dad *no*." Disgust soured Billy's tone. "Until we offered him money."

Tamara gasped, remembering the money that had been in the trunk of the Taurus. "A hundred thousand dollars."

"That's right. He sure enough paid attention when we produced that cash. Said it'd come in handy to pay for some swanky rehab place in Arizona he wanted to go. Seems Doc got himself addicted to pain pills after he hurt his back last fall."

Clay's face registered recognition, acceptance. At least parts of Billy's explanation rang true for her ex, even if that truth was hard to hear.

"But Tess only died a couple days ago. And Doc…" Clay looked to Jack now, confusion knitting his brow.

"He backed out once he got the money, the sorry thief," Jack grumbled. "He took off with the cash we gave him and headed out of town."

Billy's grip on her arm had slackened. But the gun at her head still posed the most immediate threat. She listened to the Akerses explain their actions while she mulled possible means of disarming and subduing Billy. He was desperate, and their friendship would mean little if he thought she'd betrayed him, if he panicked and tried to escape.

"Even before Mama got sick, we didn't have that much money," Billy picked up the tale. "As it is, we cashed in most of my account and Dad's retirement savings to get Doc the money he wanted. I couldn't just let him take off out of town with all our money!" Billy's breathing grew more rapid and shallow. Tamara felt his hands shake harder. "So I followed him. He must have been stoned that night 'cause his driving was erratic. He was all over the road, and he finally veered off across your pasture. When he crashed into those mesquite trees, I thought that might be the end of it." Billy sighed, and the gun wavered.

Tamara glanced at the Akerses' kitchen clock, trying to gauge how long it would take the sheriff to arrive. *Please, God, let Jericho be on the way!*

"I figured I could just confront him, scare him. I'd get our money back and that'd be the end of it." Regret tinged Billy's tone.

Jack wiped a hand down his face and heaved a ragged sigh. "Oh, Lord, it wasn't supposed to end like this. It was all just an accident, Tamara. Really."

Clay had a sharp eye on Billy's gun, but he coaxed, "What went wrong?"

"I grabbed a knife when I went after him." He waved the gun toward the butcher block on the counter.

Tamara saw Clay stiffen as if getting ready to pounce on Billy now that the gun wasn't aimed at her head. She caught his eye and gave her head a subtle shake. She wanted Billy's full confession. Wanted to keep him distracted until help could arrive. "But you never intended to hurt Doc, did you, Billy?"

"Of course not! I'm not a murderer! I only wanted to scare him, make him give the money back. But he tried to grab the knife from me, and we struggled. Like I said, he musta been stoned 'cause he was really unsteady on his feet and, well, he fell." Billy's grip tightened again, and his rapid breathing told Tamara how reliving the nightmarish events stressed him. Billy's voice sounded choked, and she knew without looking that he was crying. "H-he stumbled and fell. He landed on the knife."

"You see," Jack pleaded, his hands spread in appeal. "It wasn't Billy's fault! My boy's not a murderer. It was all just a tragic accident!"

"Why didn't you call the police?" Tamara asked. "You could have told them the truth."

"What truth? That we'd bribed the doctor to help my mother die? That I'd brought a knife along to scare the man into giving our money back?" Billy scoffed. "Not stuff I wanted to admit to, Brat."

"Better than murder charges," Clay said.

Billy tensed and swung the gun toward Clay.

Tamara sucked in a sharp breath, fear for Clay turning her blood to ice. "No! Billy, just put the gun down. Please! Don't make things any worse for yourself."

"They're already worse." The gun moved back to her temple. "Thanks to you." He scoffed. "As a kid, you were always running to tattletale to our parents and getting your brother and me in trouble. And you couldn't leave this alone either. I saw you pick up my cigarette the other day at the funeral. I knew you were up to something. That's why Dad and I were getting out of town. I knew it was only a matter of time." Billy huffed his frustration and shoved the gun against her head. "If I'm going down for murder, I at least oughta make it worth my trouble. What do ya say, *Brat?*"

"William, stop this now!" Jack sobbed. "Let her go. Please."

"I'd covered my tracks," Billy grated as if not hearing his father. "I hid Doc's body in a tunnel I remembered playing in as a kid, wiped up the car, even faked a call to his switchboard to make people think he'd gone out of town. I had everything under control…" He grunted, and his grip on her wrist wrenched tighter.

A lightning ache flashed up to her shoulder. She gritted her teeth against the pain.

"If you went after the money, why did you leave it in the trunk of the Taurus?" Clay asked, edging a step closer.

Tamara held her breath, trying to signal Clay not to try anything that could backfire. *Where was Jericho?*

"After I moved Doc's body to that old tunnel, I heard something. Thrashing or crashing. And something sounded like voices."

Clay nodded. "Probably when my neighbor came to investigate the commotion he'd heard and found a steer caught in the fence wire."

Billy harrumphed. "I thought I'd been found out, and I panicked. I just wanted to get the hell outta there. I was already home by the time I realized the money was still out there. I'd planned to go back the next night after it was dark to get the money, but by then the cops were already crawling all over the scene. The money was in police custody.

"Then when I saw you at Doc Mason's clinic, and you said you'd fallen in a hole on Clay's property…" He groaned. "I knew I had to move the body. I went straight out there, wrapped it in a sheet to move it. Buried it in a shallow grave out by the landfill."

Clay rubbed a hand down his face. "Doc deserves a decent burial. Do you think you can find the place again?"

Billy jerked a nod.

Jack wiped his face on a sleeve. "When he told me, I… I didn't know what to do. Billy's my son. I love him and had to protect him. I… It's my fault. I started this mess when I asked Doc to help Tess die. I never thought…" He sniffed and turned away.

Billy drew a long deep breath and muttered a curse. "I'm sorry, Dad. I let things get out of control. I only wanted to help. Only wanted to get the money back—"

A knock from the front door reverberated through the house.

Billy jerked. Tamara could feel every muscle in his body stiffen and vibrate with tension.

Then Jericho's voice rang loud and strong. "Open up, Akers! Sheriff's Department!"

## Chapter 17

Before Clay could register relief that backup had arrived, all hell broke loose.

Billy panicked. His face flushed with rage.

"No! I'm *not* going down for this! It was an *accident!*" Hauling Tamara up against his body with an arm across her throat and the gun at her head, he stumbled back a step toward the door.

Stark cold terror flooded Clay's veins. He needed the sheriff and his service revolver in here—now!

"Jericho!" Clay shouted. "In the kitchen! He has a gun!"

"Damn you," Billy hissed, his eyes narrowed to snakelike slits. "Damn both of you!" He dragged Tamara back another step, his gaze flickering restlessly around the room. "I won't let you do this to me!"

Tamara's eyes bulged as she gasped for air against his stranglehold. Her fingers scrabbled at Billy's arm, trying to loosen his grip.

Her gaze found Clay's, and the pleading in her expression raked his heart with sharp claws. Until now, he'd given Billy a wide berth because of his weapon and Tamara's signals to proceed with caution. But the stakes had changed.

Caution be damned.

He wouldn't stand by and let Akers hurt his wife. He'd lost Tamara once when he'd been foolish enough to let her walk away. When he'd deferred to what he thought she wanted years ago, he lost everything that mattered. But this time, he would do what he had to. He'd take the necessary risk to save the woman he loved. Clay would rather die than let anyone use Tee as a human shield.

The front door opened with a crash.

Billy bolted for the back door, hauling Tamara in his wake. "Let me go, or I swear I'll kill her!"

Tamara's lips were turning blue. She didn't have time for Clay to hesitate.

Billy shifted his attention for a split second to find the doorknob behind him.

And Clay pounced.

Seizing the muzzle of the gun, he swung it toward the ceiling. As he lunged forward, his momentum and weight brought Billy and Tamara crashing to the floor with him in a tangled heap. The gun went off. Tamara screamed. Adrenaline pumped through Clay, numbing him to all but defending his woman.

With all his strength, he battled Billy for possession of the gun, struggling to keep the weapon aimed away from them. He'd wrestled calves into submission at the rodeo that put up less fight. But Tamara's life had never been on the line before. He wouldn't fail her. Couldn't lose her.

Moments later, the weight of another body crushed him to the floor. A third pair of hands joined the fight for control of the pistol. Clay took an elbow in the jaw, a knee in the gut, but he held on. The rodeo had taught him how to handle pain and keep going.

"Drop the weapon! Lie on your stomach with your hands on the floor!" a voice repeated over and over.

"It was an accident!" Billy screamed.

"Stop fighting. It's over, Billy. You're under arrest," Jericho grated, and Clay realized the sheriff was responsible for the added body and subduing hands.

"Billy, don't get yourself killed over this! Please stop!" Jack Akers begged. "It's too late to change things now."

As if someone had drained the life out of him, Billy grew still.

With a scuffle of hard-soled shoes, Jericho's deputies surrounded them and snapped handcuffs on Billy's wrists.

Clay groaned and rolled aside. Every muscle in his body hurt.

Lifting his head, he searched frantically for Tamara. "Tee?" he rasped. He spotted her sitting a few feet away in the mudroom. She stared at him with wide blue eyes and tears streaming down her cheeks.

Joints aching, he half crawled, half dragged himself toward her.

She lunged forward and landed in his arms. "Clay! Oh, thank God. I was so scared you were… I thought the shot…"

"I'm all right." He clasped her against his chest.

As Jericho dragged Billy to his feet and a deputy read the Akerses their rights, Clay met the sheriff's eyes. "Did you get all that?"

Jericho patted the cell phone clipped to his hip. "Every word."

Relief spun through Clay, and he pressed a kiss to Tamara's head.

Thank God she was all right. Clutching her tighter, he held her close—with no intention of ever letting her go.


"Once you've read over your finalized statements and signed them, you're free to go," Jericho told them hours later at the sheriff's office.

Tamara chafed her arms. A chill she couldn't blame on the air conditioner had settled deep in her bones.

Beside her, Clay scribbled his name at the bottom of the typed statement he'd given Sheriff Yates regarding everything the Akerses had said and done this afternoon. "What's going to happen to Billy now?"

Tamara sighed and signed her statement. Her childhood friend's future was grim. A trial. A jury. Almost certain jail time, even if he worked out a plea agreement with the district attorney's office. Jack would face much the same, thanks to his silence. What he'd done out of fatherly concern and protection made him an accomplice in the eyes of the law.

Jericho shrugged and stroked a hand over his mustache. "They've got a good lawyer. Beyond that, it'll be up to the courts."

Tamara slid her signed statement across the desk to Jericho. Compunction pressed down on her. Knowing evidence she'd gathered would be key in convicting Billy and Jack weighed heavily in her thoughts.

Clay reached for her hand and squeezed her fingers. "Hey, Miss Long Face, they brought this on themselves. They had ample opportunities to come clean about what happened with Doc Mason and earn themselves some leniency. Instead they tried to cover it up, and their trouble snowballed."

"I have to wonder…" when Clay stroked the inside of her wrist with his thumb, Tamara almost forgot the question on her tongue "…why Doc was in a stolen car that night?"

Jericho grunted and crossed his arms over his chest. "Good question. We may never know for sure, but best we can figure, he'd already decided he was going to take off with the Akerses' cash and head for Arizona. In case the Akerses reported him, he didn't want to be in his own car. Guess he thought the stolen car would give him anonymity a while longer. But if he was hopped up on drugs as Billy claims, there's no telling what his warped reasoning was."

Clay shifted uneasily in his chair, shaking his head. "I should have realized there was more to his odd behavior and shaky hands than just fatigue. He denied anything was wrong, and I believed him. If I'd been a better friend—"

"Clay, he hid his addiction from a lot of people," Jericho countered. "Easy to do when you live alone like Doc did. From what Dr. O'Neal and his nurse told us earlier when we questioned them, they only learned of the addiction recently themselves when drugs started disappearing from the locked narcotics cabinet at the office."

Tamara raised her gaze to Jericho's. "That's what I overheard them talking about the day I was at the clinic."

He nodded. "I'd say so. O'Neal said he was trying to keep his suspicions on the down low to protect Doc Mason and the clinic's reputation. Dr. O'Neal was buying into the practice, planning to take over for Doc when he retired. He was afraid of how revelations of the lead doctor's drug addiction might affect the negotiations and the insurance company's willingness to cover them for malpractice."

Clay tapped his Stetson back and scratched his head. "That's why they were so jumpy when we asked questions about Doc's whereabouts."

Jericho quirked an eyebrow. "Likely. They did mention they were afraid all the questions about his long absence were related to a drug investigation. They truly believed he was in Arizona, getting clean."

Deputy Rawlings approached the sheriff and handed him a sheet of paper. "Sheriff, this just came in. Thought you'd want to see it."

"Thanks."

While Jericho scanned the report he'd been handed, Tamara and Clay exchanged a long look. He squeezed her hand again, and she sent him a tremulous smile.

She had so much she wanted to tell Clay once they were alone. When she'd had Billy's gun at her head, thinking she could die at any moment, her main concern had been for Clay. She'd seen the damage a gunshot wound could do at point-blank range. If Billy had shot her, the sights and sounds for Clay would have been nightmarish. She shuddered at the thought, and Clay's eyes darkened with concern.

Jericho glanced up. "This is the autopsy report on Tess Akers. ALS didn't kill her. She had a massive heart attack."

Turning her attention to Jericho, Tamara digested the news with a heavy heart. "It's just as well she died when she did. Learning of Billy's part in Doc Mason's death and his attempts to cover it up would have devastated her. At least she was spared that grief."

"Or *did* she find out and the stress of it brought on the heart attack?" Jericho suggested.

Tamara gasped, and her chest squeezed at the possibility.

Clay glanced from Tamara to Jericho and scowled. "You couldn't have just kept that theory to yourself?"

Jericho winced and raised a palm. "Sorry. Guess I'd better get back to it. Lots of paperwork to do before I go home tonight."

Clay shook his hand. "Thanks for everything. I hate to think what could have happened if you hadn't shown up when you did."

"Well, we were already on the way over after talking to Tamara's lab about the tests they'd run. But thanks to your smart thinking and that cell phone trick, we knew the volatile situation we were facing when we arrived, knew the urgency of getting to the Akerses quickly."

Tamara scowled. "What cell phone trick?"

Jericho grinned and shuffled away. "I'll let your ex explain."

She tilted her head and gave Clay a querying glance.

"Jericho was the last person I'd talked to before we headed to the Akerses. I had my cell clipped on my belt as usual, so when I saw how things were getting out of hand with Billy, I punched redial and left the line open. Jericho heard everything Billy said, knew what was going down in the Akerses' kitchen."

A grin warmed her face. "I always knew you were smart."

He touched the brim of his hat. "Why, thank ya kindly, ma'am." He slid his lips into a lopsided grin. "Shall we go home?"

*Home.*

A rock settled in her stomach, and her smile faded. She wished she could consider the Bar None her home again. But the simple truth was, she no longer belonged there. She may have made love to Clay, but he'd never said he loved her. She may have indulged in a walk down memory lane these past several days, but her future didn't include Clay. Not if his attitude toward their relationship and his feelings for her hadn't changed.

She ducked her head and stared at her fidgeting hands. "Yeah, I should go home. To my apartment in San Antonio."

Clay didn't answer. Didn't move.

Finally she mustered the courage to meet his penetrating dark eyes. "I'm essentially healed now, and Eric wants me back at work in the morning. With the case involving Doc Mason solved, I have no more excuses to stay."

Clay nodded with a jerk of his chin. "Fine. I understand."

"I have a few things to collect at the ranch before I head back, so—"

"Okay. Let's go." Shoulders back, his gait stiff, Clay strode toward the door.

Tamara frowned. He acted mad, upset with her that she was leaving tonight. Yet he'd known all along she'd have to go home eventually. They'd talked this weekend of her starting work again Monday. So why was he acting so angry?

She followed Clay out to his truck, her heart heavy. After the cherished memories they'd made the past several days, she didn't want to part on bad terms. She stewed over how to make things right with Clay all the way back to the Bar None and while she gathered her few possessions into a grocery bag.

When she walked back downstairs to tell him goodbye, she found Clay at his desk, pen in hand, hovering over a notepad with a pained expression dimming his face.

"Clay? Are you all right?"

His head snapped up, and his gaze went first to the bag in her hand before meeting her eyes. "All packed?"

"Yeah, I just wanted to tell you thanks, and…" *I still love you.* She fumbled with the handle of the bag. "And goodbye."

A muscle in his jaw twitched, and he rose from his seat. "Yeah, well, take care and…" He sighed and scrubbed a hand over the day's growth of stubble on his jaw. "Hell, Tee, I… I'm not good at this kind of thing."

She set the bag on a lamp table and stepped into the room. "What kind of thing?"

He turned to stare out his office window at the setting sun. When he didn't answer right away, she approached the desk. "What did I interrupt?"

He angled his head to look at her then dropped his gaze to the paper on his desk. "I was writing a letter." He paused. Sighed. "To Ryder."

Tamara inhaled sharply. "Clay, I… I'm so glad. What changed your mind?"

"Lots of things. You started me thinking about it with the things you said about me cutting people I love out of my life."

Her chest squeezed, remembering the harsh words she'd had for Clay last week, wishing she could take back the angry accusations.

"Then yesterday I talked to Meredith about Ryder and…" he hesitated, a touch of color rising in his cheeks "…other things. She made me see a lot of things in my life with a fresh perspective. Like Ryder. I thought I'd failed with him so I gave up. But I only failed *because* I gave up." He furrowed his brow. "Does that make sense?"

As his words sank in, something deep inside her shifted, and her breath caught.

"Perfect sense." Tamara bit her bottom lip. Was she guilty of the same sin? Had she given up on her marriage, on Clay's love too soon?

"Anyway—" Clay rubbed his hands on the seat of his jeans and released a deep breath "—I'm hoping it's not too late to fix things with Ryder. As much as his incarceration hurt and disappointed me, he's still my brother, and I can't give up on him."

She lifted a corner of her mouth in a melancholy smile. "The other day in your truck, you told me it was never too late to do the right thing. You and Ryder will sort things out. I have faith…in both of you."

His gaze clung to hers. "Thanks, Tee. That means a lot to me."

She lingered another moment, reluctant to break eye contact, hating the awkwardness of their parting. When the grandfather clock in his foyer rang the hour, she finally turned and gathered her bag. "Well, I should let you get back to your letter. Thanks again for everything, Clay. I appreciate—"

"Tee, I—"

She held her breath, waiting, wishing.

Clay shuffled his feet, clearly searching for the words he wanted to say. "It was good to see you. Drive carefully."

Her heart sank. Even when she was leaving, he couldn't say the words she needed to hear. Tamara nodded and backed toward the door as Georgie's words from Saturday tickled in her mind. *Clay only keeps things that are important to him.*

Her feet stopped. She needed one answer before she left. "Clay…"

His expression brightened a degree. "Yeah?"

She took a breath for courage. "Saturday, when Georgie and I were looking for the tablecloth, I found in the closet the curtains I'd made for the kitchen and the lithographs I bought for the living room."

His eyebrows pulled together, and confusion shaded his eyes. "Yeah?"

Heart thumping, she leveled her shoulders. "Why did you keep them?"

Clay looked poleaxed. He sank back into his chair, a wide-eyed stare fixed on her. "I, uh…" He blinked and rested his hands on the desk. Ducking his head, he stared at his letter to Ryder, clearly gathering his composure, forming a response.

Tamara hated how much his answer mattered to her. She should have left well enough alone, should have left for San Antonio with the sweet memories of the past week with Clay intact. Her heartbeat pounded in her ears as she waited.

"Because I had a hard enough time letting you go. I couldn't give up the reminders of our life together when they were all that was left of you."

A bubble of hope swelled in her chest. "But you took them down. Why keep them if you're going to just hide them in a closet?"

He sighed, and his face creased with misery. "Like I told you last week, it hurt too much to look at them every day and be reminded of all I'd lost. I knew I'd failed you, knew you'd left because I couldn't be the husband you needed. It hurt like hell to let you go, but I wanted you to be happy."

Her breath caught. "You think our divorce made me happy? Clay, walking away from our marriage was the hardest thing I've ever done! It tore me apart." Her voice cracked, and she paused to swallow the knot in her throat. "But if I didn't matter to you, if you didn't love me enough to meet me halfway, I figured our marriage was already dead."

His brow puckered, and his dark eyes flashed. "Didn't love you? How can you say… Tamara, I've never *stopped* loving you."

His assertion kicked her in the chest. Her knees buckled, and she had to grab the back of a nearby wingback chair for support. "What?"

He shook his head and narrowed a stunned gaze on her. "You sound surprised. After everything that's happened this past week, I thought you understood." He stopped abruptly, and his jaw relaxed. He sighed. "But then how could you have understood something I only fully understood for myself today?"

She angled her head, her fingers digging into the upholstery of the chair. "What do you mean?"

Clay pushed to his feet and crossed the floor to her. Cupping her chin in his hand, he tipped her face up to meet her gaze. "When Billy pulled that gun on you, my heart stopped. I saw my life without you and knew nothing else mattered but you. When I thought Akers might kill you, I knew without a doubt how much I love you."

Tears pricked her eyes, and she blinked to clear her vision. "You only realized that today?"

He grunted and shook his head. "I think I knew it, but I couldn't admit it. I was afraid."

Her breath stalled in her lungs. *Fear* and *Clay* were two words that just didn't belong in the same sentence. He was the strongest, most capable man she knew. "Why were you afraid?"

Sliding his arms around her, he pulled her into his lap as he lowered himself into the wingback chair. "When we were married, I saw how restless you were, how much you wanted your own career. The ranch was struggling to survive financially, and I knew there was a good chance I'd lose the ranch and not be able to provide for you. You'd already spent too much of your life doing without, and I was so afraid of failing you."

She opened her mouth to counter his statement, but he placed a finger over her lips. "I believed you'd want more than me and the ranch one day, and so I was afraid to give you my whole heart. I pulled away, built a wall to protect myself."

She released a huff of frustration. "But that distance, that wall was what made me feel I didn't matter. You stopped saying you loved me, stopped asking for my input, stopped sharing your innermost thoughts with me. I felt alone, lost. When you withdrew from me, what else was I supposed to think but that you didn't care anymore? Especially when you didn't do anything to fight the divorce."

Conviction flared in his eyes, and his jaw tightened. "Not fighting for you was the biggest mistake of my life. Like with Ryder, I didn't fight, because I thought I'd already lost you." He plowed his fingers into her hair, and his dark gaze drilled into hers. "But my real failure was in letting you walk away without telling you how much I wanted you to stay. I did love you, Tee, but I was afraid my love wasn't enough for you."

Her heart tripped. "Clay..."

"All I ever wanted for you was your happiness. I thought leaving the ranch and following your dreams was what would make you happy. That's why I let you go."

A tear spilled onto her cheek. "All I really wanted was your love, to feel I mattered to you as much as the ranch. That I was important to you."

His fingers curled against her skull, and he pulled her face down to his. "*Nothing* is more important to me than you," he rasped.

His warm breath teased her lips, sent a wave of longing rippling through her.

"The past few days," Clay murmured, "I've learned that sometimes you can make painful choices—even difficult sacrifices—for all the right reasons, for the good of the people we love, but the decision is still wrong. You can make mistakes even when you have the best of intentions."

She closed her eyes and sighed. "Like the Akerses. They wanted to spare Tess the pain and deterioration of her ALS, but went about it all wrong. One bad choice led to another until they'd created a nightmare for themselves."

"Tamara, tell me it's not too late to try again. Forgive me for not fighting for you, for ever letting you think I didn't love you. I'll do whatever it takes to win you back."

Fresh tears streamed from her eyes, and she pressed a kiss to his lips. "You don't have to win me, Clay. I've always been yours."

"But what about your job? I don't want you to give up your career. You're good at forensics, and it's obvious what it means to you."

"My work *is* important to me, but not as important as you. I love you, Clay Colton, with all my heart. I'd give up my job to be with you."

Clay pulled back and scowled. "Tee, you can't."

She interrupted him with a kiss. "I'm not! I'm just saying I *would*. For you." She smiled broadly and ran her fingers through his hair. "As your very wise sister pointed out, San Antonio is close enough for me to commute. I can live on the ranch *and* keep my job with the CSI."

A seductive grin spread across his face. "Then you're staying?"

"All I need is to know you love me, and you want me in your life again."

His mouth opened then closed. Without warning, he shifted her off his lap and dropped to one knee in front of her. "Tamara Brown, I've loved you since high school, and my love is deeper now than ever. I've made some terrible mistakes in the past that hurt you, and for that, I'm truly sorry. I promise never to let another day pass without telling you, without showing you how important you are to me."

Joy like golden rays of sunshine spread its warmth through her. If his words weren't enough to convince her of how he felt, the passion and sincerity that shone in his espresso eyes vanquished any lingering doubt. But he wasn't finished.

"The past five years without you have been the darkest of my life, Tee, and I want nothing more than to have you back on the Bar None with me. I want to ride the range with you and make babies with you and grow old with you. Will you marry me…again?"

The eager anticipation that lit his face tugged her heart. Did he really think she could say no to a proposal like that? "Well…" She fingered the collar of his shirt and angled a coy glance at him. "Do you think you have a place at this masculine ranch for my dry flower arrangements and homemade curtains?"

He caught the hand that toyed with his shirt and pulled her close for a kiss. "Absolutely and forever."

She leaned into his broad chest and stole another kiss. "Then, yes, I'll marry you…again."

Her cowboy's eyes were suspiciously damp as he drew her into his arms. "Welcome home, Tee."

\* \* \* \* \*

THE COLTONS: FAMILY FIRST *continues!*
*Don't miss the next book of this exciting miniseries with*
*Linda Conrad's*
*THE SHERIFF'S AMNESIAC BRIDE,*
*available November 2008 from*
*Silhouette Romantic Suspense.*

*Here's a sneak peek at*
***THE CEO'S CHRISTMAS PROPOSITION,***
*the first in* USA TODAY *bestselling author Merline
Lovelace's* HOLIDAYS ABROAD *trilogy coming in
November 2008.*

American Devon McShay is about to get the Christmas
surprise of a lifetime when she meets her new client, sexy
billionaire Caleb Logan, for the very first time.

*Silhouette*
*Desire*

*Available November 2008*

Her breath whistled out in a sigh of relief when he exited Customs. Devon recognized him right away from the newspaper and magazine articles her friend and partner Sabrina had looked up during her frantic prep work.

Caleb John Logan, Jr. Thirty-one. Six-two. With jet-black hair, laser-blue eyes and a linebacker's shoulders under his charcoal-gray cashmere overcoat. His jaw-dropping good looks didn't score him any points with Devon. She'd learned the hard way not to trust handsome heartbreakers like Cal Logan.

But he was a client. An important one. And she was willing to give someone who'd served a hitch in the marines before earning a B.S. from the University of Oregon, an MBA from Stanford and his first million at the ripe old age of twenty-six the benefit of the doubt.

Right up until he spotted the hot-pink pashmina, that is.

Devon knew the flash of color was more visible than the sign she held up with his name on it. So she wasn't surprised when Logan picked her out of the crowd and cut in her direction. She'd just plastered on her best businesswoman smile when he whipped an arm around her waist. The next moment she was sprawled against his cashmere-covered chest.

"Hello, brown eyes."

Swooping down, he covered her mouth with his.

Sheer astonishment kept Devon rooted to the spot for a few seconds while her mind whirled chaotically. Her first thought was that her client had downed a few too many drinks during the long flight. Her second, that he'd mistaken the kind of escort and consulting services her company provided. Her third shoved everything else out of her head.

The man could kiss!

His mouth moved over hers with a skill that ignited sparks at a half dozen flash points throughout her body. Devon hadn't experienced that kind of spontaneous combustion in a while. A *long* while.

The sparks were still popping when she pushed off his chest, only now they fueled a flush of anger.

"Do you always greet women you don't know with a lip-lock, Mr. Logan?"

A smile crinkled the skin at the corners of his eyes. "As a matter of fact, I don't. That was from Don."

"Huh?"

"He said he owed you one from New Year's Eve two years ago and made me promise to deliver it."

She stared up at him in total incomprehension. Logan hooked a brow and attempted to prompt a nonexistent memory.

"He abandoned you at the Waldorf. Five minutes before midnight. To deliver twins."

"I don't have a clue who or what you're…"

Understanding burst like a water balloon.

"Wait a sec. Are you talking about Sabrina's old boyfriend? Your buddy, who's now an ob-gyn doc?"

It was Logan's turn to look startled. He recovered faster than Devon had, though. His smile widened into a rueful grin.

"I take it you're not Sabrina Russo."

"No, Mr. Logan, I am *not*."

\* \* \* \* \*

*Be sure to look for*
*THE CEO'S CHRISTMAS PROPOSITION*
*by Merline Lovelace.*
*Available in November 2008 wherever books are sold,*
*including most bookstores, supermarkets, drugstores and*
*discount stores.*

# nocturne™

**ESCAPE THE CHILL OF WINTER WITH TWO SPECIAL STORIES FROM BESTSELLING AUTHORS**

# MICHELE HAUF

## AND

## VIVI ANNA

---

# WINTER KISSED

In "A Kiss of Frost," photographer Kate Wilson experiences the icy kisses of Jal Frosti, but soon learns that this icy god has a deadly ulterior motive. Can Kate's love melt his heart?

In "Ice Bound," Dr. Darien Calder travels to the north island of Japan, where he discovers an icy goddess who is rumored to freeze doomed travelers. Darien is determined to melt her beautiful but frosty exterior and break her of the curse she carries...before it's too late.

*Available November wherever books are sold.*

# REQUEST YOUR FREE BOOKS!

## 2 FREE NOVELS PLUS 2 FREE GIFTS!

Silhouette® Romantic

# SUSPENSE

### Sparked by Danger, Fueled by Passion!

**YES!** Please send me 2 FREE Silhouette® Romantic Suspense novels and my 2 FREE gifts (gifts are worth about $10). After receiving them, if I don't wish to receive any more books, I can return the shipping statement marked "cancel." If I don't cancel, I will receive 4 brand-new novels every month and be billed just $4.24 per book in the U.S. or $4.99 per book in Canada, plus 25¢ shipping and handling per book plus applicable taxes, if any*. That's a savings of at least 15% off the cover price! I understand that accepting the 2 free books and gifts places me under no obligation to buy anything. I can always return a shipment and cancel at any time. Even if I never buy another book from Silhouette, the two free books and gifts are mine to keep forever.

240 SDN EEX6    340 SDN EEYJ

| | | |
|---|---|---|
| Name | (PLEASE PRINT) | |
| Address | | Apt. # |
| City | State/Prov. | Zip/Postal Code |

Signature (if under 18, a parent or guardian must sign)

Mail to the **Silhouette Reader Service:**
**IN U.S.A.:** P.O. Box 1867, Buffalo, NY 14240-1867
**IN CANADA:** P.O. Box 609, Fort Erie, Ontario L2A 5X3

Not valid to current subscribers of Silhouette Romantic Suspense books.

**Want to try two free books from another line?**
**Call 1-800-873-8635 or visit www.morefreebooks.com.**

\* Terms and prices subject to change without notice. N.Y. residents add applicable sales tax. Canadian residents will be charged applicable provincial taxes and GST. Offer not valid in Quebec. This offer is limited to one order per household. All orders subject to approval. Credit or debit balances in a customer's account(s) may be offset by any other outstanding balance owed by or to the customer. Please allow 4 to 6 weeks for delivery. Offer available while quantities last.

**Your Privacy:** Silhouette is committed to protecting your privacy. Our Privacy Policy is available online at www.eHarlequin.com or upon request from the Reader Service. From time to time we make our lists of customers available to reputable third parties who may have a product or service of interest to you. If you would prefer we not share your name and address, please check here. ☐

SRS08R

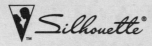

## Romantic SUSPENSE

**Sparked by Danger,
Fueled by Passion.**

# Lindsay McKenna
# Susan Grant

*Mission: Christmas*

Celebrate the holidays with a pair
of military heroines and their daring men
in two romantic, adventurous stories
from these bestselling authors.

Featuring:

**"The Christmas Wild Bunch"**
by *USA TODAY* bestselling author
**Lindsay McKenna**
and
**"Snowbound with a Prince"**
by *New York Times* bestselling author
**Susan Grant**

*Available November wherever books are sold.*

# Silhouette®
## Romantic
# SUSPENSE

# COMING NEXT MONTH

### #1535 MISSION: CHRISTMAS
**"The Christmas Wild Bunch" by Lindsay McKenna**
**"Snowbound with a Prince" by Susan Grant**
Celebrate the holidays with a pair of military heroines and their daring men in two romantic, adventurous short stories from these bestselling authors.

### #1536 THE SHERIFF'S AMNESIAC BRIDE—Linda Conrad
*The Coltons: Family First*
When a woman on the run shows up in his life, Sheriff Jericho Yates takes her in. The trouble is—she can't remember who she is or why someone was shooting at her! As "Rosie" and Jericho uncover bits about her past, they must dodge the goons who are after her, all while trying to ignore their undeniable attraction.

### #1537 MANHUNTER—Loreth Anne White
*Wild Country*
Isolated in the Yukon with 24-hour nights and endless snow, Mountie Gabriel Caruso is forced to team up with Silver Karvonen, a local tracker, to hunt down a sadistic serial killer bent on revenge. While the murderer plays mind games with them, Gabe and Silver face their biggest fears while growing ever closer…one footprint at a time.

### #1538 TO PROTECT A PRINCESS—Gail Barrett
*The Crusaders*
When Roma princess Dara Adams teams up with reluctant mountain guide Logan Burke to find a lost artifact, their lives—and their hearts—are on the line. But they're not the only ones searching for the treasure, and danger lurks around every corner. Harboring secrets that could change everything, Dara and Logan battle their desire for each other while fighting for their lives.